A Dr. Marcos

Vengeance OF THE Vanished Ones

BOOK ONE

Lee Orlich Bertram

Black Rose Writing | Texas

The author grants the final approval for this literary material.

First printing

This is a work of fiction. Names, characters, businesses, places, events, and incidents are either the products of the author's imagination or used in a fictitious manner. Any resemblance to actual persons, living or dead, or actual events is purely coincidental.

ISBN: 978-1-68513-518-8
PUBLISHED BY BLACK ROSE WRITING
www.blackrosewriting.com

Printed in the United States of America
Suggested Retail Price (SRP) $20.95

Vengeance of the Vanished Ones Book One is printed in Calluna

*As a planet-friendly publisher, Black Rose Writing does its best to eliminate unnecessary waste to reduce paper usage and energy costs, while never compromising the reading experience. As a result, the final word count vs. page count may not meet common expectations.

To Jack Hill, Jim Hill, Tim Hillebrand, and Susan Bordofsky

ACKNOWLEDGMENTS

I thank my dear friend, archaeologist Timothy Shaw Hillebrand, PhD, and my brother-in-law, anthropological archaeologist James Newlin Hill, PhD, former professor and chair of the Anthropology Department at the University of California, Los Angeles, for their years of brilliant research and fieldwork in their respective areas of archaeology and anthropology. Their professional quests for knowledge coupled with their exciting and often unbelievable reports from the field, provided background and inspiration for me to write the tales of the Mexican-Swedish-American archaeologist, Dr. Marcos Andersson.

Jim and Tim, rest in eternal peace smiling, my cherished friends.

VENGEANCE
OF THE
VANISHED ONES
BOOK ONE

ONE
Secret Mission in Guatemala

————————

In a ramshackle, Army transport DC-3 miles above the magnificent, Guatemalan rainforest, the idea dawned on archaeologist Dr. Marcos Andersson—he should not equate looking with seeing. Immersed in thoughts about the enigmatic meaning of the mysterious, ancient cave paintings of Baja California, he craned his neck to peer through a bulged window at the landscape below. He softly grumbled, "Oh, what the hell." The meaning had eluded him for over two decades. Perhaps Baja would reveal yet new answers this time when Marcos concluded his business in Guatemala. Sitting back, he was fairly bolstered by the thought in a few more days he would rejoin Susan there.

Marcos stretched his six-foot, five-inch frame deplaning in Flores, towering at least a head and a half above his old friend and guide, Oscar Williams. Oscar greeted him enthusiastically with open arms at the end of the timeworn runway. Planting his size fourteen boots in the dirt to steady himself after the turbulent flight, Marcos felt the suffocating, moist heat instantaneously cling to every inch of him. He removed his stylish outback hat and ran his fingers through his wavy mop of matted, dark auburn hair, with hints of gray at the temples. His rumpled safari suit hung loosely, splotched with patches of sweat. Marcos thanked Oscar for the cold bottle of water he tossed his way, gulping some down and pouring the rest over his face and head.

Perched on the edge of the jungle, Flores offered the perfect entrée. Traveling over deep ruts full of thick, viscous mud, Marcos and Oscar drove as deep into the jungle as the road allowed in Oscar's beat-up Land Rover. They parked the vehicle at a small Maya village comprising a dozen thatched huts with rounded ends, the style unchanged in a thousand years. As was their habit, they greeted the villagers before they took off on foot with their sharpened machetes, necessary to hack their way through and defend themselves against the jungle's vegetation.

"Where are we heading this time, Oscar?" Marcos cringed inside. He already knew the answer.

Oscar, reasonably proficient in English, smiled and pointed forward. "Trust me," he said, laughing.

"Don't I always?" Marcos said as he brushed a solid snarl of mosquitoes away from his face. Having learned his lesson the hard way on previous expeditions, he tenaciously scanned for deadly insects and snakes above and below as they slashed their way through the unrelenting flora, grunts and groans passing between the two men as their only conversation. The intense February heat and rain of the *verano* season brutally assaulted their senses. Thick, oozing mud threatened to swallow Marcos' boots with each step.

After several hours and much to Marcos' relief, Oscar signaled a rest. Gingerly laying down his machete on the jungle floor, Marcos said, "Thanks, man. I thought you were going to march me to death."

"*Nunca.* If I wanted you dead, I would have let that pit viper back there have his way with you," Oscar said as he nonchalantly drank a few sips of water.

"You're kidding, right?" Marcos laughed lightly, but Oscar didn't. Glancing around, Marcos sidled up to Oscar before taking a drink himself and toweling off his dripping face.

The two sat quietly, enjoying the lively soundtrack of the jungle—howler and spider monkeys, scarlet macaws, and raucous, keel-billed toucans. The squawks, hoots, and rustling of leaves rang comfortably familiar in Marcos' ears, preferable to any human or technological interference.

Whispering to avoid disturbing the natural sounds around them, Oscar explained the route ahead. Their destination, a newly discovered Maya site of colossal dimensions astride the border of Guatemala and Belize, lay hidden deep within the rainforest. Oscar had triumphantly made the stunning discovery, one that promised phenomenal contributions to the archaeological world. Marcos had already optimistically concluded its long history held clues to the origin of the Maya civilization.

An archaeological pursuit, however, had not prompted Marcos' visit this trip, as Oscar believed. The U.S. Drug Enforcement Administration, the DEA, had confidentially retained his services to locate and disable an airstrip carved out of the jungle. The airstrip served as the conduit to smuggle contraband arms to the Guatemalan guerillas in exchange for drugs that ended up in the hands of the cartels and from there onto the streets in the United States. Having worked with Marcos before, the DEA directed him to stage an expedition posing as an archeologist, locate the airstrip, and set up a transmitter to target it for destruction. He had perfunctorily convinced himself it would be a quick in-and-out operation—just a few days, and he would return to Baja and Susan. During the DEA's briefing on the location of the airstrip, Marcos was delighted to learn that it lay near the temple complex Oscar had discovered. An expedition to an existing archaeological site became the perfect cover for Marcos' visit to the jungle. Besides, his academic side tugged at him to lay eyes on the site if only for a few minutes.

***

After grinding hours of hacking, sweating, and cursing their way through the selva, Marcos and Oscar made camp near the bank of a small river. Hanging up their machetes, they settled to rest and eat. Darkness descended rapidly in the tropics. Marcos' team at the DEA had supplied him with all the latest, authentic field gear and modern equipment for the expedition—moisture-proof backpacks filled with breathable, lightweight clothing and sleeping bags, a tiny radio, semi-automatic pistol, digital camera, pocket computer and camcorder with power packs, field implements with mapping and recording tools, and assorted camp meals and water. A first-aid kit at the bottom of Marcos' backpack housed the DEA's neatly disguised transmitter, precisely nestled next to his bottle of Patrón Extra Añejo Tequila. From the outside, everything appeared as it should for an archaeologist embarking on an important, initial site study. Marcos assured himself they were set for several days.

An unexpected rustling in the surrounding jungle startled Marcos, and he reached for the semi-automatic pistol in his backpack, but it was too late. Six, dark-skinned men clad in filthy, ill-fitting, camo fatigues emerged from the forest with their automatic weapons drawn, swiftly surrounding him and Oscar.

"¡Alto!" shouted the leader. "¡Manos arriba!" The People's Liberation Army of the Republic of Guatemala had just arrested them.

Looking red-faced at Oscar, Marcos put up his hands as ordered. Oscar followed suit. A short, forced march later, they arrived at the guerillas' already established camp.

After shouted orders, no food, but thankfully, a little water, Marcos and Oscar were shoved to the ground, and everyone began an unsettled night in the tropical rain. Marcos and Oscar, their hands secured behind their backs, slept not at all. But when their captors nodded off, the slightest attempted whisper between the two men roused at least one of the six guerillas, usually followed up by an uppercut or a swift kick to their ribs. By night's end, they were bruised and broken and compliantly silent.

With the sun full overhead the following day, they stopped to eat lunch—canned peaches and cold tortillas. "How much farther?" Marcos asked in Spanish. "Where are you taking us, and why?"

"You will find out when you get there, gringo. Now, shut up and eat! We soon go," bellowed the leader.

Marcos shrugged it off and made the best of the break. He leaned over unobserved and whispered to Oscar, "Any idea where we are?"

"I am certain we are near the archaeological site, Dr. Andersson," Oscar said.

Lucky, Marcos thought. *At least we'll be near the airfield. But some good that'll do in the present circumstances.* He thought about Susan and was glad he hadn't allowed her to accompany him. Berating himself for agreeing to this little side trip, despite his feelings of patriotism, he wished he had remained in Baja with Susan. In reality, however, he would never refuse these assignments, thrilled with the adrenaline rush of such clandestine activities.

After lunch, the captors retied Marcos' hands behind his back, making it impossible to combat the constant strafing by insects as their forced march began again in earnest. Lost in thought, he expected the worst, hoping he could buy enough time to devise an escape plan.

Just before nightfall, they came to a thoroughly garrisoned compound. Beyond the vegetation, however, Marcos caught a glimpse of a clearing—the airstrip he sought. He had completed that part of the DEA's mission at any rate, he realized with a quiet snicker. As expected, the strip lay near a huge ceremonial complex the Maya had built as a plaza within a ring of temples and palaces. Marcos was astounded by what he could see of it and was thankful for Oscar's detailed description of the site. The dense overgrowth of vegetation partially cloaked the entire area.

The guards ushered Marcos and Oscar into the largest hut where they stood before a tall, uniformed man sitting alertly with arms spread, palms down behind an oversized desk. He had a long, droopy mustache and thick, oily black hair slicked straight back from the prominent scar on his high forehead. With accuracy, Marcos judged him to be in his late thirties. He had a commanding presence, and

Marcos counted six different makes of large handguns displayed on the desk, two within the man's immediate reach.

"*Hola, ¿cómo están?* I welcome you to our humble headquarters, gentlemen. I trust you will enjoy your stay with us," said the man in surprisingly accurate English. "Allow me to introduce myself. I am General Luis Montoya of the People's Liberation Army of the Republic of Guatemala. You are our guests as we arrange for your release."

"For your sake, I hope it won't be too long," said Marcos stridently in Spanish. His eyes never abandoned their steely gaze at the general.

"Ah. It all depends on the cooperation we get. In your case, Oscar Williams, I hope you are as valuable to your boss as we think you are, but we expect very little ransom for you. On the other hand, Dr. Marcos Andersson, we expect you to be of great value to our cause. I think it not very smart of you to come here pretending to be an archaeologist. However, we are extremely pleased you came into our little nest. It is our good fortune, no? Our people of Guatemala will owe you their thanks when we, at last, take control of the country. *Sí*, you will be happy to know, if things go well, you had a hand in our victory. Now, we contact the right parties and we see what happens. In the meantime, you will be confined to your quarters with posted guards twenty-four hours a day."

"I'm afraid you've made a big mistake, General Montoya," said Marcos calmly. "I *am* an American archaeologist, and Mr. Williams is my guide, taking me to an important site for study. I have no idea why you think I am of any particular value. Exactly who would be willing to pay for my release?"

"I make no mistake, Dr. Andersson. It is you who have miscalculated working with the DEA to spy on us, playing archaeologist. Now we see just how valuable you are to your government. *Sí, sí.* I think you are worth at least two million American dollars." The general sneered mockingly. "It does cost us nothing to find out. *Bueno.* For Mr. Williams, I ask for 100,000

American dollars. Don't you think you are worth that much to that rich capitalist tour operator, Señor Aguilar?" General Montoya said to Oscar.

"What have I done?" Marcos muttered, fixating on the fact he had not been honest with Oscar. Closing his eyes, he recalled the recent phone call from the director of the Swedish archaeological team inviting him to join the new Pompeii project. Sarcastically, he had snapped back, "*Helvete*, Anne-Marie, what could you possibly still dig up in Pompeii?" unable to conceal his professional disdain for classical archaeology. *I could have been in Napoli*, he thought as the face of Folke Andersson, his famous Swedish archaeologist Father, stared at him sternly in his mind.

General Montoya's breath collided with Marcos' cheek as the general stood only centimeters away, glowering at him. Marcos removed his thoughts from Napoli and opened his eyes.

***

The jungle rain had thoroughly drenched everything in the camp. General Montoya's guards sluggishly moved Marcos and Oscar at gunpoint in the mud through dank vegetation to a primitive hut at the end of the airstrip. They could see other men carry off their backpacks and deposit them in a thatched roof supply hut some thirty meters away.

"It looks like we're going to get to know each other even better before this ordeal is over, like it or not. I'm so deeply sorry I dragged you into this mess," Marcos said. "If we do manage to escape, can you lead us out?"

"I can, Dr. Andersson. We're actually on the outer edge of the archaeological site I discovered. We could go in either direction, Guatemala or Belize. I have friends in both who can help us. But how are we going to escape without guns?"

"Need to think on it. In the meantime, try to get friendly with the guards. Maybe we can learn something useful."

Three days passed before the general summoned them. He said to them curtly, "Señors, I am afraid I have bad news. Neither of your employers values you as much as we expected. We've given them four more days to come up with the dollars we have demanded. If they do not, we will first kill you, Oscar Williams, because you are of less value to us. Then we take your head and deliver it to Dr. Andersson's friends to show we take our business seriously. I am sure your friends are doing everything possible to find you, but I assure you even if they do, no one will get out alive." The general shoved writing materials in their hands and commanded them to write letters to their supporters, begging for their lives.

After playing along and writing their demand letters, guards returned Oscar and Marcos to the hut. But in those three intervening days, they had been busy. The same three guards took turns standing watch outside their hut, and Marcos and Oscar had become personally familiar with each.

In whispered consultation, they had agreed to target the night guard, Jorge, because if they were going to escape, they would have to do it under cover of darkness. "Maybe we can persuade him to help us," Marcos said. He didn't say it, but he knew if it didn't work, he was going to have to kill Jorge.

Marcos' efforts paid off. He learned via constant conversations that Jorge desired above all a university education to help his family and "other peoples" rise out of poverty. General Montoya had seduced him into joining the guerillas with the promise of money to buy such an education. Marcos recognized intelligence and ambition in Jorge fortified by a keen sense of social justice. After changing tactics a few times, Marcos finally convinced Jorge to help him and Oscar escape in exchange for a university education in the United States, all expenses paid. Marcos and Jorge discussed many alternatives for escape knowing that the guerillas had already set many traps. *"Debemos apresurarnos, estamos en peligro.* We have a lot to do before we take off," Marcos said to Jorge, and then the general had summoned them, cutting their time even shorter and putting them on edge.

After listening respectfully to the final conversation with Jorge, Oscar interrupted, "Dr. Andersson, I don't see how we can escape. Sorry, it just seems impossible."

He hated to admit it, but Marcos knew his guide might be right. Unless . . . "That very well may be the case," said Marcos, "but I just thought of an alternative that might work instead. Let's not escape but hide out for a couple days. We can walk away after the guerillas stop looking for us." In his mind, he acknowledged his father, Folke, as he did frequently, with *Tack, pappa*, for having repeatedly impressed on him the importance of taking a few minutes to think through all alternatives in life-or-death situations, no matter how crazy.

"Hmm. Very simple. Sounds good to me. What do you have in mind?" asked Oscar.

"Near the supply hut, I'm pretty sure I recognized a Maya tunnel capstone with a garbage container resting on top. I know, trust me. I couldn't believe my own eyes."

"*¿En serio?* You mean the tunnels priests would use?"

"Precisely. The tunnels were common in the ancient pyramids. The priests would use them to deceive the people, suddenly arriving at the tops of the pyramids out of nowhere and dazzling the people with so-called magic shows.

"I figure if we could enter that tunnel, and that's a big if, we could lie low and safely hide for a while until the guards give up and leave. How does that plan strike you?"

Oscar nodded approval. "It's *loco*, but the best plan I've heard. I have learned to trust you. I hope you are right with what you saw." He smiled broadly, giving Marcos courage.

"First, we have to get our backpacks and just hope to God that our supplies are still there. Jorge, I want you to go to the supply hut and bring them here. Go *now* and hurry back before anyone notices. Go!"

Jorge scurried off and returned in a few minutes without making a sound. He handed both packs to Marcos. Hastily, Marcos checked the contents. He could not believe everything was there. Well, almost. His automatic pistol and Tequila were missing. Guards had rifled through the packs, stuffing things back into them helter-skelter but leaving the indispensable radio and signaling device inside. Marcos mentally braced himself and breathed in deeply to calm the adrenalin, hoping both devices still worked.

While still in the hut, Marcos assembled the radio like a pro, strung out the antenna, and tapped out a prearranged code. When he finished, he shoved the radio back into his pack and removed the first-aid kit that housed a device the size of a pack of gum. Pressing various buttons, he activated it with one beep, signaling transmission. The battery life was three days, tops. Marcos concealed it delicately in the thatched roof of the hut and convinced himself the three of them could last in the tunnel that long. They had sufficient rations, but it all depended on his handlers at the DEA receiving the transmission *en seguida* and acting on it. Marcos exiled any thoughts from his mind about the horrific consequences should the device fail to do its job. He turned around abruptly to face Oscar and Jorge.

"Okay," Marcos said, "it's time to clear out. Everything's in motion. Let's climb into the tunnel and hope it's deep, or we're headed for grave trouble." He chuckled to mask his apprehension.

Ever so quietly, the three crept near the supply hut and surveyed the capstone concealing the tunnel. No man doubtless had opened it in hundreds of years. Despite jungle overgrowth, a beautifully carved surface with intricate Maya designs was visible at their feet. Marcos fought the urge to clean it off and examine it more closely, but that would surely give them away. Heart pounding, Marcos experienced a head rush characteristic of the moment of discovery which he had not felt in many years. It reminded him of how fellow archaeologist Howard Carter must have reacted when he looked squint-eyed through the peephole into the antechamber of Pharaoh Tutankhamun's intact tomb.

With somewhat rusty skills, he calculated the Maya had carved the capstone around 850 A.D. at the height of their classic period. The three attempted to pry it off with tools borrowed from the supply hut, but it would not budge. So, Marcos then showed Oscar and Jorge how to dig around it, slanting outward away from the stone, while also reminding them to be extra, extra careful not to damage the breathtaking art. Again, they met with no success.

Hearing the perimeter guards approaching, Marcos motioned for Jorge to resume his post *pronto*. They waited without breathing until the guards passed. Oscar and Marcos then re-commenced their work, prying again with no results. When Jorge returned, he threw his weight into the task. The lid lifted ever so slightly that time. They wedged it with a chisel and pried even harder, each time lifting it a little higher. At last, they released it from its ancient setting and slid it aside just enough to slip down into the now exposed, gaping entrance.

Marcos knelt reverently to cast one last fervent glance at the intricate carvings, crestfallen he didn't have precious time to interpret the story they told. He closed his eyes and lightly caressed the capstone with his fingertips. "I will be back to study you soon," he promised. Bidding it *adiós*, he efficiently smothered the capstone with dirt and placed the garbage container back on top just as it had been before. Aware of making no sounds, the three men eased themselves into the tight passage one at a time. It took every ounce of their remaining collective strength to push the capstone back into place over their heads, especially with the added weight of the garbage container.

Mission accomplished, Marcos thought, relieved. He switched on his flashlight and gave his eyes a few moments to adjust, realizing that light was the first illumination in the tunnel since ancient torches. He could barely make out steps carved into the limestone bedrock glimmering with dense, greenish scum. With much caution, they descended the slippery stairs in the stillness, trying to keep their balance as they went deeper underground. *That was good*, he thought, *the deeper the better*.

Finally, the passage leveled out. They proceeded cautiously since the floor was also very slippery. Dank and musty the fetid air threatened their lungs. The sound of footfalls from their sticky boots broke the mausoleum-like silence. Marcos had to restrain himself from stopping to examine the mounds of ancient Maya artifacts heaped mostly in corners. *At least this is a different field experience than I've endured before*, he thought. *Folke, I wish you were here. Sorry, jag önskar att du var här*.

After moving forward another forty meters, maneuvering sharp-angled twists and turns, they entered a ten-meter-square chamber with undulating plaster floors and grimy walls whose crevices emitted a chilly draft. The tunnel, he could see, continued on the other side. "Let's stop here," Marcos said, almost afraid of his own voice as it echoed around him. "I'll be right back." As a precaution, he set a well-concealed booby trap at the last turn before the entrance to the chamber, using a priceless little kit from his pack disguised as camp food. *That ought to discourage any intruders*, he thought. He grinned as he rejoined Oscar and Jorge.

Exhaustion heavily weighing them down, each found a spot to get some sleep. It was the middle of the night. *The guards will surely not discover our disappearance for another two or three hours*, Marcos calculated, just as he shut his eyes and imagined the Maya priests whisking past.

***

Marcos could not temper his growing impatience the next morning despite trying to index the ancient rites and rituals of the Maya in his head. He was a man of action. The three men had decided to stay put and rest some more instead of going any deeper into the tunnel and getting further trapped, but not knowing what was happening above ground drove him beyond crazy. Simultaneously, he hoped his contacts had received his signal and the ordeal would soon be over. However, as a realist by experience, he knew their situation would doubtless not turn around for a few more days, if at all. As he often did, he shifted gears and turned his thoughts to the developments in his interrupted Baja expedition to conquer any fatalistic notions.

"And what makes our Dr. Andersson so quiet?" Oscar asked.

"I'm sorry, Oscar. I was thinking about getting back to Baja to continue what I started there. I have a fantastic woman patiently waiting to help me who is no doubt wondering what has happened to me. I promised her I'd be back in a few days, and it's already been a week. I'm racked by guilt about the worry this little side trip is causing her."

"Archaeology and a woman—a pleasing combination. I'm not surprised a handsome fellow like you would be involved with at least one woman. I wouldn't be surprised if a dozen women were chasing after you now that your wife, Carole, has passed, God rest her soul."

"Tell me about Baja. Besides the woman, what awaits you there?"

Marcos had never revealed his interest in the archaeology of the ancient cave paintings of Baja to Oscar. As far as he knew, Oscar possessed no clue there was anything of any archaeological significance there—not like the Maya, in any case. "Just a curiosity."

Oscar laughed. "*De acuerdo*. Your face says it is more. We have time while we wait. Tell me. It will keep your mind off our troubles."

"Well, okay. You'd be surprised. Of course, there's nothing like the civilizations here in Mesoamerica with their writing, architecture, and highly specialized societies in contrast to Baja. The people in Baja existed at the simplest level of social-cultural integration imaginable, but they produced some remarkable, large-scale cave paintings, perhaps the finest in the world. The problem is the art's creators have long *vanished* along with their culture. To make matters worse, it's impossible to derive any meaning or association with rock art from the rather scant, archaeological remains. It is something that has frustrated me for years. There just isn't much correlation between the archaeological remains and the creative thinking processes of the natives that resulted in the pictographs and petroglyphs." *Perhaps we'll never know, or we may be on the verge of an important breakthrough soon. Could go either way*, Marcos thought.

Oscar nodded toward Jorge, whose expression was one of confusion. "Let's speak Spanish. He may not be interested, but at least he won't think we're hiding things from him." Switching to Spanish, Oscar said, "And . . . what else?"

"Yes, you're right." In Spanish, Marcos said, "The story of the cave paintings in Baja may very well be a tale worth telling, but it's far from finished. Somebody has been dynamiting the precious sites and destroying the ancient rock art. Local tourists discovered my longtime friend and colleague, Dr. Davis Pearce, an internationally renowned anthropologist and archaeologist, dead at one of his dig sites. Oscar, I mentioned Dr. Pearce to you long ago. His death prompted me to go to Baja. Then I met Susan, and things went from interesting to dangerous, to deadly serious and a bit terrifying." Marcos visibly winced recalling the many unexplained occurrences thus far.

"*¡Caray!* don't stop there, Dr. Andersson. The whole story, *por favor.*"

Marcos figured sharing the whole story would be cathartic for him. He began four weeks prior when he received three extraordinary phone calls on the same morning. The first one came when he was sitting in the local diner in the peacefully quaint town of Salmon, Idaho, where he had moved and purchased a ranch after Carole had passed away the year before. That call was from Ramiro Martinez Alarcón, the present governor of Baja California del Sur and his old friend and college roommate at the University of California.

"A governor called you, but why?" Oscar asked with piqued curiosity.

"He's the one who told me about Dr. Pearce being discovered dead by local tourists at a rock art site. Dr. Pearce was a mutual friend of ours. Not only that, but someone had already blasted the site and ruined the priceless, ancient art."

"Who would do such a horrible thing, Dr. Andersson?" asked Oscar in disgust.

"*Por Dios*," Jorge said. "At least when people rob our ancient sites here, they usually sell the treasures for money. They don't blow them up."

"That's why Ramiro called me, to find out what's going on."

"But why did he call *you*?" asked Jorge. "I mean, he's the governor. He has armies and *policia* for such problems, no?"

"Yes, but he doesn't know who he can trust in Baja, and he knows he can trust me because we are old school friends. He, Dave, and I made a pact to discover the meaning of rock art one day, no matter how long it took."

"And you really take this pact seriously?"

"Unconditionally. *Sin duda*."

***

Ramiro was the person who had initially introduced Marcos to Baja. Countless times, they had joined each other in Mexico on vacations. In truth, the Alarcóns had accepted Marcos as a member of their family. Together, Ramiro, Dave, and Marcos had explored the remote areas of Baja, discovering and recording many extraordinary pictograph sites. Marcos had constantly attempted to persuade Ramiro to pursue a career in anthropology, arguing he could do far more to help his people as an anthropologist than as a lawyer. Ramiro had vociferously disagreed, arguing that was not the case in Mexico, and more importantly, his father *expected* him to be a lawyer. That was exactly what he had to do out of obligation. As governor, he was a political novice and very naïve. Because Marcos knew Ramiro well for years, he had pegged Ramiro early on as a fast learner, especially when it came to whom he could or could not trust.

"He's a young governor at forty-five, swept into office on his boyish good looks and enthusiasm reinforced by his family's money and influence," Marcos said. "Ramiro considers himself the champion of the people despite his upper-class background. His family accumulated a fortune in the fishing industry over the years and owns a large fleet of boats. He told me he wanted to run for governor to obtain a platform to make meaningful changes in the social order, and he assumed office with high expectations." Marcos shrugged. "However, he has had limited success with bucking the system. That has proven frustrating and more difficult than he expected. He hadn't counted on encountering so much opposition to change. But despite all that, he is outraged to learn of the destruction of his beloved rock art."

As governor, Ramiro had solemnly held himself out as the custodian of this natural treasure of his people—an important link to their heritage. He could turn to nobody for help, so he contacted Marcos.

"But Dr. Andersson, what were the other two calls?" asked Jorge.

"Wait," said Oscar, holding up his hand. "First, back up. Dr. Andersson, you said in Baja things went from dangerous to terrifying. What was that about? Then I want to hear about this woman in your life."

As he paced, slightly agitated, Marcos admitted to Oscar and Jorge that he was unable to shake a crushing feeling of dread that Dr. Pearce had meddled with something unseen during his excavation that should have remained undisturbed in Baja. "I've also had horrible nightmares."

"Wait a minute, *mi amigo*. Are you referring to something supernatural, Dr. Andersson? Please explain."

"Yes, I guess so, Oscar. At first, I didn't want to think that. But I had an experience I can't explain any other way. An unproven, psychic approach to understanding rock art came to me after what I can only describe as a force catapulting me into the spirit realm. Even as I say it, it's hard to fathom. But I need to pursue that theory. However, if I could come to some reasonable understanding about it, it would not be verifiable scientific data."

Marcos did not reveal to Oscar and Jorge that he detested the thought of his former colleagues heckling him and discrediting his work should he advance what many considered pure psychobabble, especially after his twenty arduous years of serious study in the field.

"Dr. Andersson, you're right to be worried about roaming around in the dangerous spirit world. I know because I've grown up surrounded by the power of voodoo and the ancient Maya spirit world. Both are threatening forces to be reckoned with, please believe me," Oscar said.

Marcos nodded. But he struggled with the concept all the same. In his intellectual world of academics, he had always written such things off as superstition and nonsense. But Marcos knew Oscar held a tremendous head start over him in the spiritual world. He had grown up believing such things.

"Don't for a minute dismiss it as superstition," warned Oscar as his face flushed. "The spirit world is as real as the world you call your physical reality. There will be a large price to pay by those caught in the spirit world unescorted or without proper knowledge. Unimaginable things can happen. It's a real possibility that's how your Dr. Pearce got himself killed. He very well could've even innocently unleashed the forces of vengeful spirits. You must be so very careful, Dr. Andersson. The trouble caused will be unending if you don't make peace with the angry spirits. But first, you must find out what set them off."

"God, Oscar, you're convinced the things I described were caused by angry spirits? That is off-the-charts farfetched."

"No doubt about it," said Oscar, making the sign of the cross.

"And so how do you make peace with an angry spirit?" Marcos asked half-seriously.

"Depends. There are many ways and countless spirits. You must find out exactly what's making them mad, Dr. Andersson. Then it'll be your job to make them happy. Don't think you can ignore it because the problem won't go away, and you can't run and hide even in a Maya tunnel. No sir, you have to make the spirits happy again by setting the world straight and restoring the balance."

Marcos shook his head, feeling remarkably helpless, and he hated it. Frankly, it all sounded quite menacing to him. "I'll see what I can do, but this is way, way out of my area of expertise. What I know, though, is some kind of trouble is brewing for sure. Maybe Susan can help."

"Maybe she can help, but it's you who must make it right. There's no doubt in my mind that digging around or digging something up has made the spirits angry and altered the balance somehow. *You* must figure out what to do and then fix it. But can we forget the spirit stuff for a minute? Tell me about this Susan woman. You in love with her?"

"I don't know, Oscar. It's way too soon after Carole's death to be thinking of that." That was Marcos' code for his fear of never finding a replacement for Carole and being alone for the rest of his life.

"Every man needs a good woman, Dr. Andersson. *Are* you in love with her?"

"Perhaps so, but there's something not quite right, and I cannot put my finger on it exactly. Despite the fact that we've enjoyed each other's company in Baja, I sense that she's holding something back from me. I'll just have to cross that bridge at an appropriate time." Marcos' self-talk convinced him he and Susan were not ready for any kind of commitment with their worlds galaxies apart. "I must be cautious, that's all."

"Now, don't you go worrying about that, Dr. Andersson. I believe if the forces want you together as a couple, it will all work out when the time is right and you've each done what you need to do. Sounds to me like you need to quit grieving your dead wife and get on with your life. Let Carole go, Dr. Andersson, she's dead. Now take a chance, live your life, and live it with a good woman like Susan. I believe she came into your life at just the right time. What you need to learn is acceptance," Oscar said unabashedly. "It's time to let sink in what your heart tells you. Accept new sources of knowledge like you have always done and taught me and your students to do with archaeology."

Emotionally and intellectually drained, Marcos thanked Oscar for his insights on all fronts. "I have much to consider." He stood on the rim of a vortex, about to hurl himself in with his head and heart on different planes.

"*¡Oiga!* I'm still waiting to hear about the other two phone calls," said Jorge with an impatient tapping of his foot.

"Ah, yes, the other two phone calls."

TWO
Phone Calls

———

Four weeks earlier
Salmon, Idaho

Marcos faintly heard the phone ringing in his home office when he returned from the local greasy-spoon diner. He hustled inside, plopped with a thud into his shabby swivel chair, and punched the speaker button.

"Hello, Dr. Andersson?" asked an unfamiliar, professional female voice. "This is Dr. Cohen. I'm a psychiatrist practicing in Los Angeles. I'm calling about an urgent matter to discuss with you."

Puzzled, Marcos replied hesitantly. "Okay. How can I help you? I only have a few minutes because I'm getting ready to leave on a trip."

"That's exactly what I wanted to talk to you about, your trip. Straight to the point, I'm not only a psychiatrist, I'm also a psychic with the ability to communicate with the spirit world and have helped many, many people—"

Marcos interrupted curtly, chuckling. "Dr. Cohen, I don't see what that has to do with me. I'm trying to leave. Perhaps we could discuss this when I return, and I—"

"Please, Dr. Andersson, allow me to continue. I'll be brief. In a word, I'm calling to offer my services."

"Sorry, Dr. Cohen, I didn't realize psychiatrists were into telemarketing, but I'm not in the market for a shrink or a psychic."

"Please don't hang up yet. If I understand correctly, you have been interested in the ancient rock art of Baja for many years now. Correct?"

"Yes, but—"

"Please hear me out. I also understand that nobody knows for sure how to interpret the art or what it means because the producing culture is extinct."

Rifling through bills and mail on his desk, Marcos answered, "Yes, but—"

"I can only imagine how that must frustrate you. Wouldn't you like to gain some insight into the significance of that marvelous art?"

"Obviously, but—"

"So, do you anticipate any breakthroughs on the horizon from your current techniques and archaeological excavations? Haven't your digs only left you with more questions rather than answers?"

At the gut punch, he snapped back, "I suppose you could say that."

"All right, now bear with me. Bluntly stated, I am offering to accompany you on your trip to Baja. I will attempt to contact the spirits of those who produced the art. If I am successful, and I expect to be, I can tap into knowledge from the universe, providing you with information your archaeological deposits will never give you because it isn't there. However, you must take me to the sites where the voices will be strong so the access will be easier. Thoughts, Dr. Andersson?"

"That's a no-brainer. I must decline your offer under any circumstances. Just picture me becoming the standing joke of the academic community," Marcos said, voice rising.

"As I understand it, though, Dr. Andersson, you have not been a member of the academic community for some time now. What do you care what they think? This could finally be your chance to gain understanding, to think outside the box of current theories and practices, and make a groundbreaking contribution beyond what the usual digging in the dirt would provide."

"Thanks, but no thanks. This is truly nuts. There's absolutely no way to verify whatever information you might claim to receive concerning rock art. It would all be pure speculation, flight-of-fancy. There's no place for that kind of nonsense in scientific inquiry. Tell me how you know who I am and that I'm going to Baja."

"I have sources in different realms, Dr. Andersson. That's not as pressing as other aspects right now. What's most important I think, is you allow me to accompany you on your trip. I *must* see those sites, and you are one of a small handful of people who can guide me. Of course, I'll pay all my expenses and yours for that matter. Whatever it takes."

"That's absolutely out of the question. The plain reality is that it may very well be dangerous. Tourists recently found an archaeologist friend and colleague of mine dead at one of those sites. I suspect you already know that, however."

"I know . . . I mean . . . Dr. Andersson, I urge you, please, let me come along. It's vitally important to my work, and it should be to yours as well."

"What part of *no* do you not understand, Dr. Cohen?" Marcos asked while he instantly attempted to calculate why the rock art would be so important to a shrink.

"I have advanced greatly in my work. People from all over the world including celebrities have sought me out because of my reputation. They seek solace and knowledge in communicating with their departed family and friends. I have successfully breached the barrier between the worlds, providing them a source of peace, happiness, and comfort. It is truly life-altering."

"Well, hurray for you, but I fail to see any connection to rock art."

"Don't you see? My goal is to gain respect for the use of psychic data in scientific research. If I could make some breakthroughs with archaeological inquiries, it would advance my cause and lend credibility to the methodology. I have thought about this long and hard. You and I could establish an entirely new discipline—*psychic archaeology.* Do not forget, Dr. Andersson, I, too, am a person of science."

"Good lord! I don't want any part of it. I'm sorry, Dr. Cohen, but I really must be going. I must pack, and I have a tiring, long drive ahead of me. Goodbye."

Marcos hung up before she could utter another word, shook his head, and roared. "Unbelievable. What a quack!"

In the bedroom, he began laying out items he would need on his trip. On top of his underwear, next to a multi-function Swiss army knife, he placed a container of pepper spray and a stun gun. He considered taking at least a pistol. He felt more comfortable with a .357 Magnum, but it was illegal in Mexico, and he didn't want any problems with the authorities. He knew that scenario, and it never ended well.

***

Marcos' home had morphed into a rambling six-bedroom, four-bathroom, ranch-style residence once he had remodeled and expanded. He had proudly completed much of the work himself, considering it good therapy, the kind that didn't cost three hundred bucks an hour or whatever shrinks like whacko Dr. Cohen charged in Los Angeles.

He had remodeled the kitchen meticulously to foster his talent as a gourmet chef. From his treks all over the world, he had collected hundreds of international recipes. Friends and colleagues affectionately named him the original culinary anthropologist. He preferred to call it the social anthropology of food, an emerging field.

A fully equipped office with state-of-the-art, high-tech operations had also been added. Marcos had performed quite well as a commodities investor and could afford to buy anything or do whatever he wanted, for that matter. He cherished that freedom and enjoyed his cash. His former life in academia rarely crossed his mind.

In his private wing, he had installed a sauna, hot tub, and an exercise room. As a final touch, a small Japanese garden in a private courtyard resided conveniently off his bedroom for easy access. People constantly commented that his home was more like a museum than a residence. Nearly every available surface displayed an artifact he had lugged back from some adventure. Each object told a story and represented a piece of Marcos' history as an archaeologist and world traveler. No doubt, he could wax nostalgic for hours about each find. Dr. Davis Pearce, his biggest fan, had affectionately cherished his stories.

**

The third call that morning came from Joyce Pearce, Dave's wife, in tears.

"Marcos, you must know about Dave by now. Ramiro said he'd call you earlier this morning. I was too distraught to call you myself." Joyce sobbed, gasping for breath. "I'm numb. And to make matters worse, the preliminary report from the Mexican authorities lists Dave's death as a suicide. If that is the case, our life insurance company won't pay me a dime. I'm going to lose our home. We are deeply in debt after putting all the kids through college. With Dave gone, I only have a meager monthly income, and I haven't worked in years. He even cashed in on most of his retirement to help subsidize his work. Oh my God, I don't know what I'm going to do. For heaven's sake, I don't want to ask the kids to help."

"Joyce, you need to remain calm and not panic. The bloodsucking insurance companies never want to pay out. It will all sort out. Come on, we both know there's no way Dave would commit suicide, right? So, I'm getting ready to leave for Baja any minute now. I promise you with all my heart, I'll find out what happened and set things right."

"I know you're going, and truthfully, I'm worried about you. Marcos, promise me you'll be careful. Dave was on the verge of some kind of breakthrough in understanding the rock art. You know him. He wouldn't tell me details, but he hinted it would be dangerous, and he certainly didn't sleep well before he left, experiencing horrible nightmares. He was on-site alone, Marcos, because his graduate students hadn't arrived yet. No obvious witnesses to what actually happened."

"Joyce, hang in there for Dave," Marcos said in the most soothing voice he could muster. "Everything will be fine. I just need a couple weeks to investigate and sift through the evidence. I'll keep you posted."

"Thank you, thank you. But please, watch yourself. There's something rather sinister going on. Dave knew it, and I can sense it. I even begged him not to be on-site alone."

Marcos reassured her again before hanging up. Feeling lightheaded, he ate a quick bite and managed to finish packing. Grabbing his checkbook, he wrote a check to Joyce for twenty-five thousand dollars. *I hope that will tide her over until things become clear*, he thought with concern.

When pressing family obligations and personal struggles had compelled Marcos early in his career to leave academia, Dave had passionately appealed to him not to do it. Despite that closed door, however, Marcos remained current with the scholarship in the discipline. As time passed, he and Dave had shared the utter euphoria of archaeological exploration and discovery in Baja. This time, however, Marcos felt an unfamiliar knot in his stomach as he faced the trip to Baja. *Dave would never have killed himself,* he reassured himself. *But I haven't a fig of a clue about who could have killed him and what circumstances I am about to get into down there.* Uncertainty and fear gnawed away at his reserve of self-confidence.

Gathering up his travel gear, Marcos remembered at the last second he had not checked his voicemail in two days. He entered the code and listened—a couple of commodity brokers wanting his account followed by a faint, garbled recording, barely intelligible. *I can't believe it. That's Dave!* The cryptic message said, "Marcos, this is urgent. I'm alone and seriously need your help. Meet me in Mulege as soon as possible . . . I'll explain all later . . . please, you have to trust me." The next part was corrupted then something that sounded like *bopow*, maybe *Bhopal?* "Don't know how much longer I can hold out. Please, Marcos, please!"

Marcos drew in a deep, raspy breath and tried to collect his darting thoughts. *If only I had heard this message two days ago. I could have done something!* Marcos thought with an elevating sense of guilt and foreboding. *I could have chartered a plane and flown down. I can't imagine what kind of danger Dave encountered. What could have caused his death? Nightmares?* Head throbbing in his hands, Marcos swore to find out and vindicate his friend.

THREE
Long Trip to Baja

———

Marcos drove for three straight, sleep-deprived days to reach the California-Mexico border, laser-focused on his mission. The trip was uneventful but enjoyable until he hit gridlock on the Southern California freeways to the border. *One of the primary reasons I fled California*, he noted. Culture shock assaulted him hard after the quiet solitude of Idaho with wall-to-wall cars, drivers talking on phones and reading newspapers, deafening noise, and smog soup. The same small, black Japanese car had followed him from Idaho, at least he thought. *Unlikely. There are a million of the cursed things on the road. No one would follow from Idaho, surely*, Marcos thought.

Thirty miles from the border, he pulled over and called Joyce. "Hi, Marcos here, checking in. I'm about to cross the border. I would have stopped to see you but didn't want to disturb you so early in the morning."

"Good. Thank you so much for the check, Marcos. That was such a welcome surprise."

"Wonderful. So glad you got it. Please don't worry. Everything's going to be fine, I promise. That's why I'm going to Baja. We'll get this whole thing unraveled, and that disgusting insurance company is going to pay."

"I'm so happy you called," Joyce said, sobbing. "I just received a fax from the insurance company stating they'll close our case in thirty days unless there is new, compelling evidence to consider. Boy, they didn't waste any time dropping that bomb."

"Thirty days! Good Lord, Joyce, that's not very long. I'll do my best but see if you can get an extension to buy more time. The situation demands it since the location of Dave's death is in Mexico, for heaven's sake. You are painfully aware of the utterly bureaucratic situation there. I have no idea what I'm going to run into."

"I'll certainly try, but I must tell you something else. Ramiro said, by Mexican law, a body must be disposed of in no more than fifteen days. Also, the authorities won't allow the removal of Dave's remains from the country under these circumstances. That gives you less than two weeks to get there and have medical personnel examine the body and perform an autopsy, if indicated. If you don't do that, you might not be able to prove it wasn't suicide."

"I'll be in Mulege where Dave's body is in plenty of time. Umm . . . so sorry to have to ask you this, but what do you want me to do with Dave's remains?"

"I want you to have him cremated and his ashes spread over the site where he died," Joyce stated with resolve. "I think Dave would like that despite the unexplained, bizarre circumstances. No denying as *you* are so *painfully* aware, Dave sunk a lot of his career and life's blood into understanding rock art."

"Joyce, I *so* agree. I'll figure out some way to carry out your wishes."

"One more thing, Marcos. Do you know a Gustavo Figueroa?"

"No."

"Well, you might want to look him up. Dave told me he was going to see him. Mr. Figueroa has a large ranch south of Mulege."

"Thanks for that clue. I'll try to call later. *Adiós.*"

***

Marcos detested the thought of interacting face-to-face with anybody at the University of California, *the bastion of ingrained bureaucracy and administrative overreach.* As a colleague, Dave had observed the department chairman test Marcos to his limits and pulverize all desire to continue in academia. Dave stood by as Marcos fell headfirst from the ivory tower too many times. Out of devotion to his friend and to archaeology, however, later that afternoon Marcos phoned several faculty members and graduate assistants in the Departments of Anthropology and Archaeology to inform them personally about Dave's death and to tease out any leads. Not surprisingly, he received repeated comments of shock and incredulity. Marcos felt guilty that he was relieved about avoiding everyone's wounded reaction in person and any accompanying, residual sneers aimed at labeling him—the maniacal professor in the imitation Indiana Jones hat.

Dave's colleagues all concurred that he had appeared excited lately but at the same time distant and more anxious about his work than usual. As a former professor himself, Marcos considered that Dave's work in Baja must have been important enough for him to leave campus in the middle of the quarter. To a person, each adamantly had agreed that it was absurd to think he would have contemplated suicide let alone actually taken his own life. Dave had held boundless love for his precious family and archaeology. Marcos subtly mentioned Gustavo Figueroa, but nobody at the university knew anything about him. *Damn. Into the black hole I roam,* Marcos thought as he shook his head.

Eager to cross the border and leave Tijuana and civilization behind, Marcos would head south into the *real Baja.* He had not been there for several years and looked forward to his reclusion. It would be good for him and would give him a chance to recharge his batteries. *Maybe crazy Dr. Cohen was half-correct in a sense. Baja certainly holds a certain metaphysical allure,* Marcos thought. *If Dave had finally had a breakthrough, I owe it to him and his colleagues to figure it out. A new technique? A new site? Uniquely different art? What? Dave, after all this time, I'm ticked off you didn't confide in me, my friend.* These thoughts offended Marcos deeply despite Dave's phone call. Now, he had to get out of his state of irritation and accept that Dave *had* tried to communicate with him, albeit too late.

Cycling methodically through his CDs, he settled on Linda Ronstadt's *Canciones de mi Padre.* Normally, he would have listened to a few well-chosen selections from his vast collection of classical music and opera, but Linda's full-spirited, throaty interpretation of the classical Mexican *música ranchera* was just the ticket for his re-entry into Mexico.

***

Marcos loved eating almost as much as archaeology and traveling. He considered each trip a gastronomic extravaganza, and his chronicles of local cuisine had become legendary. As ardent as he was to head south, he could not pass through Tijuana without getting a fix of the famous, authentic Caesar salad at Caesar's Palace. He headed for Avenida Revolución, admiring the undeniable gentrification. As he pulled into the parking lot, a small, black Japanese car crept by, reminding him again of his earlier sightings. *Ah well, I'm just super fatigued and need food,* he rationalized.

On his way to the restaurant, he passed a donkey painted with black zebra stripes attached to a gaily colored cart, politely declining the opportunity to have his photo taken. A barker, lurking in the doorway of a dingy bar hemorrhaging thunderous, live music, promised him beautiful naked women and invited him in for a free peek. *My, the citizens of Tijuana are certainly enterprising,* he thought, admiring their entrepreneurial spirit. Next to Caesar's, a new arcade overflowing with shops offering a myriad of folk-art items enticed him. He decided to meander through there after lunch. Each trip, the creativity never failed to amaze him, as the merchants never failed to produce new items to sell to tourists.

An adorable, diminutive Indian girl with a sad, sunburned face and worn lavender barrettes matching her misbuttoned, dirty lavender sweater, held her hand out beseechingly. Against his better judgment, Marcos handed her a five-dollar bill.

"*Gracias*, señor," she whispered almost inaudibly and scampered off to her mother sitting a few meters away selling Tarahumara baskets to tourists.

It was noon when he entered the lobby of a once-grand hotel, famous during the days of prohibition, and was at once hampered by the long line of lunch patrons. Marcos didn't mind the wait, using the time to refresh and relax a bit. An authentic Caesar salad was virtually impossible to find, despite the fact many restaurants had it on the menu sans any clue as to its origin. That affronted the chef in Marcos. *Doesn't anyone know that a person first created the Caesar salad in Tijuana? I ought to publish a letter in at least the Los Angeles Times giving credit where credit is due!* Marcos thought.

Amusing himself by people watching as he waited, he noticed a beautiful, svelte woman enter the lobby unescorted, ear pressed to a large cell phone. He heard her say something like, "Can you speak louder? I can barely hear you. Thank you. That will be all. I can take it from here."

The woman wore very stylish, strappy wedge sandals, khaki shorts, and a rather low-cut, form-fitting purple top, accentuating her cleavage. While she fumbled with her phone and purse, Marcos could not stop checking her out, soaking in every detail. She carried an upscale, overstuffed backpack slung over one shoulder. Her shoulder-length, attractively styled, chestnut hair framed her delicate oval face accentuated by plump lips, piercing, sea-green eyes, and a perfectly proportioned nose. *Something that perfect has to result from a skilled surgeon's work,* he thought. Stealing one last look, he guessed she was in her mid-thirties, a bit young for him even if he were in the market, which he was not.

Marcos finally averted his eyes to avoid the appearance of gawking and focused on the hideous, Aztec calendar representation on the ceiling.

"Excuse me, sir. Do you speak English?"

He felt a light tap on his shoulder, turned, and locked eyes with the attractive woman with the sea-green eyes standing next to him.

"I apologize. I hope you don't think me rude, but it looks like it's going to be a long wait for a table. I was thinking it might speed things up a bit if we shared one. Do you mind?"

"Uh . . . no, of course not. Great idea. I'm Marcos Andersson, by the way."

"I'm pleased to meet you, Marcos. I'm Susan," said the woman politely while extending her hand. "Excuse me while I bury my dumb cell phone at the bottom of my purse and forget about it. The reception is so hit or miss." She rolled her eyes. "I have no patience for it, and I forgot my charger on top of that. You from California too?"

Amused, Marcos observed as Susan threw her phone into her purse with a flourish. "Back in ancient times. I live in Idaho now," he said while obviously trying not to stare at her *décolleté*.

After a few minutes of general chitchat, the maître d', a grandfatherly gentleman who possibly could have been present when Caesar created the famous salad, seated them near the window with a wonderful view of the street below. Marcos politely waved his menu away, stating he just wanted a Caesar salad and a bottle of Santo Tomás *blanco* with "*bolillos y mantequia también, por favor.*" Although the waiter spoke English, Marcos ordered in Spanish to impress Susan, if he was being honest.

"I always dine here for the Caesar salad," Marcos told Susan. "I highly recommend you try it. You know this is the very spot where the owner, Caesar, created it. Nothing like returning to the scene of the crime, I always say. Lots of bad imitations out there these days, which offends me greatly." Marcos touched his heart.

"You mean *the* Caesar salad originated right here?"

"Yep. The inventor, Caesar Cardini, fled the States because of prohibition and ended up opening a restaurant here where he created his namesake salad. You most likely noticed the place has seen better days. However, the salad survives in all its awesomeness."

"Great. I will follow your recommendation and have the salad, if you will order it for me in Spanish."

Marcos gladly complied. "Please share the wine with me. So, are you down here for the day and some shopping, Susan?"

"No, I've come to join a tour, but I have to catch up with it. I understood they were going to have lunch here, but I have obviously made a mistake. Oh well, I can catch up with them tonight in Ensenada. I'll just take a taxi."

"Hold on. Ensenada is 105 kilometers away. I'm going that way and would be more than happy to give you a ride."

"You would? Fantastic—I accept," she said, batting her lashes with exaggerated coquettishness.

"By the way, what kind of tour is it?"

"Supposed to be a natural history tour, some birds, plants, geology, stuff like that."

"That's not bad stuff. It could be quite interesting."

"I guess so. I just really wanted to see some ancient rock art. Baja has some magnificent paintings and murals. My tour includes only a few sites, but it was the only tour I could find, and I just needed to get away for a while. What about you? What exactly are you doing in Baja, Marcos?"

Taken aback, Marcos said, "No way! You're not going to believe this. I'm here in connection with rock art."

"What do you mean, *in connection with rock art*?"

"I'm an archaeologist and have been interested in the rock art here for years. You are right—it's magnificent and much, much more. I've explored and found many sites over the years with close colleagues. I've excavated associated deposits looking for information about rock art but with no success. You see, there's no way of determining if any given deposit truly relates to the paintings. Consider if we had a picnic on the surface of a rock art site and left various items behind. It doesn't mean they're connected with the paintings."

He shrugged. "The world might never know the intended meaning of the rock art because, unfortunately, the people who produced it are long since dead, erasing any trace of their culture." Marcos blushed as he realized he had just delivered a lecture to a stranger.

"I sense your concern and frustration. But there must be a way to figure out the meaning of that art. Why are you here then? Do you have some brilliant, new technique you plan to test, or are you primarily exploring new sites, hoping for a breakthrough?"

"Tragically, an archaeologist friend and colleague of mine was found dead recently at one of the sites. I'm down here to find out what happened on behalf of his family."

"Oh God, Marcos, that's unbelievably terrible about your friend. I'm so sorry for you. If you don't mind me asking, how did he die?" Susan's voice grew softer.

"I have no idea. That's what I'm here to ferret out."

***

It wasn't too long by Mexican standards before the *mesero* arrived with the wine and a cart stacked with all the ingredients for the salad. First, he poured enough wine for Marcos to taste along with the cork to sniff. Marcos nodded while the *mesero* obviously enjoyed pouring wine for him and Susan. Next, he wiped the huge, well-seasoned, wooden bowl thoroughly inside with garlic cloves. In the bottom of the bowl, he placed a generous amount of fresh minced garlic, a dab of mustard, a pinch of salt, some olive oil, and several slabs of anchovy. Marcos' taste buds stirred. Then, with one hand, the waiter deftly cracked an egg, added the juice of several limes, and with great precision, mixed and mashed the ingredients thoroughly together as Susan watched intently. *Looks like the same fantastic fare*, Marcos thought. The waiter heaped shiny leaves of romaine lettuce in the bowl, gently but masterfully tossing the salad to distribute the dressing evenly over each leaf. He smiled widely with professional pride as he worked. Nobody would have ever suspected he had tossed the same salad a thousand times before.

Next, the *mesero* melted butter in an old skillet and cut up small loaves of bread into substantial squares to make the specially seasoned croutons right before their eyes. Piling their plates high with generous portions, he served Susan and then Marcos, but not before garnishing with freshly shredded Parmesan cheese, toasted croutons, and freshly ground pepper to complete the presentation. Indeed, it was quite a show by any standard.

Susan poised her fork tentatively over the salad and said, "It looks scrumptious, but I wonder if it's a good idea to eat fresh lettuce in Mexico?"

"Don't sweat it," Marcos said. "A huge percentage of the lettuce and tomatoes consumed in the U.S. comes from Mexico without us knowing it. You likely eat Mexican lettuce every time you have a salad."

"I have never tasted anything like this Caesar before," Susan said with a toothy smile and twinkling eyes.

"I told you. Hey, don't want you to miss out on more of the incomparable, Mexican *bolillos* and fantastic margaritas."

"Count me in," Susan said.

Marcos ordered more *bolillos* and a round of margaritas and effusively complimented the waiter on the excellent salad made possible only by his expert preparation. Flushed with pride, the waiter accepted Marcos' credit card and floated away, no doubt expecting a large tip.

"Hold it, Marcos, when I invited you to share a table, I didn't expect you to pay for everything. Please, let me pay for my lunch."

"Let's just say you owe me one sometime. I'll get this one, and then later you can take me out to an *expensive* place. How's that?" asked Marcos, charmingly amused.

**

As they wound their way out of town, the abject poverty reflected in the cardboard houses and makeshift dwellings lining the outskirts still depressed Marcos. *If only I could do something to improve the human condition here*, he thought. They passed the new bullring descending the hill toward the coast. Heading south on Mexican Federal Highway 45, Marcos noticed a growing number of beach resorts and condominium developments undoubtedly constructed on speculation for gringos. They would reach Ensenada in an hour, the last outpost of civilization before the road collided with the interior remoteness of Baja.

Marcos broke the silence. "Do you know how California got its name?"

Susan shook her head.

He never passed up the chance to teach a history lesson to a captive audience. He began with how Hernán Cortés had named California in 1533. Some years earlier in the late fifteenth or early sixteenth century, the Spanish writer Garci Rodríguez de Montalvo had written *Las Sergas de Esplandián*, a sequel to a set of chivalric romance novels, *Amadís de Gaula*. The subject was an imaginary, fantasy island named California inhabited by amazons and griffins. The first explorer had convinced himself that the Baja Peninsula was an island—hence, the name California.

"Later, after further explorations, our California became Alta California for Upper California and theirs Baja California for Lower California. Fast forward, Baja was pretty much a neglected territory of Mexico until 1976 when officially granted statehood and divided into two states, Baja California Norte and Baja California Sur," Marcos said with a flourish.

"No disrespect intended, but it appears to me it's still much neglected."

"Wait 'til you get further into the interior. It can get desolate. There wasn't a paved road until 1976. That road, almost sixteen hundred kilometers from the top to tip, was supposed to fortify commerce and tourism."

Marcos pointed out that a chain of charming, little hotels known as Los Presidentes, merely a comfortable drive apart, much like the old Spanish California missions, was intended to support tourism along the road. Sadly, the anticipated tourism did not materialize, and the adventurous few who visited normally did so self-contained in motorhomes, contributing minimally to the Mexican economy.

"I'm very interested to see how those wonderful little hotels have fared during the years since I've visited," said Marcos. "*Buena suerta.* The owners may as well try to run a chain of hotels on Mars. Terrible logistical problem not to mention the maintenance hassles."

Marcos pulled into the tollbooth, gave up some *pesos*, and drove south on the toll road to Ensenada, truly enjoying the view from the sheer cliffs overlooking the mighty Pacific. "I always stay at the El Presidente. Where is your group staying?"

"The same place, according to the itinerary. Thanks so much for the lift, Marcos. I enjoyed the ride very much and your company, of course. Maybe I'll see you around down the road. I understand not too many decent places to stay exist other than the El Presidente. Oh, and thanks again for lunch, too. Hit the spot."

By the time Marcos parked the car and returned to the hotel lobby, Susan had disappeared. His luggage greeted him at the reception desk. He booked a second-story room overlooking the pool, his usual choice. A siesta sounded heavenly to him as it had been a very tiring, three-day drive resulting in back and neck aches. Marcos caught himself wondering if he might bump into Susan again. *She seemed nice enough and quite easy on the eyes*, he thought, surprised at himself for noticing. *I think not. She'll likely be off with her tour group in the morning.*

Marcos relaxed for a few minutes then headed down to the pool. Floating on cool water, he noticed people stopping to stare unabashedly at a striking figure descending the stairs. Appearing poised in a skimpy, bright purple bikini, her attire left little to the imagination. *Oh my God, it's Susan.* He watched her sexily toss her towel on a chair and plunge into the pool. She came up gasping for breath next to him.

"Cripes, Susan. You caused quite a scene with your dramatic entrance."

"I hope you like my suit," said Susan, adjusting her halter straps.

Marcos nodded sheepishly. "So, want to have something to drink?" he asked, changing the subject. "I'll surprise you with a very refreshing concoction."

"Sure," Susan said still half-submerged, then sliding onto an available chair attached to the inside of the pool's wall.

The waiter could hardly take his eyes off her, but inventive Marcos distracted him long enough to order Susan a strawberry margarita and a can of Carta Blanca *con limón* for himself. With drinks in hand, they toasted one another and to their respective adventures ahead. Marcos took the wedge of lime, squeezed the flavorful juice onto the top of the can, and sipped with satisfaction as Susan watched curiously.

"The best way to drink beer in Mexico," he said. "Here, try it. See what you think."

Susan hesitated then cautiously took a sip and flashed a smile of faint approval as she handed the can back to him.

"Well, I'm going to take a few laps to work out the kinks then dress for dinner. Are you having dinner with your tour group tonight?"

"No, it's a free night. I'm on my own."

"Mind if I join you? Remember, you owe me one."

"I didn't think you'd get even with me so soon but sure. Why not."

"I know just the place," Marcos said, sure of himself. "Shall we meet up in the lobby in an hour? That enough time?"

"More than enough. I assume we don't have to get too dressed up for dinner here?"

"That's right. Very casual."

"See you in the lobby in an hour."

***

Just before time to meet Susan in the lobby, Marcos efficiently dressed in shorts, sandals, and a T-shirt with a University of Idaho logo on it. In the spotless but empty lobby, he successfully extracted Susan's room number from the reluctant desk clerk, although he didn't know her last name. The clerk merely winked when he gave the number up. As Marcos knocked on her door, he wondered if she had changed her mind and felt a pang of disappointment.

"Who is it?" Susan asked.

"Marcos."

The door opened revealing Susan in a short towel.

"Sorry I'm late. I dozed off and lost track of the time. I'll be ready in a minute. Come on in and wait if you want."

I wonder if she'll dress in front of me, Marcos thought to himself, rattled. Part of him wanted to wait inside. The fact she allowed him to see her in a towel surprised him a little but, again, maybe not after her sensational entrance earlier. He declined her offer to come in, stating he would just wait down by the pool.

Before long, Susan, dressed in a form-fitting, black T-shirt and white shorts, descended the stairs to the pool in a similar fashion as before but with her Birkenstocks flapping. *Man, what an exhibitionist*, Marcos decided.

"I took my cue from your informal attire and dressed accordingly. I take it we're not going to the ritziest place in town. Where exactly am I taking you?" she asked.

"I know this great little, intimate seafood place where a mamacita makes tortillas and cooks them over an open fire as fast as you can eat them."

"Sounds yummy."

A block off the main tourist drag and down a narrow side street, Marcos navigated by memory and ushered Susan through a brick-lined, arched doorway into a quaint, candle-lit restaurant called Tio Pepe Mariscos. The waiter seated them near the circular fireplace where tortillas browned on a large *comal*. When the waiter arrived and dutifully handed out the menus, Marcos looked at Susan. She nodded, and he waved them away and ordered *tacos de mariscos* for two with Dos Equis, his favorite Mexican dark beer. Savoring each sip of beer, he said he hoped Susan liked seafood tacos.

"What kind of seafood?" she asked, sampling the beer tentatively then reading the label.

"Well, depends on what's available. You can always count on some shrimp, maybe some clams, and perhaps a bit of bonito fish or lobster. Did you know that taco means heel?" Marcos asked.

"Heel, why heel?" she asked seemingly intrigued.

Just then the food arrived, and Marcos held up a taco and said, "Well, look at it. When the tortilla is folded in half it looks like the heel of a shoe, right?"

"Gotcha," said Susan as she attacked her food.

***

They strolled along the breakwater, letting dinner settle before retiring for the night. The moon, rising in the east, tracked its radiance on the water as they giggled and recalled the events of the day. Once back at the hotel, Marcos asked Susan if she would enjoy a nightcap then ordered two Damiana in the quiet hotel bar. Susan confessed she had never heard of Damiana.

"It's not widely known even in other parts of Mexico," said Marcos. "Comes from a sage-like plant growing only in the south of Baja. Supposedly, it contains a unique property."

"Medicinal?" asked Susan.

"Well, that depends on what's ailing you," said Marcos wryly. "Don't worry, just take a sip, and see what you think. It's not going to kill you, or I wouldn't have ordered it."

A cautious Susan raised the hand-blown cordial glass to her lips and sampled the liquid on her tongue. "It tastes sweet but quite *sagey*. I've never had anything like this before." She sipped *con gusto* until she drained the glass.

Marcos grinned as he sipped his glass and said casually, "Aphrodisiac."

"Aphrodisiac?"

"You heard me. Legend has it, Damiana is supposed to be an aphrodisiac."

"Ha!" bellowed Susan, "So, just what did you have in mind ordering me an aphrodisiac, mister?"

Shamefacedly, Marcos said, "Nothing, really. I don't think it works at all. Just local folklore."

"Well, you're right. It doesn't," said Susan, rolling her eyes.

Later, as they stood outside Susan's door, Marcos said, "Thanks for dinner and a nice evening. I certainly didn't mean to insult you with the Damiana. When do you depart in the morning?"

"We're supposed to get a godawful early start—bags out by six and breakfast in the restaurant here. On the road by seven."

"What's your next stop—San Quintin, no doubt?"

"And you knew that how?"

"It's home to the only decent hotel between here and Cataviña."

Susan bade Marcos farewell, wished him a good sleep, and thanked him heartily for everything.

***

Marcos had drowned deeply in sleep that night. At his typical breakfast of fruit, *bolillos,* and strong coffee, he reflected on his short time with Susan. *By now, she and her tour group have long departed,* he thought. While anxious to find out what happened to Dave and get back to Joyce, he could not deny his unsettling feeling of apprehension about the whole situation. It made him want to ease into his inquiries. Mentally, he compared what lay ahead to diving into icy cold water, which he had never been able to do. Marcos' inner scientist, however, urged him to get moving, clearly aware that time was of the essence. The much-anticipated breakfast sat at the bottom of his stomach like a pile of cement.

FOUR
San Quintin

On the road to San Quintin, Marcos detoured to the winery in Santo Tomás to purchase a few bottles of red and white wine for any emergencies down the road. His favorite Latin phrase, *in vino veritas,* in wine there is truth, popped into his head as he headed for the winery. He fondly recalled the substance of the many lectures to his anthropology students about Santo Tomás being the site of an old Catholic mission founded in the late 1600s. Most of the old missions the Church had founded to civilize the natives no longer survived nor did the people. The concept of missionization, according to Marcos, was in reality defensive expansionism. The prime directive had been that the Church would build missions, civilize the natives, and in ten years, cease the missionary goals, and turn the settlement into a *pueblo* to ensure Spanish tenure in the vast territories of the New World. A cold shiver cut through Marcos as he thought about how the ill-conceived and cruel concept had destroyed cultures, torn families asunder, spread disease, and enslaved free people. He had published several passionately written articles on the subject, which Dave had analyzed and helped edit.

Setting those thoughts aside, he focused on his drive. North of San Quintin, he gaped at the unending kilometers of hearty tomato plants the water reclamation project had nourished. Specialized equipment penetrated deep into the earth to extract ancient water from gravel sandwiched between layers of impervious basalt.

Hydrologists theorized that the water would not last forever, but billions of gallons were available to green up the desert.

He headed west after turning off the highway in the direction of the Lagoon of San Quintin. He drove along windswept borders of tall cypress trees, passing hectares upon hectares of cornflowers. Growers dried the beauties year-round for use in flower arrangements worldwide. The road turned south a few kilometers after the cornflowers ended and soon led him to the side parking lot of the El Presidente-San Quintin Hotel. His stomach sounded the lunch alarm at the noon hour, unfashionably early by Mexican standards.

He checked in and homed in on the bar in search of a cold beer. The place was dead. A lively, extended Mexican family overflowed at a corner table in the restaurant, the adults watching joyfully as their children ran around, shouted, and generally behaved like children. Their boisterous kid talk echoed back and forth in the cavernous restaurant. The noise did not detract from the hotel's allure of being poised on a vast, white, sandy beach textured with Sahara-like dunes.

Marcos glanced at his watch, wondering when Susan's tour group would arrive and what sites they had seen, detailing in his mind what he would have shown them if he were the tour guide. *Yeah, they no doubt ate a crummy bag lunch and will stay out in the field for as long as possible. But they should for sure be at the hotel for dinner. There's no other place to eat.*

He waited for a half-hour, nursing his beer, then ordered lentil soup and chicken tacos. As he sat surrounded by his silence, he remembered the trips he and Dave had made here on their way to the rock art sites. They had dug hundreds of clams together. Competing feelings of anger and sorrow brought tears to his eyes. *Dave, my friend, I can't bear the thought you intentionally did this. I refuse to believe you just checked out and left us, old buddy. I need help to deal with this,* Marcos reluctantly admitted to himself.

Leaving the hotel, he walked a few kilometers down the beach to stretch and combat the attack of sleepiness, spontaneously deciding to try his luck at clamming. Although he hadn't brought the traditional pitchfork along to help capture the elusive creatures, he would rely on his sheer determination and skill. The huge clams measured fifteen to seventeen centimeters in diameter. It didn't take long to lose himself in the pursuit even as the wind buffeted him in gusts and the surf crashed and pounded the shore. With the tide massaging his ankles, Marcos dug in the sand like a lunatic. He fell over in his elation, got up, and continued to excavate the sand like the trained archaeologist he was.

All at once, he stood up and yelled gleefully, holding up a flat object skyward. "Success!" He raced toward the beach and was pleasantly surprised to spot Susan observing him. He ran over to her and asked her to keep an eye on his clams until he came back. Turning on his heels, he raced back into the water, twice repeating the digging ritual.

Marcos, exhausted and drenched in sand and surf, finally flopped down beside Susan, grinning widely. He caught his breath, pulled out his handy Swiss army knife while grabbing one of the enormous clams, inserted the blade between the lips, severing the muscles at each end, and pried the hinge open. He produced a lime and a thin bottle of salsa picante from his magic pocket and sprinkled the salsa liberally over the clam. Last, he diced the meat into small tidbits and squeezed some lime over it, offering the shell to a very perplexed Susan.

"Hmm, quite a boy scout," she said.

"Have some. It's delicious," urged Marcos. "Here, let me show you." Marcos scooped some of the gooey stuff out of the shell with his fingers and popped it into his mouth with a look of ecstasy. "Go on, try it. You'll love it."

Hesitantly, Susan pinched a small piece, staring at it close up, then with eyes shut, tasted it. She took another small piece, that time savoring it.

"Hey, that's not too bad, just a bit hot and rather chewy. My God, that's the first time I've ever eaten raw clam. What would my mother say?"

"Thanks for guarding my clams. Fancy meeting you here. By the way, we're going to have the best clams for dinner tonight you have ever had in your life, bar none. What was your day like so far?"

Susan's tour group had just pulled in when she decided to take a break and soak in the beautiful beach. She admitted to thinking Marcos was a beached seal or something from a distance and was quite surprised to find him there. "It was pretty humorous watching you dig clams. Was that an archaeologist's crude method to tune up his excavation skills?"

Marcos shook his head and laughed good-naturedly. Then, out of sincere interest, he asked about the tour group's activities for the day.

"Bird watching, mostly shorebirds. We saw brant, lovely creatures, and pelicans, and we went to a tomato farm where we sampled various kinds."

"You mean to tell me you didn't go to the lagoon looking for whales, or to the mudflats for oysters, or the English settlement, the old mill, or the cemetery?"

"Huh?"

"Susan, I honestly don't think your tour company is giving you the best Baja experience, at least so far. I hope it'll get better. Please tell me you at least stopped at La Bufadora near Maneadero?"

"What's that?"

Marcos explained La Bufadora was a famous blowhole that gushed seawater into the air with a fearsome rumble when the tide rushed into the cliffs along the coast. Visitors young and old considered it quite an extravaganza with its unearthly sounds.

"Jeez. Maybe you should be our tour guide, Marcos."

"Ha! Yes, I should. Well, need to pass these to the chef to prepare for dinner tonight. Can you join me, or are you stuck dining with your tour group? You witnessed firsthand how hard I worked for these clams."

"I think I can manage joining you. See you at seven o'clock?"

***

Marcos sipped at his second glass of wine when Susan appeared in the dining room looking ravishing in a long wrap-around skirt displaying a colorful *tapa* cloth print and a brown V-neck T-shirt. He stood and held out the chair for her, complimenting her on her nice *pareu*.

"What the heck's a *pareu*?"

Marcos pointed to her skirt, assuming she had traveled to Tahiti and purchased it there.

"I bought this at a little boutique in Santa Monica. It's just a piece of cloth really," Susan said.

"I know. It's from Tahiti. The Polynesians have all kinds of clever ways to wrap a *pareu* to make everything from skirts to full-length dresses. Wine?"

Susan nodded and asked about the night's offering, whereupon Marcos mentioned Santo Tomás Winery and its *vino blanco*, fruit of the land. "Bet you didn't stop there today, either."

"Nope. I'm truly beginning to think I bought a substandard tour, Marcos."

A tall, lanky, fifty-something, in-charge-kind-of woman burst into the dining room clad in skintight, pink pedal pushers. A white cotton blouse revealed her tanned midriff. Fancy sunglasses perched on top of her head complemented her blonde ponytail. *Not bad*, Marcos noted. The woman surveyed the almost empty room and made a beeline for Marcos' table.

"Mind if I join you?" she asked, pulling out a chair and sitting down. "Always good to see fellow Americans. You are Americans, right? Hi, Andrea Becker," she said with a wave as she gestured to the waiter. "I'm on sabbatical. Teach at Southern California

University—history, Central and South American areas of concentration."

Intently, Andrea informed them she had been visiting Baja for years, finding her trips very inspirational and altogether spiritual. During her many adventures, she honestly felt she had communicated a few times with the ancient spirits, subjects of her research, as she put it, "that must still roam this forsaken peninsula." Andrea's husband, who had recently left her for another man, had labeled her a bona fide head case because she believed in spirits.

"Do you guys believe in spirits?" she asked, peering at Marcos and then Susan.

"I certainly don't," said Marcos. He turned to Susan for her reaction to the boisterous interloper.

Susan remained non-committal and said nothing as she raised an eyebrow at Marcos.

"So, what brings you folks to Baja?" asked Andrea as the waiter placed a Carta Blanca in front of her on a vintage Bohemia coaster.

Marcos' and Susan's eyes locked for a split second. He wondered how much he should tell the intrusive, garrulous professor who appeared to be slightly off center.

"Oh, come on," Andrea said, "is it some secret government mission?"

Marcos cleared his throat with a nervous laugh. "No, I'm an archaeologist. I'm here to look at some rock art. I'm Marcos Andersson, by the way, and Susan is on a tour of natural history. We just met in Tijuana."

Ignoring Susan, Andrea shot off questions like rounds. "Archaeologist, huh? Rock art? Fascinating, right? You know, I've heard of some incredible cave paintings down here, but I've never actually viewed them in all the years I've been coming to Baja. How do you locate them, Marcos? Where *are* they located? Any around here?"

Marcos felt neck pain coming on. Out of sheer politeness, he instructed her that the closest examples were certainly around the Cataviña area, not far south of their present location.

"I'm headed there. I adore that place. Any chance of seeing some cave paintings while I'm there?" asked Andrea flamboyantly, waving her arms around widely.

"Sure. No doubt you'll be staying at the El Presidente. Inquire at the front desk for directions. There's a small cave not far from the hotel approximately a mile up the road and a short hike up the hillside in a rocky outcropping to the east. You'll have to search around a bit, but you'll find the cave, eventually."

"Fantastic. I'm off to Cataviña in the morning," Andrea said, leaning in closely, lowering her voice. "One cannot be too careful while in powerful places like that. Things can turn dangerous because the spirits may be prowling around and up to devilry. I've studied this area and have heard true accounts in which forces lure people to the other side into the spirit world, and they cannot return. You have to know what you're doing when you deal with spirits, let me tell you. I absolutely can assure you spirits are present here, and I don't think they're very content. Something or someone has stirred them up. I can feel it. In my learned opinion, we all must be extremely mindful out there."

Marcos could not tolerate yet another person blathering on about spirits. He tapped on the table, ill at ease, experiencing some relief when the clam cocktails finally arrived. Although he felt obligated to invite Andrea to join them, he found her exhausting. Thankfully, she declined the invitation as she planned to dine with some new friends she had met on the beach that afternoon. As precipitously as she had appeared, Andrea bid them adieu, heading for the bar.

The *cocinero* delivered the cocktails himself with a flourish and hovered quietly while Marcos sampled his work.

"*Sabroso, magnifico, que rico. Es perfect*," Marcos gushed while the chef bowed charmingly.

Susan attacked her cocktail hungrily and commented that she liked it much better than her clam sample that afternoon.

"Well, on a similar note, it's a shame your tour guide didn't take you out to the oyster beds in the bay today. They are rife with beautiful specimens. We could be having oyster cocktails, too."

"Yuck. I've eaten oysters before. They were slimy and smelly."

"You mean you don't know oysters are powerful aphrodisiacs?"

"Honestly, Marcos, again with the aphrodisiacs!" Susan smirked and shook her head. "So," she said, changing the subject, "what do you think of Professor Becker?"

"She's got a great body for a mature broad," said Marcos eyes twinkling.

"Not that. What a motormouth. Don't you agree?"

"Yeah, five more minutes and she would have rolled out her life's story. Her mouth aside, what do you think about all the spiritual stuff, huh? Absurd, right?"

"Well, I don't think it's absurd in the least," Susan said in a rather academic tone. "There is no doubt in my mind that spirits exist. Andrea's right. Evil spirits can exist at the same time as good spirits who could be friendly and beneficial guides."

"Oh great, not you, too. Are you now telling me you're an expert on the spirit world? Perhaps you and the vociferous professor should team up?"

"I read a lot," said Susan, catching Marcos' eyes over her margarita glass.

Thankfully for Marcos, they dropped the topic and sidled into safer conversation, enjoying their food along with the company. After dinner, they sauntered along the beach listening to the pounding surf, marveling at the reflection of the moon dance on the lucent water. When Marcos walked Susan to her room, she thanked him for a lovely evening, softly grazing his cheek with a kiss. Marcos stood motionless for a moment in front of her closed door, touching his hand to his cheek to preserve the kiss a little longer.

He retired to his balcony to contemplate the moonlight on the waves caught in their endless cycle of death and resurrection as they beached themselves like helpless whales only to begin the cycle again. As he absorbed the display, he likened it to the ancient Egyptian sun god Re, reborn at dawn each day. Re rose in the eastern sky each morning and traveled across the sky throughout the day. As he traveled, he fought with the serpent, Apophis, who later died in the west, swallowed up by Nut, goddess of the sky, at the end of the day. Re was reborn again the next dawn after having vanquished the evil serpent.

At the same time, he thought about the excitement of introducing Susan to the whales at Guerrero Negro, but the cycle of the waves also reminded him of individuals who engaged in harmful behavior. His thoughts turned serious as he speculated. *If the ancients here had believed in reincarnation, they wouldn't have thought it mattered what they did. Indeed, Dave could have done something stupid and harmful like the ancients, thinking it didn't matter.* He brought out a bottle of robust, red Santo Tomás. With his Swiss Army knife, he easily pried out the cork, sniffed it with flared nostrils out of habit, and poured himself a glass while his overactive mind still raced.

Savoring each sip of the unique bouquet, Marcos let out a loud sigh. It was good to be alive and back in Baja after a long absence. True to form as a scientist, he analyzed the meaning of Susan's kiss. *Now, don't read too much into a friendly thank-you kiss, Dr. Andersson. Face it. You're out of practice. Don't make anything more of it than that.* Settling on the bed, he warily thought about all the earlier discussions of the spirit world. He forced himself to make sense of it all. The thought that there could be something to it nagged at him as he imagined Dave trapped on the other side. *No, of course not—no science in it*, he reassured himself.

＊＊＊

Marcos greeted the day by pounding down a delicious plate loaded with *huevos rancheros* and observing Susan's tour group amble in. After everyone had scattered in all directions, Susan finally sauntered in with a rather corpulent redhead sheathed in a bright yellow muumuu decorated with red and orange hibiscus and accessorized with a giant, straw handbag. Red tennis shoes further accessorized the garish outfit, peeping out beneath the hemline. Susan came over to his table with her companion, who in her apparent mid-thirties had an imposing but affable presence with a pretty face and delicate porcelain complexion.

"Morning, Marcos. This is Emily, a member of our group. Emily is a mining engineer from Montana. Loves rocks. Thought you two might have something in common. May we join you?"

Marcos stood and helped seat the women while inquiring about the day's itinerary.

According to Susan, the group was heading to the badlands of El Rosario. Then to an onyx quarry at El Marmol and some sandstone formations near Cataviña where they were to overnight. Roadrunners, quail, and dove were on the watch list du jour.

"Well, that's all very well and good, but there's so much more to see like rock art, old missions, fossils. For that matter, several plants you'll start seeing today don't exist anywhere else on this planet, and far more interesting birds inhabit the area than those you just mentioned," Marcos heard himself say with authority.

"You mean we're not going to see all that other stuff? What a crappy tour, Marcos, unbelievably omitting the rock art site. The main reason I signed up for this trip was to see rock art. If I hitched a ride with you today, could you show me the rock art? Please! You know I'm dying to see it, and it would be such a shame to come all this way and miss it," said Susan.

Marcos had not contemplated taking a companion with him on his mission to discover clues about Dave. "Hmm, I don't know. I plan to visit sites Dave and I recorded—a way of reconnecting with him and maybe gaining some insight into his activities here."

Susan turned puppy dog eyes on him, and Marcos, although protective of Dave and reluctant to share his personal experiences, gave in and agreed to show her some of the rock art. "All right. Although the local rock art we'll see pales in comparison to what's in the central part of Baja. I'd hate for you to miss the mission and the plants as well." She maintained her sexy smile for him, and all resolve was lost. "Okay. I was going to stop at Cataviña tonight, regardless. I think Dave would have been thrilled to know I shared Baja with a total novice. He loved doing that—such a wonderfully patient teacher. We'll make it a tribute to him."

"Sounds very appropriate. I'll think of some excuse for not continuing with the tour."

"So, Emily," said Marcos, "you're a mining engineer. Where did you earn your degree?"

"Doctorate. University of Wisconsin."

"What's your specialty?"

"Gold."

His curiosity piqued, Marcos said, "That's interesting. But I know gold is almost non-existent in Baja. So, what brings you to Baja?"

"You're right. I'm just looking at the geology. I am comfortably at home with the volcanics, hailing from Montana."

"Well, I'm your neighbor to the west in Idaho. I escaped from California."

At the mention of California, Emily's eyes lit up, and she seized the opportunity to regale the strangers with the sordid tale of her married life. Her story did not lack drama. In addition to geologic pursuits, she had traveled to Baja to help heal the deep wounds festering from a marriage that ended badly.

"My stuck-up in-laws couldn't stand me, you know, never good enough for their little boy. Thought I was too dumpy and didn't have enough family wealth, and I embarrassed them and their Newport Bay, Southern California Yacht Club elites. Hubby and I did a crash and burn from the constant disapproval. The jackass caved and chose Mommy and Daddy over me. Crank forward, I've made enough of my own, separate money in gold over the past couple years to buy and sell them all a hundred times over. Revenge is even sweeter than I had ever imagined."

Her tale left Marcos and Susan speechless. Finally, Susan excused herself, leaving Marcos to deal with Emily, while she tracked down her tour guide to tell him about her planned departure from the tour.

"Archaeologist, huh? Cool! I suppose we share some interest in rocks but from very different perspectives. What brings *you* to Baja, Marcos? There can't be too much exciting archaeology here. Observing the environment tells me a lot about the lack of sustainability for any kind of civilization, right?"

"Correct. No civilizations have flourished here in the restrictive environment. However, the ancient cultures did produce some of the most incredible rock art seen anywhere in the world and on a prodigious scale. Some of the murals are larger than life-size."

Their conversation flowed easily. As a fellow scientist, Emily intelligently probed his plans, and before long, he was spilling the story of Dave's tragic death and his own quest to get vital information for Joyce and himself.

Emily touched Marcos lightly on his shoulder. "I'm very sorry about your friend, Marcos. The field can be very dangerous at times. Please let me know if there's anything I can do to help."

Marcos shook Emily's hand and offered what was a genuine thank you. "Aside from the ex-husband, where does your geology fit into this trip?"

"Oh, just getting a lay of the land and scouting for zeolites."

"Zeolites?"

"They're formed along with volcanics."

"Yeah, so what's the allure? That's the stuff of kitty litter, isn't it?" Marcos said, chuckling.

"I have found that the zeolites here in Baja contain special qualities. They could likely alter the world economy, possibly bring OPEC to its knees, and shift the balance of power. These special zeolites . . ."

Marcos stood abruptly when Susan returned to the table with a huge grin on her face. "What's so amusing?" Marcos wanted to know.

"I ticked off Tim, our tour guide, with my alternate itinerary. He went off on me as if I were an errant child and said he couldn't be responsible for me if I was going to go gallivanting off with every man who came along. I think he considers me to be a bit of a *slut*."

Emily dismissed Tim with a flapping wave in his direction. "Just ignore him," she said. "Truthfully, if I could find a good man, I'd be off with him in a flash. You go and look at all the rock art you want, sweetie, and do whatever else you want. Don't worry about Tim. I'll take care of that creep." She pulled a can of SlimFast from her straw handbag and slapped it down squarely on the table with a grin of satisfaction.

Emily knocked back the SlimFast and scowled. "I almost forgot to mention this earlier, Marcos," Emily said.

"A geologist contact, Robert Powell, told me he'd been working with some super famous archaeologist in locating the zeolites sites. I was planning on meeting up with him in Guerrero Negro, and I'm sure he's aware of the rock art sites as well. If we connect the dots, could that famous archaeologist be your deceased friend? You might want to talk to Bob. What was your friend's name?"

"Dr. Davis Pearce."

"Yes, he's the one. I remember his name because one of my exes has the last name Pearce."

Marcos' ears perked up. "Tell me about this Robert Powell."

"Not much to tell. Competent but not formally trained as a geologist, but lots of practical field experience all over the world. Tells everyone he graduated from the College of Hard Rocks. Terribly bad joke, I know. I get the impression he's quite the opportunist, for sure pitting one side against the other. In this case, I'd guess my acquaintance, Minister of the Interior Carlos Delgado, and me. Carlos is a huge opportunist first and a rapacious politician from Mexico City second. I think Bob is working for Carlos to help extract zeolites for big government contracts while negotiating similar deals on the side for personal gain."

Marcos did not look forward to meeting the unsavory pair of Bob and Carlos but badly needed any information they might supply about Dave. He thanked Emily for her tip and anxiously expected encountering the pair in Guerrero Negro.

FIVE
Discoveries

———

"Care for some music?" Marcos asked. He and Susan were headed south to El Rosario in his new Lincoln Navigator.

"Depends on what. I can't stand country crooning or rap. What's on your playlist?"

"Mostly classical, and I concur with your dislikes. I brought a nice sampling along—consider it a touch of civilization juxtaposed with primitive Baja. The music can come in handy, like the time I got caught in the dark searching for a cave in a remote canyon." Later that day, Marcos had finally found the cave he was looking for when he realized darkness was descending rapidly. If he explored the cave, the canyon would be full dark when he emerged, and he might not be able to make it back to his truck. Thinking smartly, he had grabbed his portable CD player and turned on Jussi Björling, his family's favorite Swedish tenor, full blast and left it in his truck while he had explored for the cave.

"The brilliant sounds of Mozart's *Don Giovanni* guided me safely back to my vehicle in pitch blackness even from two kilometers away."

"Very resourceful of you," said Susan. "But then, I suppose one has to be resourceful as an archaeologist working in remote places under stressful conditions. I can just envision you battling with insects, wild animals, unfriendly natives, and worst of all, government bureaucrats."

"That's the unromantic story of my career in the field in a nutshell."

As Marcos concentrated on the road, Susan thanked him for allowing her to tag along, promising not to pester him. She vowed to help him out however she could, impressing Marcos with her sincerity and concern. *She's certainly sharp*, he conceded to himself. "Well, señorita, here we are, and I don't even know your last name."

"You want to know my last name? In what language?"

"Jeez, English, of course, silly."

Susan closed her eyes and paused, a strange reaction to a simple question. "Susan?" Marcos asked.

"Okay, Marcos ... it's ... Priest—Susan S. Priest."

"What's the *S* stand for, Susan Priest?"

"It stands for *something*," said Susan winking.

"Come on, what's your middle name?"

Hesitating, Susan blurted out, "Sarah. It stands for Sarah. Sorry, that's what I used to tell my friends when I was in the first grade. Guess I feel young again being here. Or perhaps it stands for sister, the sister I never knew," Susan said under her breath with a distant look in her eyes.

"And just who is Susan Sarah Priest? I mean what does she do when she's not hitching rides in Baja?"

Susan stared out of the car window before responding. "I'm just traveling around Baja on a personal and professional quest to find myself," she said without looking at him once.

"Then I truly hope you find whatever it is you're looking for. Baja is good for that. I used to travel here frequently to recharge my battery and nourish my soul. It's so good to be back again. I've missed it. But I've had other things going on in my life."

"Like what, for instance?" Susan asked, finally turning to look at him.

With more openness than she had offered, Marcos recounted how after much contemplation and soul searching, he had made the decision to segue from archaeology and teaching into investments to make money and run his own tech business. He even shared that just over one year before, he had lost his wife, Carole, to cancer. After her death, Marcos had given up on all archaeological pursuits, sold his business in California, moved to Idaho, and bought a small ranch. "I've been remodeling the house for the past six months. Honestly, this trip signifies my escape from crippling depression."

"I'm sorry to hear about your wife. Are you comfortable telling me about her?"

Susan skillfully shot Marcos question after question about Carole.

Feeling comfortable talking about his wife, Marcos revealed the two had met at the Universidad de Guadalajara when he was a graduate student and Carole was a teaching assistant in British literature. She spoke near-native Spanish. During her academic career, Carole had earned quite a reputation as a brilliant professor of English and as a Jane Austen scholar. His Swedish father's Andersson family and his Mexican mother's Becerra family had experienced heights of elation when the two wed. Marcos teared up.

"Sorry to be so inquisitive. I can tell you loved and admired Carole very much. She sounds wonderful and is a lucky woman to have had such a devoted husband. From your detailed and intimate description of her, I feel as if I know her, almost as well as I know my own sister. So, do you ever think you'll get married again?"

"No, no." Marcos felt certainty in his heart that he could never replace Carole and committed not even to try. "I've decided to devote myself once again to my first love, archaeology, and to those humanitarian projects which help to improve the human condition. That should give me a full and busy life. I want to help people become more self-actualizing. I think being able to reach one's potential is a key ideal that will make a real difference in the world."

"Any children, Marcos?"

"No, we couldn't have children. I think it almost broke Carole's heart when she found out it was impossible for her. We discussed adoption but never followed through."

"Adoption?"

"Yeah, adoption. Why?"

"Oh . . . nothing," Susan said, her voice trailing off.

Marcos eagerly awaited his turn for twenty questions. His curiosity about the woman sitting next to him had grown, and he wanted to know all about her. He cut right to the chase. "And what about you? It appears you aren't married. Ever been married? Anyone significant in your life right now?" Marcos prided himself on his blunt manner.

Susan filled in that she was not married, had never been, but had come close a couple times. She had written it off as never having found the right man. However, she clarified that she had not given up looking by any stretch and still hoped for marriage in the future. Marcos listened intently.

"Hey, if it's meant to happen, it'll happen when it's supposed to. I'll just have to trust the universe on that and go with the flow, to use a familiar phrase," Susan said.

A man would be totally crazy to pass her up, Marcos thought. He realized he knew nothing about Susan's profession, education, or background up to that point and seized the moment during precious travel time to ask her about all those things, trying not to offend her.

After a series of rather innocuous questions, Marcos found out she had attended Millview College in California, graduating with a degree in sociology. *Not much you can do with a bachelor's in sociology*, Marcos thought. Susan turned to him and let him know she was searching for something to do with the rest of her life but needed to gain some perspective first. He let out a loud, "Hmm," and cleared his throat to queue up for the next question.

"I don't want to talk about it now. Maybe later."

Marcos found Susan's explanation vague and too dismissive for his liking, but gave her the benefit of the doubt, for the moment. "Well, in that case, why don't we sit back and enjoy the scenery. Hey, we're not far from El Rosario, considered to be the birthplace of the northern state of Baja California. Quite a place. I had an *outrageous* adventure there, even got myself arrested."

"Whatever for? It couldn't have been for theft. It doesn't look as if there's anything around here to steal," Susan said with a smirk.

"I guess you could say it was for attempted theft in a way."

Susan took the bait. "What happened?"

Marcos' long face turned glum. It was one of his first expeditions to Baja with Dave, sponsored by National Geographic. A few students had accompanied them. It was a joint expedition, both paleontological and archaeological. His esteemed colleagues, Dr. Ross Stewart, the paleontologist, and Dave, had not arrived yet when they set up camp. The local *policia* had arrived on site and accused the team of seeking lost treasure, treasure belonging to his country. Marcos had clearly explained to the officer that they were there solely looking for bones and artifacts and had gained the necessary permission from Mexico City.

The officer had found the explanation unacceptable and arrested Marcos, incarcerating him in the local clink. Marcos sent word to his students to bring two bottles of his best Tequila, which he then shared with the arresting officer, who was also the police chief. When they were roaring drunk, the chief granted permission to the team to dig for treasure if Marcos agreed to split it with him, fifty-fifty. Marcos could not agree to the arrangement fast enough to buy time to make his next move. It was not the first time hard liquor had bailed him out of a jam.

"So tell me, did you find any treasure?" Susan asked.

"In a way. Dr. Stewart was ecstatic when the team uncovered the skull of a giant duckbill platypus-like dinosaur. He clutched it like it was a treasure. I dug up a few arrowheads, quite ordinary. The archaeology turned out to be paltry. I wanted to hire guides to go up into the mountains to look for sites, but the El Rosario natives were scared to death of the mountains." Retelling the incident brought details to mind he'd forgotten. The natives had thought evil spirits of the ancient ones lurked in the mountains and refused to step one foot closer even when the team threw lots of money at them. A blinding flash of insight suddenly struck Marcos. *Oh my God! That was my first encounter with spirits here, which I hadn't realized until this instant. ¡Dios mío!*

"That's fascinating, but why did the chief believe the team was treasure hunting?" She appeared bothered by that notion.

Marcos promptly explained that many legends had circulated for years about pirates coming ashore and hiding treasure in caves.

"Any truth to such stories?"

"Sure, historically speaking. A lot of treasure traveled from the New World back to Spain in those days. Pirates could certainly have confiscated some of it which then ended up in a remote place like this."

"Marcos, do you think Dave was looking for treasure and got mixed up in something that killed him?"

"Anything's possible, I suppose. But what hurts terribly when I think about it is Dave didn't include *me.* I knew zero about what he was doing down here. That's not like him. We were very close. He would have told me. He should have told me. Why didn't he, for heaven's sake?"

Susan blurted out, "Maybe he wanted to communicate with the spirits to learn about the rock art. You wouldn't have supported that, I assume?"

"Correct. That would be ridiculous," Marcos said with a shrug.

Dissipating the tension in the air, they hit a bump in the road, and the CD skipped a bar. "Por un Amor" by Linda Ronstadt played right through Susan's protests about the condition of the road.

Marcos pivoted gladly into a detailed history again. "This road is a miracle. Before paving the so-called old road, a trip from El Rosario to San Quintin could take as long as eight hours. With thick dust and mud during certain seasons, you may as well forget it. Dave, the current governor Ramiro, and I came down here when we were graduate students before paving. It took us an entire summer to travel to La Paz and back to Los Angeles."

The pair descended into a deep, eroded ravine or *barranca* called Malpaís—the badlands. Thanks to the erosion, it was an excellent place to search for fossils. As they entered El Rosario, Marcos pointed out the empty jail, a single room with iron bars over the heavy wooden door, where the local law enforcement had incarcerated him. Susan demanded Marcos stop so she could get a picture of him behind bars, hinting to him teasingly if he did not behave himself, she would send the incriminating photo to his local newspaper. It felt good to laugh together.

Marcos easily slipped into the role of tour guide. After the jail, he drove along the river west of town to La Bocana, the bay on the Pacific Ocean. After that, Marcos showed her the adobe walls melted down from groundwater that were once a Dominican mission. Finally, they bought cold drinks from a tiny, modestly supplied store. Ancient glass cases proudly displayed fantastic, giant ammonites exceeding forty-five centimeters in circumference, straight from the badlands. A few arrowheads were scattered about display shelves.

"We'd better get a move on. We have a lot more to see today," said Marcos, ushering Susan out the door toward the car.

Susan spoke briefly about the little town being remarkable and wanted to know if the people had any plans to restore the mission. The townspeople had a fund to restore it, Marcos explained, to which he had often contributed. "Want to donate something to it? Just go back inside and give your money to Señora Espinosa."

Marcos escorted her back inside and introduced her to Sra. Espinosa. Marcos found himself truly impressed with Susan's generosity when she pulled out two crisp hundred-dollar bills and handed them to the señora, who graciously accepted the donation. She wrapped up some freshly baked empanadas and handed them to Susan with a big hug.

"That was very generous of you, Susan. Or did you just buy some very expensive empanadas?"

She shrugged and gave him an enigmatic smile.

"It won't be long now. Let's see who can spot the first boojum tree," said Marcos, childlike, as he rolled the window down. "Loser has to buy the winner dinner tonight. Dave and I always used to play this game. Takes me back. What do you say?"

"I'd say I'm buying dinner tonight. I don't have a clue what a boojum tree looks like."

Marcos assured Susan that spotting was easy if she could envision a giant upside-down carrot with prickles on its skin—or perhaps a parsnip because they were whitish characters straight out of Dr. Seuss. When the trees aged, they developed branches resembling grotesque arms curled outward from their bodies. He suggested they ought to have a prize for who could spot the most grotesque one as well. Marcos was fiddling with the stereo changing CDs when Susan exclaimed, "There. I see one. A boojum, Marcos, is that a boojum?"

"Yep. You got it. Congratulations. Guess I owe you dinner."

"Now what? These are fantastic. You're right. Look, now there's a whole valley of them. They're all over the hillside and off into the distance as far as I can see. I've never seen anything like them."

"Have you been to Arizona?"

"Yes, once to a meeting in Phoenix."

"What kind of meeting?"

"Oh, just a meeting, nothing special."

"Well, anyhoo, do you remember what saguaros are?"

"Yes, they're big cacti with arms reaching upward, right?"

"Yes, well here we don't have saguaros, we have *cardones*. They look something like saguaros, but they're four times larger and quite incredible. We'll start seeing some soon. Want to go for cocktails on who sees the first one?"

"You're on. Hey, Marcos, do you have any Vivaldi CDs?"

Marcos reached into the back seat to retrieve a case of CDs. "Aha, found it!"

As he triumphantly popped *The Four Seasons* into the player, Susan exclaimed, "Aha, yourself! I win. Look at the saguaro, I mean *cardón*, over there."

"Well, what do you know. You slyly tricked me. You play dirty."

"Yeah, but you needed a handicap. You've been here before and surely know where each one is and given each a name to boot."

"Fine, I buy the drinks too," Marcos said at the same time as he slowed his vehicle and made a sharp turn west into the desert onto a dirt track.

"What's going on?" asked Susan.

Like a professional train conductor, Marcos announced they were approaching San Fernando Velicatá, the only mission Father Junipero Serra of Alta California had ever founded in Baja. He had done that while traveling on his way to Alta California. Hardly anything of the mission remained beyond its historical significance, which attracted thousands of tourists yearly. In a cloud of chalky dust, they headed west for several kilometers.

Marcos stretched his arm out the window indicating they had arrived at San Fernando Velicatá. "The usual convention in those days was to give the mission a saint's name first, followed by an Indian name, usually that of the village where the mission was located," Marcos said.

Marcos pulled over and parked. As the two got out and strolled down the quaint road, he surveyed the landscape thoroughly, abruptly halting near an extensive outcropping of basalt. "See anything else of interest?" he asked.

"Well, I see other plants, but I don't know what they're called."

"I'm not talking about plants. Keep looking."

"I don't know what you're talking about."

"Keep looking," urged Marcos as he walked over and stretched himself across a basalt boulder, tapping his toe on a rock surface.

Susan continued to look around 360 degrees. In growing exasperation, she turned to Marcos with her hands planted on her hips and begged him for a clue.

He tapped his toe more rapidly. "I am giving you a clue," he said.

"Oh brother, Mr. Archaeologist," said Susan bending down over the spot, "is that what I think it is? It looks like a drawing of a man with a bow and arrow shooting a deer or some kind of animal. Holy moly."

"You got it. Never thought you'd see it. Congratulations, finally."

"Look. What's that? There's another one. Over there—another one."

Susan set off like a kid on a birthday scavenger hunt as she threw out caution and clamored over every rock, examining every surface. When Marcos calculated she had exhausted the inventory, he rewarded her with a bottle of cold beer from the cooler in his car, some fruit, and the bag of Señora Espinosa's empanadas. Leaning against the car, the two enjoyed their lunch together.

"Wow! Señora Espinosa sure can make mean empanadas. And the beer and fruit are great complements. Thanks, Marcos. I worked up quite an appetite climbing around and searching for rock art." She took a big bite of empanada. "Oh, and you're not a half-bad tour guide, by the way."

"Voilà, the thrilling but exhausting world of archaeology."

"Oh, Marcos, this is way beyond exciting. I'm so grateful you brought me here. Tell me everything about this place."

Marcos didn't wish to quell Susan's ardor but knew there wasn't much to tell. "Well, you have noticeable examples of pictographs the ancients painted and petroglyphs they carved. It is rare that both exist at the same site."

"And the figures?" Susan asked like an excited student.

"Yes. Those are anthropomorphic figures represented by hunters with bows and arrows, as well as zoomorphic figures in the form of deer, sheep, dogs or perhaps coyotes. I suspect the dogs aided in the hunt."

"Please, tell me more."

"You see rectilinear, curvilinear, and geometric designs are also present. We moderns lack knowledge as to their significance. In some places, like the Southwest, we can sometimes correlate contemporary symbols with ancient ones, but here any descendants of the people are gone, and we can't ask them." Marcos sighed.

"What a shame. Do you know anything about their age?"

That was another difficult question for Marcos due to the problem of dating them directly. "Do you see that lichen over there? It's growing over one of the petroglyph designs. That means it's younger than the underlying petroglyph. I've dated the lichen here. It stretches back three hundred years. Therefore, we know the rock art is older than that. It was here when the missionaries arrived, and it doesn't appear the natives were producing it at that time or after the mission period, at least not at this site."

The setting for the rock art was staggering. Marcos and Susan stood reverently to drink in fully the gorgeous site with the basalt walls flanking the valley with its meandering stream, like Marcos and Dave had done so many times before. As they casually turned to observe behind them, remnants of the dam constructed by missionaries were visible in the side canyon.

History had not recorded why the beautiful oasis had failed. Marcos had opined for some time that the natives had very likely revolted because the missionaries had treated them like slaves. Marcos and Dave had recorded that very site together many years ago. Dave had predicted as he stood in the same spot that one day they would both finally discover the key to understanding the meaning of the glorious rock art. It had been of utmost importance to him—to both of them.

"Who knows, maybe Dave discovered the meaning—I mean, I certainly hope he actually discoverd the key," said Marcos wistfully.

"Perhaps he did, Marcos. For Dave's sake, I hope so."

"I have to wonder, however, if it was worth dying for?"

With a noticeable change in mood between them, Marcos pointed in the direction of the car and suggested they head out. They retraced their steps in silence back to the car. Several kilometers down the main highway, Marcos slowed and pulled into a sandy creek bottom, stopping the car and motioning Susan to follow. They headed on foot, continuing up the canyon toward another rock art site nearby that he and Dave had discovered a very long time ago.

Pointing out various plant species in the picturesque but unlikely oasis, Marcos said, "Susan, look at the *torotes*—elephant trees. They dominate this whole area. I have my own private collection of baskets woven from their bark. The Seri Indians on the opposite side of the Sea of Cortez made them. Aren't they something else? Take these beauties in. This is the only area where they grow."

"The elephant trees make this area incredible," said Susan. "I bet your baskets are fantastic."

Susan and Marcos hiked up the watercourse, encountering several deep depressions in the rock called *tinajas*, which trapped an astonishing volume of water. They scaled the side of the arroyo and headed toward a large, granite outcropping. It was a steep climb, especially the last ascent before Marcos signaled a halt while he stood in front of a crevice in the rock. He squeezed in, motioning for Susan to follow. Once inside, the enclosure opened up to a small chamber approximately five meters by one and one-half meters wide and less than two meters high at the tallest point.

"Aha!" exclaimed Susan, "I see pictographs—they're painted."

Marcos watched his awestruck student study the colors of the cave—reds, blacks, whites, yellows, and blues all over the walls. However, there were no naturalistic designs at this site, only meanderings, concentric circles, and geometric forms. It was unusual since most sites depicted people and animals—naturalistic representations.

Not surprisingly, Susan asked, "What does it all mean?"

He shrugged in frustration. "The world may never know the meaning of all the designs." Numerous archaeologists predating him and Dave had attempted to associate designs by ethnographic analogy from the explanations of living natives. That was risky business because of cultural differences and changes over time, coupled with the sad fact there were not any living ancestors of the people who produced the art. Thus, with no progress at all in unlocking clues, the meaning had remained a mystery in the field of archaeology.

"We can't determine what went on in the minds of the people, even though what you see here are psychological statements frozen in time."

"What you need, Marcos, is a fresh method of *seeing* this art, so you can finally capture the meaning."

"No kidding, wouldn't that be nice," Marcos said. "I'm driving myself mad wondering what Dave was up to when he came down here. He was on to something. I can feel it in my bones. He quite possibly *saw* something. Next up, Cataviña."

Not far to the north of Cataviña, they entered a picture-postcard valley landscaped with huge granite boulders. The wind had riddled the stone with carved-out caves. Marcos named it his enchanted rock garden, and for good reason.

Like a hidden sanctuary, a charming, little hotel with its fitting Mexican architecture cropped up suddenly. Frank Lloyd Wright would have approved how well it fused with the environment. The staff greeted them effusively since few guests visited that remote corner of the world. Marcos asked for two, commodious corner rooms each featuring a special alcove where he liked to sit, think, and imbibe.

"Dr. Andersson," said the desk clerk, "we have one other guest in the hotel, a Dr. Andrea Becker, history professor from Los Angeles. She checked in earlier and asked for you. That's how we knew you were coming. Then she asked about any caves with paintings. I told her about the one about a mile up the road, and she took off to see it without even taking her luggage to her room. She was in a real hurry."

***

Later that afternoon after the traditional siesta, Marcos knocked on Susan's door. "Want to go for a hike?" he asked when Susan came to the door yawning.

"Where are we going?" she asked, stifling another yawn.

"Time for more rock art—some truly unique pictographs."

In a dither, Susan threw on some clothes and met Marcos in the lobby. They headed north in the Navigator a mile or so, crossing a ravine that had water in it. *Very unusual for Baja this time of year*, Marcos thought. He parked on a little rise next to another vehicle with California plates. They were about to have company.

"Must be Andrea. Where is it exactly? I don't see any cave from here."

Marcos pointed up at the hillside looming in front of them about one kilometer away. Crossing a dry arroyo, they threaded through the maze of sagebrush and began the ascent. Marcos stopped at the edge of an overhang. It didn't take Susan long to discover the contents of the rock shelter.

"Aha," said Susan, "pictographs—painted in—red, black, white, yellow, but only meanderings and circles, no humans, no animals." Susan had caught on brilliantly and apparently had learned by now just to behold and not to ask Marcos about the meaning of the rock art. "Well, can you at least tell me how old these are?"

"Not exactly," was his classic response. "I once scraped off a small amount of the pigment, which has an organic binder, and took it to the C14 lab at the University of California. Unfortunately, there was not sufficient material for an accurate reading. You need to have at least one gram, but I didn't want to destroy the painting to get more. Creating pictographs is an ancient tradition though, possibly extending back ten thousand years. In my opinion, the ancients still produced them right before European contact in the 1600s."

Marcos and Dave had discovered two more small sites of pictographs but no petroglyphs in this area a decade ago. He clarified for Susan it was likely attributable to the geology other than anything else. The sea covered the Baja Peninsula at one time, but due to a violent cataclysm produced by volcanic eruptions, Baja rose out of the sea. The whole peninsula connected to the mainland of Mexico but eventually separated about twelve thousand years before. The older, exposed surfaces were composed of granite while the younger rock was basalt. Chemically, they were the same, both having a volcanic origin. The only difference was that the granite had cooled more slowly, allowing for the formation of the characteristic large crystalline structure as opposed to the different, uniform composition of basalt. When basalt cooled rapidly, the result was obsidian, or volcanic glass. The area where Marcos and Susan stood was all granite, which accounted for the weathering and odd sculptures of Marcos' enchanted rock garden.

"There's still another small cave in the same formation to the northeast of here. Let's go check it out."

Scrambling over huge boulders and dodging menacing cholla, they came to the entrance of the small rock shelter hidden from view until they practically fell into it. Marcos bowed like a knight, and gallantly motioned for Susan to enter first. He was admiring her adroitness when he heard her gasp. "Marcos! Come quick!"

Marcos ran toward the sound of her voice and found Susan with her chest heaving. She met his eyes then held out a shaky hand, pointing. Barely one meter in front of her sat Andrea—or rather Andrea's corpse, with head back, mouth twisted in an exaggerated, open position, a look of terror defining her face. She resembled Edvard Munch's painting *The Scream* with her hands clenched in fists at the sides of her head, her face contorted in an endless, now silent scream. Even the walls of the cave evoked the background of the Munch painting. Susan collapsed, trembling into Marcos' arms. He pressed her to his chest and held her until she settled down. He incredulously peered around the cave looking for something, anything.

Still holding her, he asked, "What do you suppose caused this?"

Susan surprised Marcos, not taking long to regain her composure somehow. She examined Andrea, apparently looking for signs of a cause of death. She checked for broken bones, snakebites, and any obvious contusions, finding nothing. "Marcos, I think she was scared to death. Perhaps she should have followed her own advice and been more circumspect of the spirits," she said gravely. "I find no physical trauma indicated here. Looks like a heart attack, which can be agonizing and frightful. The question is, what are we going to do about this, Marcos?"

Marcos all the while had stood by while Susan worked. Her thoroughness impressed him under the macabre circumstances. "We need to leave her as is and report the death to the hotel. They can take care of things through the local authorities. The less we have to do with it the better. It might even be a day or two before the authorities get here, given the remoteness."

Hurrying back, Marcos and Susan informed the hotel staff about Andrea's death. The horror-stricken, young clerk said, "You know, Dr. Andersson, even the people who live around here are afraid to go into those caves. They believe ghosts of the ancient ones inhabit them. I warned Dr. Becker about it, but she just ignored me and turned her back. Now look what's happened. How did she die?"

"We think she was scared to death," said Marcos.

The desk clerk, ashen-faced, nodded his head grimly in complete understanding.

SIX
Cataviña

Marcos stole a few moments from the day to rest quietly and collect his thoughts. He sat alone at a table in the bar nursing a Modelo beer. With the obvious exception of the horrific end to his afternoon, he decided it had been a productive day re-visiting the sites he and Dave had discovered in what seemed now another life. The visits had re-connected him to Dave until he and Susan had discovered Andrea's hideous corpse. He had seen plenty of dead bodies in the past, but the two deaths associated with his beloved rock art were now dragging him against his will into the realm of the existential.

Marcos looked up to see Susan burst into the dining room with the geologist, Emily. Instead of her bright yellow muumuu, she was wearing electric blue. It made him smile, a much needed smile. *Boy she's a force unto herself,* he mused. Members of the tour group began seating themselves at the reserved tables. Susan saw Marcos, waved, and headed toward him with Emily.

"Mind if we join you?"

Marcos stood to greet them and motioned for them to sit as he queried Emily about her day.

"It was okay for a geologist type, but it sounds like you and Susan had a much more interesting one. Too bad you're not our tour leader, Marcos."

Marcos realized Susan had not told Emily about Andrea's death, which was best at this point. "Yeah, just what I need," said Marcos, "a tour guide gig."

Susan ordered a glass of wine while Emily stuck to a Diet Coke. Soon after their drinks arrived, the tour leader, Tim, came over with a peeved look plastered on his face and asked the women to join the group, "please," so the wait staff could serve dinner. Marcos disliked Tim immensely. *What a jerk*, he thought as he shook his head.

Susan rolled her eyes, shrugged, and got up to rejoin the group with her untouched wine in hand.

A disgusted Emily said, "I don't know how many hundreds of employees I have working for me who call me boss all over the world, and I'm paying good money to be treated like a child here by that *moron*."

As Susan and Emily departed leisurely, Marcos stood with a wry smile and encouraged them to enjoy their meals as his thoughts turned to his plans. He craved his standard Mexican fare—a large combination plate with a taco, chicken enchilada, chile relleno, and the inevitable rice and refried beans. He enjoyed washing it all down with another Modelo. All that was bound to abate his increasing hunger from the day's activities, providing him comfort and relaxation.

Marcos attacked his food and was finished eating while most of the tour group lingered over their meals, complaining about this or that. He signed the bill, left a hefty tip for the servers, and went out to enjoy his after-dinner coffee and Kahlua by the pool. The cacophony created by the people talking with their outside voices, scraping their chairs on the tile floor in the restaurant, caught up with him after he sat for only a few minutes.

The guest rooms of the hotel all faced onto open courtyards. Marcos could clearly hear conversations in the corridors with doors opening and banging shut as people returned to their rooms for the night. The noise disturbed him more that night than usual. He was attempting to enjoy his solitude when Susan came across the lawn to where he sat, piercing the silence.

"Mind if I join you for a moment?"

"No problem. I was just thinking about taking a walk to visit a spot where Dave and I used to camp before the hotel was built. It's supposed to be a full moon tonight. That place is enchanting at night, especially with a full moon. We won't need flashlights. Care to join me?"

Susan gladly accepted the offer. "It's still early, and I'm much too wound up to sleep, anyway."

As they walked, she unloaded a bit on Marcos, first by informing him of her total excitement about the rock art, but second, how the discovery of Andrea's corpse had drained all the joy out of it.

"Marcos, I'm deeply concerned that Andrea's death may connect to the rock art or the spirits. Have you considered yet that Dave may have died from the same cause?"

"Well, no. Of course not. Come on, let's keep going. A walk is just what the doctor ordered. Hopefully, it will clear our heads of all this nonsense."

Marcos led Susan through an ancient, rusty iron gate and a rock garden into a courtyard then through another gate that opened onto a rocky dirt path leading to the west into the desert. It took no time at all to leave behind the lights of the hotel. They no longer heard the heavy drone of the generator.

Susan looked up and gasped as a shooting star zoomed across the heavens. The air was still and cool on their cheeks—the desert scent mind-blowing.

"The stars are so bright and very close. It's a very different sky here. This does not exist by any stretch in Los Angeles," Susan said. "I can't wait 'til the moon comes up."

Up a canyon to the west, a coyote howled, and his pack members returned the call. The desert embraced them. Mirages of grotesquely shaped boojum trees and giant cacti appeared above them ominously.

"I feel transported to a fantasy world," Susan said. "Small wonder, Marcos, why you love Baja so much."

He stiffened, and she asked, "Are you still thinking about Andrea's horrible death?"

"Oh, I don't know, exactly. I guess lots of things are running through my mind, including things I miss. Baja reminds me of them."

"Can you tell me what?"

"Carole for one. Dave for another. He was my colleague and best friend in the world. We shared a special passion and enthusiasm for Baja I can't find words to describe. Discovered sites together. Dug together. Camped out, explored, dreamed, and got blotto together. Made an honest-to-God blood pact that one day we would discover the meaning of the rock art. His wife intimated to me Dave was onto something, a breakthrough. I believe her. He had an overwhelming compulsion to return here, and . . . and it killed him."

"I understand you miss Carole and Dave, Marcos," Susan said gently. "Maybe it's time to let them go, remember them fondly, and be thankful for all the love, support, and friendship they gave you. Let them go, Marcos."

"I've been trying, but it isn't easy. First Carole, now Dave. Who's next, for heaven's sake?"

"This too shall pass. You must believe that. The grieving is a process we must all endure, a part of life, a life in which you at least had known them both well."

"Of course I got to know them. What do you mean?"

"Oh, nothing."

Regrouped, Marcos suggested they not dwell on the losses right then but try to live in the moment. A visible glow appeared in the sky just as they looked eastward. The moon was rising over the mountain. The pair sat snuggled together in wonderment, gazing at the moon as it gradually emerged and ascended as a towering globe illuminating the entire desert. As it rose higher, the moon decreased in size, leaving the landscape basking in its bright, bold glow.

Attempting not to break the mood, Marcos leaned in and whispered, "Come on, I want to show you something. It's the place Dave and I used to camp that I told you about."

He left the dirt road, snaking his route skillfully, skirting treacherous cholla, and working south encircling a low ridge. After a while, they came into a thicket of cottonwoods fed by a stream that burbled lyrically in the night. Marcos pointed out the remains of a long-abandoned, adobe ranch house. Nearby, the rusted remains of a Model-T truck lay in the last throes of decomposition. He bade Susan follow. He had something further to show her.

Marcos lightly grasped Susan's hand and led her up a small slope northeast of the house. They reached a flat below the crest of the ridge running behind the home. There stood a cemetery. They could see a half-dozen graves with mounds of rocks and markings in various stages of decay. The earliest marking was 1898, the most recent, 1916. Most were illegible. The family name Soto cropped up on rock faces several times.

"Shush," Susan said, holding her finger over her lips.

The two waited without a sound. The cool, dry air surrounding them grew noticeably still, absent any vibrations. The frogs ceased croaking in the stream, the coyotes yipped no more, and the insects suddenly had nothing to say. The atmosphere braced in anticipation of something portentous, unfamiliar, and foreboding. Susan reached for Marcos' hand, and they both squeezed hard in reaction to the unnatural silence. A faint, pale purple light appeared before them, lustrous. As if in pursuit of them, the light swept close and focused as it glowed brighter and more intensely, illuminating them. It was simultaneously calming and frightening. Neither of the two could move nor speak. Marcos contemplated screaming and running away fast to loosen the grip of the incomprehensible presence, but he couldn't move.

Susan slipped into some kind of altered state. Marcos, frozen in place, was only able to observe her through his anguish, powerless to act. After an incalculable moment—it could have been five minutes or five hours—the dimension of time ceased to exist in that level of being, the purple quintessence faded, and Susan gradually returned to the present. The aberrant stillness waned, and the normal sounds of the night recommenced. They sat stunned, clasping hands tightly, not daring to look or speak to each other for a long time.

"Susan, my God, are you all right?" asked Marcos, visibly shaken.

"Yes, I think so," Susan said bewildered, obviously not quite fully oriented to the present level of reality.

"What was that strange episode all about?" asked Marcos anxiously. "Where in the world did you go?"

"Didn't you experience it? Did you feel or experience anything?"

"It scared the crap out of me, but other than that, nothing until the purple flash went away. So, what happened with you?"

"I can't talk to you about it right now. Please take me back to my room. I need to sleep. Maybe we can talk about it in the morning."

Marcos couldn't pull anything meaningful out of his archaeologist's knowledge bank to explain the strange occurrences that night and worried that he had lost his grip on reality. *I have never been that scared on any of my expeditions*, he admitted. *What is going on? I can't deal with this rationally. Vad tror du, pappa?*

Both unnerved by the ordeal, they walked hurriedly hand in hand back to the hotel, agreeing to meet early for breakfast the next morning to talk honestly about the occurrences. Marcos did not like it one bit. *Dave, do you hear me? Not one tiny bit!*

***

"For the love of God, what was that?" Marcos cried out in a panic as he bolted upright out of a fitful sleep some hours later, knocking his head against the wooden headboard. Beads of sweat covered his face as he tried to recall the details of what he would come to refer to as a nightmare. Squinting, he remembered seeing bright colors swirling so fast around him that he still felt dizzy. Somebody or something had tortured him with a bright purple light in his eyes. Dark, shadowy figures pulled at him, trying to drag him down. He couldn't move. "Damn, Dave. Is that what you endured?" he mumbled. "Did you somehow cause this to happen? Jeez, I'm afraid to fall asleep."

**

Marcos boasted often about never having headaches. The next morning, however, he suffered from what could only be described as the mother of them all, affecting his eyes. He was dog-tired as he stumbled into the dining area, disheveled, to root around for coffee to nurse the headache. He had heard that caffeine worked well on certain types, and he needed relief badly. Plain old Advil had not made the slightest dent. He felt like plucking his eyes out.

Marcos looked around the empty room and then at his watch, noting the 4 a.m. hour. *Jeez! The stupid chickens aren't even up yet.* He lurched toward the coffee display, grabbed the hot carafe, and poured himself a cup, spilling a large quantity on the floor. *Certifiable klutz! I'm in no mood for this.* He slumped into a nearby chair feeling overwhelmed from a fitful sleep and walking the floor. His thoughts were random, and he was nervous and grouchy.

As he sat and sipped at his coffee, clinking his fingernails on the cup, he conjectured in advance about permutations of what Susan could tell him about their encounter. He had no clue about classifying it as a brush with the dark side in a nightmare, some weird kind of out-of-body transcendence, a religious experience, or entirely his mind playing tricks. Correction, their minds both playing tricks. He made the decision to keep quiet about his personal nightmare for now. He was not altogether certain he had the mental wherewithal to deal with Susan. Therefore, he sat in silent pain.

He was surprised when he looked up and saw Susan, unkempt, as she walked toward him, penetrating his space in the dining area. *Great! Must have somehow conjured her up since it's still way too early for breakfast. So much for gathering my thoughts.* He instinctively poured her a cup of coffee before she sat down at his table. She drank it black and smiled her appreciation over the brim.

"Couldn't sleep either?" he asked.

"Not really. You?"

"Can't remember a worse night, ever. As much as I hate to admit it, that purple light thing haunted me. Genuinely scared me."

Susan leaned in close. "Tell me, Marcos, *now* do you believe in the supernatural, in spirits, that sort of thing?"

"Well, I believe it's a reality for some people, some cultures."

"No, no, no, I mean, is it a reality for you?"

"I am a scientist and historian. I don't dwell on alternate realities very much. But, if you are referring to religion and such, I lack patience with the whole darn concept—too many wars, too much misery, too much divisiveness in the name of religion, too much intolerance."

"Okay, Mr. Archaeologist, then how do *you* explain what happened last night? Enlighten me, please." Her tone was gruff.

"Susan, I don't know. I'm still sorting through the evidence, as it were. Right now, I am too tired to face it at all. In a word, the experience remains incomparable."

"Well, there you have it. As you would say, welcome to evidence of the supernatural world," Susan said dead serious, eyeball-to-eyeball.

Marcos predicted the proverbial freight train was due to hit him any minute. He turned the conversation back on Susan, demanding an explanation about her experiences the night before, the part she had declined to tell him then.

Never dropping her gaze, she said, "I have many things I need to tell you, among them a confession. But first, I must ask you a huge favor."

"All right, what is it? You can ask but no guarantees from this end."

"Marcos, I want to quit the tour group. I want you to take me with you. I want to *see* the rock art with you. I want to experience Baja through your eyes. I'm just wasting my time, otherwise."

"Hold on a minute! I told you I'm here on serious, personal business that could turn dangerous. I don't even know how long I'll be here in Baja. Admittedly, I've enjoyed your company, thank you. Now, I must get down to business. And I have tight time constraints."

"Marcos, please, I can help you. I won't get in the way. I'll be an asset, I promise. This is very important to me."

He grew irritated at Susan's presumptuousness. "I didn't come down here to be a tour guide. I have some life and death matters I must attend to. Dave's wife is anxiously awaiting information to send to her insurance company. I'm sorry, but it just wouldn't be appropriate under the circumstances. Besides, I need to be alone to connect with Dave by visiting some of the sites we both cherished for years."

"Okay, fine, Marcos, I'll tell you what happened to me last night. Please focus and hear me out. A presence, an anthropomorphic vagueness, appeared before me. I knew it was Ignacio Soto, who had first settled this land in 1856 along with his wife, Consuela. He told me they had eight children, three of whom died young. Of the remaining five, two boys and three girls, only one of the sons remained behind to help run the ranch. The others moved away as they married.

"Pepe Soto, the one who stayed, married a girl from a little *rancheria* called Dos Piedras, twenty-five kilometers to the east. They had six children. Again, all left except Juan, who remained behind, married and produced five children. A flash flood killed two of them. The authorities recovered their bodies days later a mile downstream. After that, a boy, Julio, stayed to continue the family ranch operation along with his seven children, all of whom eventually left. Life had been too difficult here and the seduction of the larger towns too strong."

Marcos stood by without a sound, astonished. The first thing that came to mind, typical for him, was that somebody needed to verify historically what Susan had presented.

"There's more, Marcos. Julio finally died in 1916. His wife went to La Paz to live with their daughter, abandoning the family homestead after four generations of barely eking out an existence. What had kept the family going was Ignacio's dream of *buried treasure*. He had a vision as a young man that treasure hunters had buried a vast trove in the region of the Jesuits' settlement before the locals had expelled them. Neither he nor his sons ever found it, if it ever existed at all. However, the thought of treasure had been enough to keep them here, searching, hoping, existing."

Marcos didn't know whether to feel impressed, relieved, or freaked out. "I can't believe you received all that information. I was right there with you, and I got nada."

"There's more information. Try not to wig out. You said you and Dave had a connection with that place. You used to camp there, right?"

"Yes."

"Well, just as the saga of the Soto family was fading away from me, I had a distinct feeling Dave was attempting to communicate from the other side. I felt his presence, faintly, but we didn't make contact. The connection was broken."

The color drained from Marcos' face as she spoke of Dave. He rested his head in his hands, propped up by achy arms. He could not muster enough energy to look up at her as he warily expressed his incredulity about what she'd just said. "Get real, Susan, how can you expect me to believe what you said about Dave?"

"There's a reason I received that information. Brace yourself, here comes the truly difficult piece. God, I surely hope you will not hate me. I wouldn't blame you if you did." Susan paused to look straight at Marcos and took a deep breath. "You see, I haven't been altogether honest with you." She let out her breath, nervously.

"Honest about what, exactly?"

"My name for starters."

"What, so you're not Susan Priest?" asked Marcos confused.

"Sort of, but not really. My first name is Susan and my last name is Priest in English. That's true. However, in Hebrew, my last name is Cohen. Does that name ring any bells?"

"Susan Cohen? No, should it? Are you a former student?"

"How about Dr. Cohen?"

There it was—the freight train about to collide with Marcos' reality. "Whoa! You're the bizarre doctor who called me at my home in Idaho. The shrink—the psychic! All this time I thought that person was old . . . I mean, your voice on the phone sounded old. What the heck, Susan!"

"My professional voice, I guess. I'm so very sorry, Marcos," Susan said sounding sincere. "I wanted to tell you, but we were getting along so well, and I've been having such an incredibly wonderful time, I didn't want to ruin it. Then it got harder and harder to say anything until now." Susan hung her head. "I didn't want to keep up the charade any longer. And I am so sorry for how I've hurt you. I only hope it's not irreparable." A tear trickled down her cheek.

"I must tell you, lady—you have some set of *cajones* on you. I ignored the red flag when you conducted what appeared to be much more than a nonprofessional investigation of Andrea's body. How non-scientific of me. How did you know about me, that I was traveling to Baja and would be eating in the special restaurant in Tijuana?" Marcos felt betrayed and duped at the same time. It was too overwhelming for him to handle while still dealing with Dave's death.

"In the interest of full disclosure, I have yet another confession to make. Why not, as I'm sure you detest me by now for good reason. I had you tailed by a private detective right up to when you entered the restaurant in Tijuana. Perhaps you saw me talking on my no-good cell phone when I came in. It was to him."

"How long has this been going on?" Marcos asked brashly. "My local sheriff told me some guy was asking about me around town in

Salmon. *Your* guy, I assume. Was he driving a compact, black, Japanese make car?"

"I confess to hiring the detective, Marcos. Yes, he drove the black, Japanese car. But the entire situation was serendipitous. Let me explain. I have recently become obsessed with the concept of *psychic archaeology* and remembered hearing something about rock art in Baja, and what a mystery it was. By pure chance, I phoned the University of California Anthropology Department chairperson who informed me about Dave and his work. The chair mentioned Dave was away on a dig but also suggested I get in touch with you. The rest is, as we say, history." Susan sighed.

"Susan, you're a doctor. Why didn't you just put on your professional, game face and divulge everything to me in the first instance?" *Weird*, he thought.

"I tried to over the phone, but you rejected me out of hand, remember?"

"My dearest friend had just died. Can you blame me? You hit me out of nowhere on the heels of that devastation," Marcos snapped back.

"No, certainly not. In any case, I needed to have you checked out to see if you would be a trustworthy person with whom I could travel to Baja. You could have been some kind of pervert for all I knew. You checked out okay, in case you're interested." She smiled faintly before gazing down at her shoes.

Marcos fought back the fury rising inside him as the redness increased in intensity from his neck to his scalp. Rarely that angry, he let it rip. Sputtering, he managed, "I ought to strangle you! I feel so . . . so . . . invaded and utterly deceived! How could you?" *Helvete!*

"I humbly ask for your forgiveness. I realize how inconsiderately I have handled everything from our initial encounter in Tijuana. Truthfully, I've been going through some bad times lately, and I can't seem to do anything right. I strongly feel the personal need to be here in Baja, to gain some perspective on what path to take next in my life's journey. Again, please, forgive me."

Marcos fumed with anger and frustration and didn't care if Susan knew it. He hadn't felt that brand of hurt since Carole died, doubting if he could trust Susan again. "Susan, I *don't* know," Marcos said. "This is way beyond upsetting."

Susan, much more composed, asked Marcos repeatedly to please take her with him to view rock art sites. She assured him that if she became the slightest pain in the neck, he was free to abandon her at the side of the road, no matter where they were.

"News flash. You passed pain in the backside three cups of coffee ago. I can't believe you did what you did. You used me, plain and simple, and I can't forgive and forget." Marcos knew himself well. He would have to deal with residual distrust at some point.

"Come on. I'll make it up to you, I promise. You'll see. Please quit making me beg like this. I'm not used to begging, and I'm not very good at it." She sounded sincere enough.

"Yeah, I'll bet you're used to getting whatever you want. Spoiled rich kid, I presume? You come off like a real princess," said Marcos scornfully. He felt conflicted and doubted his real feelings. At that moment, he was incapable of separating thoughts of Susan using him from intense thoughts colored by the loss of Dave. In either case, he deplored his loss of control.

"I assure you, Marcos, I'm no princess."

He measured his response in a heartbeat and consciously attempted to remain safely on an intellectual plane. "Sorry about that, but I clearly expressed my opinion of psychic archaeology to you before I left Idaho. There's just no way to verify it. Therefore, what good is it?"

Susan paced back and forth right in front of Marcos a few times before she spoke. "Lest you forget, I have shown my ability to communicate with the spirit world. You observed me firsthand yesterday evening. Please go ahead and check the accuracy of the information about the Soto family I received psychically. I am certain the historical records will provide you proof."

"I neither have the time nor the inclination. Besides, that's all recent history you recited." Marcos suspected, based on her performance thus far, that Susan had already undertaken the research, and that was precisely what she had uncovered.

Susan remained undeterred. "Don't be silly. Look, I'll keep whatever psychic clues I retrieve from the rock art private. I won't even discuss them with you if that works. Just take me with you, and let me visit the sites. I'll do any communicating with spirits on my own. You won't even know I'm doing it. Jeez, I'll carry your bags for you. I'll wash your dirty clothes. I'll pay you. Whatever you want. You're the only one who knows where all these sites are, Marcos. This is my personal and professional quest. As an archaeologist with strong research and field experience, surely you can find some modicum of understanding. We're here now, and it would mean the world to me if you let me tag along. Please, from the very bottom of my professional and personal hearts."

Marcos was in shocked disbelief hearing Susan drone on. It reminded him stingingly of so many arguments he had had with colleagues over the years, leaving him drained and discouraged. He did not tolerate conflict of any nature. It was such conflict that had resulted in his retreat to the quiet ranch in Idaho. "No, Susan. My complete focus must remain on Dave and only Dave. I have no desire at all to play tour guide for a psychic." *There. That should do it*, he thought to himself.

Next came the coup de grâce. Susan cleared her voice and stared deeply into Marcos' sad baby blues. "Marcos, consider that my skills both as a physician and psychic will come in handy for examining Dave's body and even communicating with him."

In a moment of self-doubt, Marcos turned inward and reached deep inside himself. *Despite her actions, Susan may be correct, and Dave is trying to communicate, even though I can't fathom the concept.* He had no idea whether he was at a low ebb of being worn down, he admired Susan's acumen and intelligence, or Folke had whispered in his ear never to ignore any line of inquiry, no matter how unthinkable. The possibilities struck him like Thor's legendary hammer. Welcomed relief washed over him, and he permitted himself to defer, for now.

"I cannot stand to see a grown woman grovel. All right, all right, you can come, but I reserve the right to set you out on the side of the road in a split second if you cause me even the slightest trouble. Do you understand? Those are my terms. Do not mess with me and make me regret my decision."

"Marcos, I am so eternally grateful. You won't regret it—I give you my solemn promise. I can't wait to tell Tim I'll be leaving the crappy tour group. I'll miss Emily, though. I like her. She's quite plucky."

Marcos urged Susan to have one final breakfast with the tour group as closure, especially since she had already paid for it. He bid her "*Hasta luego*," and directed her to meet him in the lobby ready to depart at nine a.m. sharp. "Don't be late. I have no patience for delays." He meant every word.

Susan squeezed both of his hands as she smiled at him with her all-knowing green eyes, the eyes that bore right through him. Oddly, he didn't feel a sense of violation but rather the sincere thanks she was somehow transmitting to him. Something stirred, catching him off guard. *Det här är så frustrerande,* he thought. *I absolutely cannot fall for this woman. I can't handle that stress right now.*

The situation had presently risen to the level of a serious case of conflicted behavior. Marcos wondered if he would regret his decision as he attempted to ignore the ache in the pit of his stomach.

Down deep inside his core, he suspected Susan was withholding additional information from him. *Sooner or later, I'm going to have to come to terms with that information,* he thought. *Susan is one determined woman. Crap, she'd better be a good doctor.*

Marcos admired her determination in a way. *Psychic archaeology? Forgive me, Folke. Please forgive me.* For now, Marcos chose to forge ahead and hope for the best. *She does remind me of somebody, however. Damn!*

SEVEN
Return to the Cave

Sadness gripped Marcos whenever he left Cataviña behind. The area with its surroundings abundant with a diversity of unique plant life was, without a doubt, his favorite. Despite Dave's death and other complications, he found new energy with the possibility of discoveries. It remained a conundrum, however. While a scattering of rock art sites existed there, sites were much more prevalent in the south. He had been unable over the years to reconcile in his mind why the comparatively lush area would not have attracted native populations and inspired the same level of awe in them as it did in him. He had played that tape a thousand times before.

"Marcos, I think we should go back to the first cave we visited yesterday."

"Oh, let's not waste our time there. I promise there are much grander sites coming up. Besides, I think we've disturbed the spirits there enough," he added in jest. "After all, look what happened to Andrea. I think it best to put some distance between the site and us. The clock's ticking with the time remaining to secure Dave."

"What in the world is that?" Susan interrupted, pointing to the ignition key with what appeared to be a red triangular-shaped fetish dangling from it. "I haven't noticed it before. Hmm."

"What? You mean this?" Marcos asked, as he fondled the object between two fingers.

"Well, that fetish just glowed bright, scarlet red. I swear I saw it glow red and then fade."

Marcos grinned. "That fetish, as you put it, is actually an amulet carved from the shell of the red spiny oyster. What you saw was most possibly a reflection from something on the car's instrument panel. Look. It's not glowing red now."

She shook her head but sat back in her seat for the ride.

When they reached the dry Pleistocene lakebed of Lake Chapala, Marcos pointed out the ancient beach terraces and launched into a snippet of history.

Interrupting, Susan lowered her voice demanding, "Marcos, turn around now. We must return to that rock shelter near the elephant trees."

Marcos turned to face her with every intention of disagreeing, but the look on her face was stone. Still tired and unwilling to wage battle with Susan and her overactive intuition, Marcos decided cooperation would be the easier route. Turning the vehicle around, he headed back north, thankful that at least it had only taken her seventy kilometers to put her foot down.

In forty-five minutes, they were back in Cataviña and in a few more minutes to their parking spot near the cave site. Susan leaped out of the car and hurriedly led the way back to the cave homing in on it with precision. That impressed Marcos greatly as it was not always easy even for him to find that cave without effort. Susan stooped down to enter and then stopped to turn around and face Marcos.

"I need to go in alone."

"Whatever," said Marcos, nonplussed. He located a suitable boulder and sat down to enjoy the panoramic view of the valley. Susan emerged thirty minutes later from the rock shelter, drained of energy and color.

"Now it's your turn, Marcos. Go in and see what happens. Just try hard to remain open to the possibilities, and let all information flow into your consciousness."

Relaxed, Marcos obeyed without comment, although curiosity about Susan's experience consumed him. *Okay, only one way to find out*, he thought unenthusiastically as he entered the rock shelter and sat on the ground. He sat and sat and sat some more on the floor of the cave listening to his breathing as time passed, but nothing changed. *No revelations. Shoot. Perhaps it would help to get into a more receptive mood*, he surmised and began deep breathing to prepare for a meditative state. Marcos understood meditation and had used it during stressful episodes in his life. He assumed the lotus position with eyes closed and hands in his lap with palms up. *Om, amazingly comfortable—I feel receptive to whatever enters my consciousness*, he thought, hoping. Minutes passed. Still nothing happened.

Next, Marcos concentrated long and hard on the artwork, attempting to discover a particular, meaningful pattern that might click in his mind. Nothing happened. Uncharacteristically, he waited patiently until reality struck him clearly—nothing was going to happen. He admitted to himself that he felt slightly foolish for even attempting to receive psychic information. *Isn't this inane scene just perfect? I have violated my own basic beliefs as an archaeologist and cheapened the very process of inquiry. I must be desperate.* He slithered out of the cave on his stomach and found Susan down the slope sitting under the shade of a *cardón.*

"May I ask what happened in there?" Susan inquired with guarded anticipation.

"Zero, nada. Not one single thing."

"Oh no, I was so hoping you'd receive the same information I did, even though I don't understand it all."

"What exactly don't you understand?" asked Marcos sardonically.

Susan's eyes lit up as she related her experience. "The pictographic figures on the surface of the cave came to life, appearing and reappearing, rearranging themselves sequentially. Some appeared like plastic, fluid, as though an invisible artist had constructed them, morphing from one shape into another. I had the distinct impression that the people had reserved this cave for the exclusive use of women, powerful women within the culture. Marcos, that was precisely why I asked you not to come in with me. I received a strong message that I should experience the cave alone *as a woman.*"

Somehow it had come to her that women only had entered the cave when they experienced their monthly cycles, a strange coincidence in itself as she had just started hers the day before. "Not just any women could visit, only those who sought ultimate knowledge. I also learned that only powerful women *dared* to enter. This wasn't a place that all women had known about—only a select few. Those women had either to discover the cave or follow a natural force that drew them to it in a natural selection process. If any men had stumbled upon this special place, the female forces would have naturally repelled them."

"Then why did you send me in?" Marcos asked.

Susan ignored his question for the moment. "I didn't receive any information about the meaning or content of the specific representations of the rock art, but I had the distinct feeling that if I re-visited over time, the meaning would somehow reveal itself to me. As I then gain insight, I, too, will feel compelled to leave behind a symbol reflecting my insight or symbolizing a token of my appreciation. The thought struck me—those symbols may not be conventional symbols with a shared meaning of the culture. Rather, they may very well represent the innermost personal testimonies of all the women who made them, representing an aspect of their new insight left behind to inspire those who came after. Unfortunately, the intensity of the message faded, and I knew the session had come to an end. Since you didn't receive any information as a man, that corroborates what I learned. I had to test it out by having you enter. Any impressions, Marcos?"

"Interesting," was all Marcos said at first as he processed Susan's remarks. "The content of these pictographs, mind you, is certainly different from that found at most of the other sites. That I have *seen* myself. It's not outside the realm of possibility that powerful women produced these figures." He couldn't believe he was going along with her, but it just felt right. "Following that line of thinking, this site could certainly have been a power place where only female shamans came or perhaps those women who sought the power to become shamans."

The information blew Marcos away. The sequence of how the figures appeared could represent what people had seen in the form of superimposition, so he could at least determine what form had existed earlier than an overlying one. Perhaps with careful study, he could then determine stylistic changes in time like a pottery sequence. *Okay, I SEE the possibilities*, he thought.

Excited, Marcos explained to Susan that it had also been the case in many primitive societies that men would banish women from the group when they menstruated. As native societal history had recorded, menses had been a time of great spiritual power when the men allegedly had feared the women.

"So, honestly, Susan, it's not unlikely that only menstruating women visited here. In some societies, the natives constructed huts for that purpose. From what I know of these people, they could not afford the luxury of a special hut. Besides, they were too nomadic with no permanent settlements. If all this were true, then I as a male am an intruder, explaining why I failed to receive any insights in the cave. But then, the fact remains I don't possess *your* gift, whatever that is."

Marcos was both shocked and impressed. He struggled to believe Susan's psychic abilities enabled her to find meaning in the mysterious rock art he had studied for over two decades. *What if she can actually communicate with Dave or with the ancient spirits? Believing in her process of discovery flies in the face of everything I learned as a scientist*, he thought. Yet his gut told him to trust her if there was the slimmest chance of helping Dave. *Herregud! I damn near did not allow her to accompany me. Thinking outside of my archaeological box is not my strong suit*, Marcos confessed. Folke would have agreed.

Susan had listened without interruption to Marcos. "What you said, Marcos, makes perfect sense to me. I am so glad and relieved you agreed to return to the site and allow me to test my theory by going into the cave yourself. At the same time, however, our different experiences tend to invalidate the working theory that the information from the universal mind was ready for tapping." Susan's voice grew softer.

"Yes, you were fairly certain about that working theory," Marcos said.

"And I admit the thought had crossed my mind that you had not been truly open and receptive enough given your skepticism. The explanation is crystal clear to me now—the special knowledge was available only to and for women. Marcos, it had never been available to men, and there was no reason to believe that it would be now—despite universal information." Susan breathed deeply.

"Well, there you have it. We can agree that we both learned something new after all. We both believe we discovered the true function of the rock shelter."

"I also know that whenever I return to the site, I will access more information. But I've quenched my thirst for knowledge about this site's art for the time being and cherish today's success."

"I am anxious, Susan, to get on with my journey. I for one have no desire to return to the other cave where Andrea met her fate—not now, anyhow."

Susan nodded as her first reply. "Marcos, you need to understand that we are all quite capable of receiving information and communicating with spirits, establishing a connection with the store of knowledge that represents the collective experience of humankind. I don't view this necessarily as a special gift but rather a receptivity to taking in knowledge. Believe me. With faith, conviction, and practice, the information will flow freely to you. I am quite certain it will flow to you as well by the end of this trip, and you will be able to access this powerhouse of data."

"Susan, don't you see? Even if that were true and everything I wanted to know about the art I was miraculously able to find out, it would make no difference. I could never share my findings practically and earnestly with any assemblage of archaeologists. Wherein lies the necessary evidence?" Marcos returned to dwelling on his academic frustration about the unrecognized discipline of psychic archaeology.

"Your reluctance is a challenge, Marcos. The evidence would come from duplicating the information and from others receiving the same information. Can't you accept that?"

The entire discussion took place while retracing their steps southward. Before they realized it, they were at the junction of highways 1 and 5, where highway 1 went south to Guerrero Negro, and highway 5 headed off to the east to Bahía de los Ángeles, situated on the stunning Sea of Cortez. Marcos turned off to the east impulsively. "You know, I hadn't planned to visit Bahía de los Ángeles on this trip, but it's only about seventy kilometers away. It boasts a phenomenal view overlooking the sea."

Halfway there, he slowed in search of a familiar, albeit barely detectable, dirt track to the south. Spying it, he swiftly engaged the four-wheel drive and took off through the desert flanked by a rich valley painted iridescent green with myriad stands of paloverde. He followed the faint track through a sandy wash on the floor of the canyon. Grateful for having the four-wheel drive in the soft sand, Marcos pulled out of its dangerous clutches by shifting the transfer case to a low range. The scene was all too reminiscent of another trip when his vehicle had sunk in the sand so deeply he had to abandon it before he went under himself. *Ah, good times,* he mused. *Bra!*

After sixteen sluggish kilometers of grinding in low range, the valley widened at last, and Marcos headed toward the tall escarpment of basalt cliffs on the west side he knew so well. He pulled up and stopped at the foot of the talus slope composed of mammoth-sized chunks of dislodged and tumbled lava in graphic testimony of the violent forces of the earth at work there ages ago.

"I've brought you to another rock art site, although I hadn't originally planned on heading this way. First," said Marcos, as they skirted the cliff looking upward, "let's just survey this site and take an inventory of what's here. I didn't get an opportunity to do that the last time I was here."

Susan happily agreed and enthusiastically pointed out an anthropomorphic figure of a well-endowed male holding a hooked stick above his head with a spear in his other hand.

"What's that stick with a hook on the end?" she asked.

"That's an atlatl," said Marcos.

"Atlatl?"

Susan was about to find out how much Marcos delighted in talking about atlatls. In his professorial mode, he lectured that atlatls were highly effective devices used to launch spears or darts. They provided an extra fulcrum to the arm and allowed users to hurl projectiles at least three times the normal distance with three times the force of an arm by itself. Indigenous people had invented the atlatl approximately 200,000 years ago, pre-dating bows and arrows by 180,000 years. Marcos was proud of the vast collection of atlatls he had acquired and fashioned himself.

"The term atlatl is derived from Nahuatl, the language of the Aztecs. However, it's a term universally applied to these types of throwing sticks. I read in a diary from one of the Spanish missionaries that the natives here had used them, which bears out these pictographic representations. However, I have yet to discover or see any physical, archaeological evidence of their existence here in Baja, other than the pictographs. It's my dream to dig one up for scientific closure, but so far, I've only found projectile points of the appropriate size normally used as tips for atlatl darts, the points being larger than arrowheads and smaller than spear points."

Before Marcos could wind up his lecture on too much information about atlatls, Susan scrambled up the cliff to take a closer look at her discovery. She had not gotten six meters up the slope when she let out a deafening screech. Marcos caught up to her in haste. Obviously frightened, she pointed to a tight crevice in the rock where a stout, nasty-looking lizard with baggy skin folds had pancaked down on his belly.

"Ah, behold the sexy chuckwalla," Marcos said with excitement. "We're extremely lucky to see one. Hey, the natives used to eat them as a delicacy. Want to try some?"

"God, no!"

"Oh, come on. Grab its tail and pull it out so we can take a closer look," Marcos said.

"Are you insane? I'm not touching that weird creature."

By now, Marcos was quite amused. Snickering, he said, "You couldn't have pulled it out anyway because their great defensive mechanism when threatened is to hide in a crevice and inflate themselves making it almost impossible to pull them out." He explained how the chuckwalla's tail easily detached, rendering it safe. Then it would just grow another. To be able to continue to enjoy this delicacy, natives of the Southwest had invented the ingenious chuckwalla hook, something like a large crochet hook used to pierce the lizards to deflate them and pull them out.

Susan interrupted Marcos' chuckwalla adventure by continuing to advance cautiously toward the pictograph. Near to it, she noticed a large petroglyph nearly the same size. It looked like a dead deer upside down with a spear protruding from it. They clambered all over the cliffs discovering more and more intriguing examples of Baja rock art.

"Remember the site we visited southeast of El Rosario at the San Fernando Velicatá Mission? Twice now we've experienced the rarity of finding pictographs and petroglyphs at the same site. I'd say pretty fantastic, don't you agree?"

"Oh, Marcos, yes! Let's spend the night here," Susan said, her green eyes aglow.

"What? Don't you want to go to Bahía de los Ángeles and dine on delicious turtle steak for dinner and meet some of my longtime friends?"

"I think it's far more important to remain on-site here. I have a strong feeling about this location. You won't be disappointed."

"But we're not equipped to camp on this trip," said Marcos, somewhat exasperated. Besides, he had a strong craving for turtle meat. In truth, however, he had learned always to carry all sorts of emergency supplies when heading out into the desert. Normally, he would have camped the entire trip, but he thought it more efficient to use hotels this time. He nodded his consent.

Due to their passionate exploration, the two had lost complete track of time. Before they knew it, the sun descended rapidly, casting the entire west wall in a dark shadow. Viewing rock art had become impossible. So, they gathered firewood, built a fire, and prepared to spend the night.

"You must be starved," Marcos said.

"Well, I can easily survive fine one night without a meal. You know, maybe we should fast to prepare for revelations during the night—unloading our unnecessary baggage, so to speak."

"Well, luckily, there's no need for that," said Marcos, as he unpacked some emergency rations from his supply locker in the back of the Navigator.

With a light, packaged-for-camping, but surprisingly tasty meal out of the way, they stretched out on a tarp close to the fire gazing up at the vast blanket of stars, feeling minuscule and insignificant in the universe. Marcos ruminated with great misgiving on what lay ahead that night. At that moment, however, he only desired to reach over and gently draw Susan closer to him. Fighting the urge, instead, he commented, "I hope no rattlesnakes are attracted by the heat of the fire, and of course, we have to keep an eye peeled for scorpions too. They pop up out of the sand seeking heat, you know." Marcos could not stop himself from trying to gross out Susan.

"Okay, Mr. Snake and Bug Authority. Maybe this wasn't such a great idea to camp out in the desert after all. I've never been camping in my life nor had the desire to do so. But I feel a strong force pulling me to be here in this very place *tonight*." She reached over and lightly placed her hand on Marcos' chest making eye contact and said, "Hey, big guy, I'm depending on you to protect me." She smiled enticingly then withdrew her hand.

"It's a deal. Of course, I'll protect you from rattlesnakes and scorpions," Marcos said, waving around his huge pistol. "I'm relying on you to protect me from any evil spirits you might unleash during one of your, let's say, *stupors*."

Susan left Marcos bewildered. There had been two kisses, handholding, a skimpy bathing suit, and touching his chest now with the come-hither smile. The intelligent beauty certainly held an attraction for him, despite her deviousness. In fact, he was surprised at how he had been able to compartmentalize his worry and anger when at the start of the day he'd been so upset with her. He knew, though, that he could not allow himself to be distracted and had to remain sharply focused on the purpose of this mission—Dave. Besides, he had convinced himself that he was not interested in having another woman in his life right now. *I have noticed that Susan possesses a few endearing traits that certainly remind me of someone*, Marcos thought. He had no theories, vague or otherwise, where that thinking was coming from.

They lay close to the roaring fire, trying to get comfortable, waiting for whatever. For Marcos to anticipate whether they would gain knowledge of the ancient secrets of the rock art that night remained impossible. *Nope. What nonsense! What the devil am I doing here?*

The enormous pleasure of being present in the desert so far from anything she had ever experienced before with the starscape and its moon rising in the east intoxicated Susan. She stole a shy glance at Marcos, finding him both strange and attractive, and tried to remember how long it had been since she had been with a man personally, not in a doctor-patient relationship. Admittedly, she took the same advice she gave her patients and went for a run or exercised whenever she needed to relieve sexual tension. Not only was it inappropriate to run or exercise now—she knew she could not allow Marcos to touch her, given the complexity of circumstances. She decided it was prudent to push any thoughts aside for right now and stay focused on the purpose of the trip. Susan ejected her thoughts and allowed her mind to go blank.

***

Hours passed when Susan suddenly let out an ear-splitting scream of pure terror. Her body shook violently as she withdrew from a meditative state. Sobbing uncontrollably, she rolled toward Marcos. "Hold me!"

As he embraced her tightly, as much for her comfort as his own, Marcos froze in place as a maelstrom drew him in like a tempestuous hurricane. He clung to Susan for dear life while peering through a kaleidoscope of flashing colors wildly tossing him about. Faces, horribly maniacal faces—red, black, white, and purple—leered at him as he plunged even deeper into the spinning, roaring vortex. Animals—fearsome beasts such as bears, mountain lions, wolves, and giant raptors with talons—swooped closely and tore at him as the storm thrust him into the ancestral spirit world of those who had created the ancient rock art.

The next scene happened instantaneously. Faintly, but unmistakably, a figure appeared, shockingly grotesque with unresolved agony chiseled on its suffering face. Dave reached out to Marcos with both arms extended then in a flash faded into the swirling chaos. Instinctively, Marcos wanted to reach out and free Dave from this world, but he could not move his limbs. He remained paralyzed, trapped in his terrifying mental image of not dying but being absorbed against his will into the other world. He lost total consciousness at the chilling thought of never being able to exit this world, exactly like Dave.

**

When it was all over, the two still held onto each other as an anchor in their normal world. Finally, Susan said, "It was beyond horrific." She carried on between sobs. "Somehow, I was transported back to this very place at a time in the distant past. At the onset, I wasn't altogether clear about what I was doing among the band of aboriginals camped at the foot of these cliffs. The sun was coming up on their second day of camping when hideous screams from both men and women abruptly awakened me. Next to me, I saw a woman's head explode—brain matter spurting out in every direction, splattering on the ground like a spent firework."

Susan meticulously described how a gigantic stone had fallen from the sky, pulverizing the child sleeping at the woman's breast. She had looked up to see men at the top of the cliffs, their bodies painted vertically half white and half red, heaving large stones down at the helpless band of sleeping people. The men of the group under attack were painted red on the top and black on the bottom horizontally. They had hastily attempted to organize and arm themselves, returning fire with their bows and arrows, but it was ineffective. The adversaries at the top concealed themselves too well.

Marcos listened with rapt attention as Susan vividly recalled the people's genuine surprise about their attackers, who she had learned had not originated from the area. The local natives had never experienced such danger accompanied by violent death before. She also learned that the outsiders had been exploring new territory due to the impact of a severe drought on the plants and game in their home range. They had migrated to this lusher area in search of food and had found an abundance. It became clear to her that the interlopers desired to eliminate the competition—the local inhabitants. Susan nestled into Marcos, still trembling. "Oh my God. I now realize I was actually an observer, a witness, smack in the middle of the violent attack."

***

When Marcos recounted his experiences to Susan, she reassured him with a big hug and told him while it must have been frightening, he should feel encouraged. This was an entrée into the spirit world. The nightmarish nature of the encounter was a reflective slice of the carnage that had unfolded there.

"As you are painfully aware, not all history is pleasant after all," Susan said.

"I know. I saw representations from what appeared to be two different tribes painted on the cliffs—the horizontal and vertical reds, blacks, and whites," Marcos said. "You?"

"Yes. I saw two types of representations during the bloody event as well. The various colors were vivid."

"I wonder if what you experienced, Susan, was like a historical documentation. Think of it being akin to quite a crude videotaping of the ancient happening. Super valuable information for our databanks despite the horribly graphic nature of the content."

The thrilling discovery, however, came as Marcos and Susan discussed the details of her revelations. She had received renderings from two opposing points of view. They surmised, therefore, that perhaps the larger the number of participants, the more information from different points of view. That certainly comported with their real-world thinking. If ten people all witnessed an event, there could be ten different points of view.

"Very interesting," they said at the same time laced with a nervous edge.

"And then there's the piece I saw," Marcos said. "Dave's tormented, without a doubt. I saw his gruesome face. He reached out to me—he longed to come back to me."

"He can't come back to you, Marcos. He must accept his situation."

"But he's obviously in a terrible situation, suffering. That's not right. What about all this heaven stuff and the blissful spirit world?"

"He hasn't reached his final destination yet. From what you described, it sounds like the angry spirits have blocked Dave's path. We must help him by assuaging their anger."

"*Attans!* How do you propose we go about that?" *Folke, vill du hjälpa mig?*

"Be patient. The way will reveal itself to us, Marcos. Trust me. It will all work out. You'll see."

Sleep was almost impossible the rest of the night and came in fits and starts. The hard ground hurt their backs and the fear of another supernatural encounter occurring haunted them. Although nothing of a supernatural nature happened, Marcos was constantly in terror of the spirits drawing him into their realm while he slept, never to return. It marked the beginning of his living nightmare.

***

At first light, Marcos awoke and instinctively looked up at the top of the cliffs to spot any enemy visitors poised to hurl stones down on them. When he and Susan both realized they must have been thinking the same thing, they broke into laughter, relieving some of the residual tension. Marcos produced more emergency rations, and they brewed tasty, full-bodied coffee over the fire while they discussed the events of the previous day. Both were quite amazed given the circumstances that they could rationally discuss everything.

"I have a nagging question for you. I'm trying to understand why you felt so compelled to summon the force again so soon. Are you able to tap into the spirit world at any time?" Marcos was dead serious.

"Just remember my experience in the rock shelter the previous morning. That suggests the summoning could happen at any time," Susan said.

"After what occurred, I prefer to leave well enough alone for the time being. Truthfully, Susan, I'm not mentally up to any more confrontations with the supernatural following the abhorrence of yesterday." The unanswered question lingered in his mind whether they had played a larger role than just being witnesses. *What if we actually took part in the events*, he wondered. *¡Ay, caramba!* If so, he recognized the distinct possibility that they could be killed or unable to return to their present.

Marcos asked Susan in hushed tones, "Do you think using Dave as bait was some kind of ploy to draw me in deeper so that I couldn't escape?"

"I don't know. I'm quite concerned too about the nature of what we experienced, but I don't have any more answers for you, yet."

"One of my premier fantasies throughout my life has been the concept of time travel. H.G. Wells impressed me as a youth to the extent that I read every book and short story available about time machines and traveling back through time. At the same time, however, the concept struck me with terror. I can recall countless episodes where I awakened in a sweat from a dream about time tripping. Each time, I worried about not waking up and dying.

"You know, we *could* die," Marcos said. "If we, or you, were to manifest in a different time plane and involve ourselves in the time and space vectors of that dimension, could we or you disengage willfully? Think about it. Of course, there's the ever-looming problem that our mere presence as observers could potentially change the course of events. As a scientist, I must tell you I have asked colleagues and myself repeatedly during my tenure in the field if it would be ethically or morally wrong to tamper with events if it would result in a more favorable outcome. I found that the consensus on the definition of a favorable outcome was difficult to pin down and was inevitably based on cultural assumptions. What may *seem* favorable may not pan out thusly in the long haul."

"But isn't everything in the universe supposed to happen for a reason?"

"That concept has always seemed a bit too deterministic to me. Besides, it's too much like one religion's interpretation of the Golden Rule, which I wholeheartedly question. On the surface, the rule appears to be a workable concept for moral behavior. But in my opinion, it has possibly contributed to too much havoc throughout history in the name of itself and religion," said Marcos, flushed. "Damn! I apologize for the lecture. Shall we take a hike?"

Marcos grasped Susan's hand firmly as they walked up the sandy-bottomed canyon. When they had rounded a point of basalt detached from the cliff above, Marcos led her over to it and helped her climb to the top where it was flat and warmed by the sun. The wind had blown it clean. Marcos lay down, savoring the moment, clearing his mind, and feeling the power of being with Susan in such a remote place, as if they were the only people in their own, private world sans spirits.

"See," said Marcos, "this is what I love about Baja. You can be so alone and exclusive here."

"Mmm," purred Susan, placing her hand on his thigh.

Marcos contentedly glanced upward at the basalt escarpment. The shimmering sun was bright, radiating dancing, heat waves. It was difficult to focus. Then he saw him—black on one side, white on the other, a hazy, intimidating figure peering over the edge down at them. For a split second, he couldn't comprehend the image above him. Staring straight at it trying hard to focus, he realized it was a manifestation of a pictograph. The figure raised his arm preparing to launch a spear. Marcos instantly yanked Susan off the rock, nearly dragging her back to the Navigator, running at full tilt.

"What's the matter, for God's sake? You're as pallid as death itself."

Marcos was speechless. His adrenaline pumped so hard that he hyperventilated while struggling to turn the car around to head out of the valley. He drove at breakneck speed to distance themselves from the apparition, reminding himself to take deep, slow breaths to calm down. As a scientist, a pretty picture he was not.

Marcos finally turned to Susan and shuddered. "Plain as day, I saw a white and black figure on the cliff above us holding a spear, poised to hurl at us. I knew I had to get us out of there fast. I'm sorry I was so rough, but there was no time to spare."

Susan grew concerned and looked straight at Marcos who was still pale. "I must say, Marcos, what you describe differs greatly from what we experienced yesterday, namely being observers. You're talking about us actually becoming part of the action, or as you put it, manifesting ourselves in the time and space vectors of the original event. That would be time travel, not tapping into the spirit world like we've been doing. We must be careful not to confuse the two. I honestly believe it's doubtful you saw what you described. I know for certain as a psychiatrist that the mind can play tricks sometimes."

Marcos drove stiffly with hands glued to the wheel, listening and trying to absorb the information.

"My opinion is you actually experienced something quite jolting yesterday evening, which might have triggered your conscious mind to produce an image transferred over from your subconscious mind. A very fine line exists between the two. When one side is super-stimulated, it could occupy a person's conscious thoughts as well. And I think you were most likely in some type of altered state when you saw what you described to me." Susan looked into Marcos' tired eyes.

"I understand that in some cultures, people are encouraged to dream and experience visions to the point of it becoming impossible for them to distinguish between reality and dream states," Susan said.

"What you say is true," Marcos nodded approvingly. "The Iroquois come to mind, for example."

"See the heat dancing out there in waves," Susan said, pointing to the sea, "which could be a mirage. I recall driving up the coast to Santa Barbara one time. When looking across the channel, I could see the islands that were not islands but fantastic forts and castles in the sea. Those were mirages, but I *did* see them."

"Maybe you're right." Marcos sounded half-convinced. "To tell you the truth, this is all freaking me out. What we need to do is push the pause button and gain a fresh perspective as we keep moving south. But first, I want to take you to a special place on the way so you can enjoy a much more beautiful, bird's eye view of the Sea of Cortez. You won't believe how blue-green and gorgeous it is, landscaped with tiny islands. It's truly stupendous."

As they stared out the car's windows lapping up every drop of the available view, Marcos interrupted the silence.

"You know, as shocking as it was, I'm still glad we came here and stayed overnight. Dave said countless times there was something powerfully seductive about this site, but he couldn't for the life of him, no pun intended, identify *the what*. My quest now is to find out *what* he found. Seems clear enough, right? I hope to dear God that he was spared the experience I had. I just hope I can somehow hold it together when we finally collect Dave's body." *Will he look like Andrea? Did both of them interfere with the spirits, each in their own way?* he questioned. *Helvete!*

EIGHT
Splitting Logs

———

Passing sparkling, white Lake Chapala, Mexico's largest freshwater lake, and heading south, Marcos told Susan about its history. He had explored all around the beach terraces many moons ago searching for artifacts and remains of ancient campsites. His efforts resulted in the recovery of a few, crude, stone-chopping tools left behind by the ancient inhabitants. It was evidence of their otherwise unknown occupation of the peninsula around eight to ten thousand years ago.

Sadly, Marcos and Susan left the entertaining cacti, boojum trees, and elephant trees behind for the occasional, tattered Joshua tree. Susan dozed as they traveled through the Desierto de Vizcaino, a bleak expanse of inhospitable land covering much of the coastal plain in central Baja. Marcos occasionally glanced over at Susan as she slept peacefully. He disguised a yawn with a chuckle just thinking about how he found her extremely fine-looking, despite her disheveled state, post-scary night in the desert. Something gnawed at him, though—she reminded him of someone he could not pinpoint. He relegated that thought to the back recesses of his mind and concentrated with eyes glued to the road and thoughts directed at what lay ahead. *Focus, old boy*, Marcos told himself. *You can do this. Remember, you're here to learn the facts and circumstances of your best friend's death. It's about Dave. You can place everything else on your park list while you sort that out.* He inhaled quietly and felt more centered.

Marcos looked over at Susan as she stirred. "You're awake. You had a nice little snooze there. Must have needed the sleep."

"It's exhausting communicating with the spirit world," she said, mouth agape with a noisy yawn escaping.

"I'm still unconvinced it's not all purely a horrible nightmare. Are you certain your psychic powers haven't seduced me into having these so-called experiences with the supernatural? Tell me it's true, oh please."

"My God, what else do you need to be convinced the spirit world is real? One person and perhaps another is dead so far because of it."

Marcos shifted and squirmed in his seat. It was time to change the subject once again. "So, what made you get involved in psychic psychiatry?"

"My grandmother. Okay, okay, it's a long story."

"Lucky you. This is going to be a long trip," said Marcos not wanting to push his luck.

As an anthropologist, he had long held the opinion that lengthy trips provided the perfect medium for people to get to know a lot not only about others but also about themselves. "In my humble opinion, if people would just travel and experience the world around them, they wouldn't have to go to shrinks." He gave her a wry grin.

"You sound like my mother who also holds a very low opinion of my chosen niche in medicine."

Marcos blushed and apologized for his rudeness and the unintended meaning of his statement. "It's just that people get so caught up in their own self-importance they lose perspective of the whole evolution of humankind and their purpose for being here in the first place." That did it, and they both experienced relief as the tension dissipated.

"Honestly," said Marcos. "I could tell you a secret that would put all you shrinks out of business, but I won't whisper a word of it to anyone else. It has zero to do with rock art or archaeology."

"I can't wait. What is it?"

"It's as simple as splitting logs, my dear doctor."

"What? Splitting logs?" Susan sputtered shaking her head and rolling her eyes. "You've reduced my entire field of medicine requiring nine years of training to splitting logs? Thanks so much."

Marcos waved his hand around for emphasis. "Not your profession, silly, the *solution* to people's problems."

"Okay. I'm listening." Susan gave him her full attention.

"Tell me, have you ever split logs?"

"Heck, no. I'm a sophisticated city girl from Los Angeles who's never even been close to a log. I have a gas fireplace in my home in Southern California, renowned for its temperate climate, by the way."

Improvising, Marcos graciously invited Susan to visit his ranch in Idaho someday where he would gladly introduce her to log splitting, although he knew that would not happen any time soon. *I'm guessing she thinks we don't even have any paved roads let alone civilization in Idaho*, he thought.

"Perhaps you could enlighten me vicariously by honestly telling me about your truth. As you know, we don't always have to experience everything personally to understand it."

Marcos sat without moving, deep in thought.

"Well, I'm waiting," Susan said.

Marcos cleared a hitch in his voice and began. "People go to shrinks to work out their self-concerned frustrations and to make sense out of things, right?"

"I suppose in a naïve sort of way that's an important part of what we do."

"I believe people wouldn't have to do that if they chose to split logs. Bar none, it's the most wonderful therapy ever discovered. I have learned that, unfortunately, very few people know about it anymore to the extent that we certainly need to reinvent it."

Marcos had often imagined himself in the shoes of the early settlers while splitting logs on his ranch. He had long ago concluded that the same kinds of modern-day frustrations and self-related concerns had not afflicted them. Their lives and energies had focused on the basics and daily survival. No time was left for elaborate phobias that clinicians had yet to label or describe.

"You see, our ancestors could get rid of whatever ailed them by splitting a few logs," Marcos said in complete earnestness. "It's hard, exhausting work but so rewarding in the end. Folks have not merely worked through and released their frustrations but also achieved a new level of understanding through the process. Meditation with cardio. When finished, people have a pile of wood to use for cooking and keeping warm. Now, what could be better than burning up the residue of your issues? By the way, Dave and I split many a log out in the field when we went days and months without discoveries. See, scientific application." His eyes twinkled.

"I'll be sure to put it on my prescription list," Susan said, rolling her eyes.

Marcos held little appreciation for psychiatry or clinical psychology. He believed the tangible results of splitting logs were far superior to paying ungodly, hourly fees for sessions likely to yield no resolution. He couldn't imagine anything more effective than putting an affliction up on the chopping block and pounding it with a maul.

"What do you say to me franchising clinics for wood splitting in large cities where all your needy patients hang out and do whatever they do? I've experienced firsthand how cities seem to mess people up. People were never meant to live in such concentrated masses."

"Thank you, Dr. Andersson, for that dissertation on *la condition humaine* and your banal cure-all," Susan said sarcastically. "I'm sure my colleagues will be eternally grateful and enlightened knowing the chopping block will relieve them of all their professional duties and responsibilities and peremptorily cure their patients. I stand in total awe."

Marcos thought for a moment. Admittedly, his theory had limited application, and people needed help from shrinks for the deeper stuff. As for dealing with plain old frustrations, he stood steadfastly by his basic premise. "Okay, so maybe I overstated it. But

I regret not finding this out until I moved to Idaho and began splitting logs for my wood-burning stove, which is my sole heat source.

"Just imagine all those years of unresolved frustrations I could have escaped had I known sooner," Marcos said.

"Sorry to correct you, my friend. People don't escape their frustrations no matter how deeply they bury them. They must let them surface and resolve them. We shrinks, as you call us, do some good in actually healing people, whether you care to admit it or not."

"Okay. So, speaking of disciplines, what do you think about archaeology? Don't be shy. Thought I'd give you an equal opportunity to bash my profession."

"I see. Umm, I wonder whether archaeology offers any real service to humankind. While I certainly find it interesting to learn about humankind's past activities, in the end, I see the science as stones and bones and assorted artifacts you and your colleagues use to reconstruct an entire civilization. I am not convinced that man is capable of learning from his past since he doesn't have a very good record of it to date.

"And you archaeologists certainly give us the barest outline of what has occurred in any case. There's very little vital force in an archaeological report, and what *is* there is mostly conjecture it seems to me," Susan said.

"Indeed, now who holds the other's discipline in low regard? I appreciate what you're saying, so I will choose not to argue. But I *do* believe we can learn something from our past, or at least we should try to learn about the process of man's cultural evolution."

"All right. I give you credit for developing some painstaking processes to find and correctly identify important artifacts and assign them relevance within a certain space and time. Let's just say I admire your work enough to want to come to Baja with you.

"Back up, though. I noticed you said *man's cultural evolution.* Typical chauvinist. I thought you would have risen above that kind of language in your own, archaeological evolution by now."

"A thousand pardons. I should have said human culture or just culture, as *man* is the only culture-bearing animal in existence."

"Once again."

As soon as his words hit the air, Marcos realized what he had said. Fumbling over his words, he said, "Let me apologize again. I'm having difficulty attempting to alter old language patterns."

"Exactly. The old patterns in all behaviors are very difficult to break. That's why people continue to act out destructive, crippling scripts. It requires intense work to overcome these habitual patterns, and it's almost impossible without a coach. Bingo! That's where we come in and can be of service," Susan said. "Back to the subject. Tell me, what good are your disciplines of anthropology and archaeology if we can't apply them and learn from them?"

"Let me remind you that one of the purposes of our trip is to seek information collaboratively leading to an efficacious contribution to our respective fields," Marcos said.

"I certainly hope so. You believe people can learn from the past. That we have in common," Susan said. "Connecting with spirits and allowing them to be our guides is so important, and archaeology holds promise as a valuable medium of contact. I predict you will appreciate that before we're done here."

Marcos could not squelch the prejudice and skepticism in his head, as much as he wanted to believe. He was unable to convey in words exactly what he desired to say.

***

As they set out for their next destination, Guerrero Negro, whose name translated as dark warrior, Marcos told Susan that local history had recorded it as having had something to do with escaped, Black slaves from a Manila galleon. They covered the eighty kilometers from Bahía de los Ángeles junction to Guerrero Negro effortlessly. Marcos nicely asked Susan to glue her eyes to the horizon to the south for an eagle. Repeatedly, he asked her if she had spotted it yet. He observed her scanning the sky high and low, near and far, with no success. Pointing straight up the road, he asked her to focus solely on the horizon.

"Look, Marcos," Susan said, pointing and grinning. "I can make out a structure sticking up above the horizon."

"Excellent! That's the eagle marking the 28th parallel—the boundary between Baja California Norte and Baja California Sur. And for us, it also signals our arrival at Guerrero Negro."

As they drew closer, they could discern the stylized, forty-three-meter-tall steel eagle gradually increasing in stature as they approached the 28th parallel. Towering over them, the eagle gave testimony to whatever progress this remote part of the world might enjoy. To the east and the west, bright green, overhead highway signs offered directions reminiscent of a major interstate freeway in the United States. At each side on the top of both signs rested giant piles of twigs. Marcos said they were osprey nests. Ospreys, eagle-like raptors, subsisted on a diet of fish. Right on cue, tiny fluff balls peeked shyly over the jagged rims of the nests. Marcos drew in a deep breath like a proud father, secure in the thought these nestlings represented yet another generation of incredible osprey who also marked the 28th parallel and had done so for over forty generations. *Some things don't change*, he thought, *and for good reason*.

"Why don't we have a good look around town before checking into our hotel," Marcos said.

"You mean there's a town here in this godforsaken place?" asked Susan sarcastically.

"Hold on, it's a bustling metropolis of almost 10,000 people," Marcos assured her. "This is home to one of the major salt-producing facilities in the world, shipping to Japan, Canada, and the United States, and it's the main source for all of Mexico."

As they cruised the main drag, the prosperity of the diminutive town, boasting many shops, two gas stations, a beautifully modern city hall, updated schools, and fine restaurants, impressed Susan. A couple of kilometers west of town, Marcos turned off to the south and headed to their hotel, promptly plunging them into a science-fiction world of endless salt ponds, *salinas*, in different states of evaporation, some pink.

"The ponds are a real tourist attraction," Marcos said. "It's amazing watching the workers load the giant crystals onto barges headed for Cedros Island where the salt gets shipped internationally. Such uniqueness for this area."

They left the strange world of pink and white to seek lodging for the night and grab a bite of lunch. Predictably, Marcos chose his favorite hotel, the El Presidente-Guerrero Negro. As they entered the largest and most spacious of all the El Presidente lobbies, a veritable museum of Mexican folk art surrounded them. Marcos, in his element, took Susan on a mini tour as he curated the objects from the Yucatan, Morelos, Oaxaca, Michoacan, Tonala, and elsewhere. He could tell he had impressed her with the life-sized statues of Mexican women holding planter pots from Oaxaca on their heads, recalling how he had toured all the pottery factories of Oaxaca to purchase such a piece for his garden.

As Marcos secured rooms at the reception desk, he inquired if Robert Powell was a guest, remembering their geologist friend, Emily, had mentioned him. If, as she had said, Powell had known Dave and they had worked together, Marcos wanted to meet him. According to the desk clerk, Powell had been there and had informed hotel staff he would return the next day from Cedros Island. He had traveled there to inquire about shipping zeolites from its deep-water port.

After checking in, Marcos and Susan retired to their rooms to freshen up. They stuffed themselves at lunch with deliciously fresh seafood, happy to be back at the coast taking full advantage of the abundant marine buffet. Drowsy from the wine, they both had a siesta after lunch. There was nothing to do but wait for Powell to return from Cedros Island the next day. So, they took a walk out into the desert for what remained of the afternoon.

***

Over margaritas in the hotel bar that evening, Marcos asked Susan about her plans for the evening.

"Oh, I don't know. I thought maybe I'd ask the concierge if he could arrange a ticket and a limo to the opera." She rolled her eyes. "You bum, you know you have me at your mercy. I wouldn't have a clue about what to do in this place other than to read a book in my room or get a good night's sleep. I'm here to experience different things and am up for something different. Suggestions?"

"How different?" asked Marcos.

"Oh, I don't know, not just the same old thing," said Susan, grinning again.

"Well, I don't know what you had in mind, but I do have a surprise for you."

"I'm game. What is it?"

"Well, if I told you, it wouldn't be a surprise, now would it?"

Susan conceded.

"Hey, let's go have dinner before we get bombed," urged Marcos, now aware of his hunger.

During the fish enchiladas, Susan applied all her skills to get Marcos to divulge his secret. Steadfast, his lips were sealed, and he would not give her a glimmer of a hint. Finally, he nonchalantly threw something in about a mating ritual.

"You're taking me to a mating ritual?" said Susan, one eyebrow raised.

"Not exactly," Marcos assured her, asking her to be patient for once.

Back in his room, Marcos began stripping the bed, bundling up the blankets and pillows. He had already instructed Susan to do the same, chuckling with delight at the look she shot back at him. He also told her to dress in her warmest clothes. He tossed the bundles of bedding in the back of the Navigator. They took off, passed through town, and kept heading west toward the ocean. Things were upbeat and going well. Marcos hoped the activity coming up would amount to a positive diversion, enough to keep their minds off Dave, anyhow.

NINE
Scammon's Lagoon

In a short while, they were at the edge of Scammon's Lagoon, a narrow ribbon of water sparkling in the moon's light. They parked the car safely on the crest of a sand dune and strolled toward the shore. Marcos found a rowboat sitting on the beach and invited Susan to get in as he shoved it out into the water, jumping in himself. Skillfully operating the oars, he propelled the boat into the middle of the lagoon where the two of them stopped and quietly sat.

Without warning, a massive amount of pulsating water off the starboard side rocked the boat, and Susan screamed. Something colossal, black, and intimidating rose out of the water. It appeared in the moonlight to be at least three meters across and triangular. Seconds later, it disappeared stilly as the water calmed, becoming smooth as glass. Both beautiful and mysterious, it enshrouded the earth in perfect, radiant stillness.

She looked at Marcos agog. Marcos smiled back. As he spoke, something broke the surface of the water, and a geyser erupted into the air, culminating in a heart-shaped spume of water and air.

"What the heck's going on?" Susan murmured looking around.

"Don't be frightened. This is my surprise for you, and you *said* you wanted to do something different tonight, right?"

"Yes, but I didn't say I wanted to get scared out of my wits! Are you trying to get us killed by some kind of sea monster or what?" Susan gasped.

"Trust me, it's quite okay. These are my friends and the gentlest creatures alive," Marcos said.

He introduced her to the gentle, California gray whales, whom they were lucky to see. They appeared in that location during a very brief period each year. *This is truly one of nature's treats*, he thought to himself confidently. Marcos bravely extended his arm over the side of the boat, motioning Susan to do the same. Parallel to the boat, an enormous snout looked up out of the sea, ten times longer than their tiny boat. Marcos reached over, giving it love pats just like his dog, encouraging Susan to do the same thing.

Hesitantly, not wishing to lose an arm but curious about the possibility, Susan reached over and stroked the behemoth, shutting her eyes tightly. "Oh my God," she said, "now I've petted a whale. If only my mother could see me now, she would die. Marcos, I don't know what I'm going to do with you."

With a charming smile, he urged Susan to sit back, relax, and enjoy it, wondering what she meant exactly by *what am I going to do with you*. He shrugged and elected to let that pass without further comment.

"I want you to know how difficult that is for me, but okay."

Marcos detected Susan's tentativeness about the whole thing and thoughtfully led her back to shore. But before he could, she stopped him with both hands and said she preferred to pet another, fantastic creature. He was pleasantly surprised. As for himself, he had long admired and observed all species of cetaceans.

"Oh my, Marcos, look at that. They're on both sides of the boat. We'll be crushed!" shrieked Susan.

Without a doubt, magic shimmered everywhere as she reached out and softly petted one and then the other. Marcos remained right beside her, sharing the moment, even if it might be their last, living out the precious time with the beasts. Noiselessly, the grays suddenly disappeared beneath the surface, simultaneously leaving Susan and Marcos with arms still stretched overboard. Their hands clasped as the moon reflected in their eyes. They both appreciated the awareness they shared at this instance, a rare experience that brought a rush of recognition of something special in the course of human existence, and the unplanned opportunity to share it made it all that much more exciting. *What a contrast this scene is to the carnage we witnessed yesterday*, Marcos thought. He cherished the peaceful moment as he had done with Dave a thousand times before.

Susan nestled into Marcos' embrace as he told her a bit about the whales. "Each year, they migrate from their icy homeland in the Bering Sea to winter, mate, and bear their young in the sequestered lagoons of Baja. The gestation period for a whale is a year. They breed in these lagoons and return to bear their young in the same place a year later." Marcos gently cleared his throat. "The mating ritual I mentioned earlier was referring to the mating behavior of the whales." He blushed slightly when he shared that the normal pattern of mating was for one male to support the female while her mate, a different male, "did his thing." He smiled shyly at Susan.

"You've presumably never imagined such a piece of anatomy until you've seen a whale in mating mode," said Marcos. He used his hands to illustrate graphically while he blushed his way through. "Those things make me feel a slight bit insignificant. My zoologist father-in-law used to have just such a specimen hanging over his home bar, the subject of conversation at cocktail parties. Of course, that was nothing compared to the conversation it caused when he brought it home on the airplane from the Republic of Chile." Marcos shook his head and howled until he observed Susan was not enjoying what he considered to be interesting, scientific details as much as he was. *Wow, she must think me odd*, crossed his mind as he changed topics.

They had drifted almost back to shore as he prattled on, and with a few strokes of the oars, Marcos effortlessly slipped the boat back onto the beach. They jumped out, retrieved their blankets, and spread them out on the sand, backs against a dune.

He placed his fingers to his lips, signaling Susan to be quiet and listen. They both heard it—a low moaning sound with modulation of intonation and intensity in a mournful entreaty, answered by deep, sad sighs from another direction. Marcos whispered that it was the whales talking dolefully but peacefully like *the ancient ones* telling of their histories and connecting with the present and future all in one. After concentrated listening, the sounds eventually lulled them to sleep in one another's arms.

***

They awoke at dawn to feel the chill of the morning touched by the glow of the first light. They stretched and greeted one another in remembrance of yet another enchanted night together, this time with the cetaceans. Not fifty meters offshore, a mother and her offspring swam along, spouting in a slow rhythmic ballet. Across the narrow channel, they spotted the other whales spouting. Their friends had not abandoned them.

Marcos declared the scene *an extended coupling* when he pointed to two males and a female clustered in a clumsy but stunning display of courtship. He wondered aloud if this act was in reality a more highly evolved expression of love and kept mulling that thought repeatedly as they observed, fascinated.

"Did you mean *extended couplings*?" asked Susan.

"Well, yes, sort of. The thought occurred to me we humans possess the capacity to love more than one person simultaneously and perhaps in different ways. Normally, our culture limits us from expressing ourselves thusly. What do you think of that, Dr. Cohen, professionally speaking of course?"

"Perhaps you're right about us having the capacity, but we aren't equipped culturally to deal with it successfully. Of course, you could say you loved all your children equally along with your spouse, but that's not the same as having multiple, primary relationships. It would likely be easier for a man to handle than a woman because a woman would need to feel special, protected, and needed. As traditional as that may sound, I have found it to be true."

"Fine, that's your professional stance. What's *your* take?"

"Well, that's a little close to home right now."

"What? You're involved in multiple relationships? Susan!"

Susan shook her head. "I really hate discussing that topic. Between my medical practice and clients seeking psychic help, I have no time to cultivate one primary relationship, let alone multiple ones. Besides, I have not yet met the man I would like to take home to meet my mother. She would never approve, in any case," Susan said.

Marcos chose not to comment about the touchy relationship issue. "Just Mom? What about Dad?"

"My father died several years ago. He was a well-respected surgeon in Beverly Hills. Now, my mother is left alone to carry out the tradition for a while longer, being a well-respected doctor herself. My father was always with his patients at the hospital and had little time for me."

"I'm sorry," Marcos said. He understood since he had lost his father, Folke, during his earlier years and missed him dearly. He reached out and gently patted her back in accord.

"It's okay, I guess. I have literally spent my entire life attempting to gain my so-called parents' approval. I was unsuccessful in pleasing them. As a result, I just stopped trying," Susan said.

Marcos had a difficult time processing the fact that Susan's parents were not proud of her despite her stature as a highly respected psychiatrist with a list of patients from the *who's who* of celebrities. "They're really not proud of you? That doesn't make any sense."

Susan let out a low snicker. "I wish I was kidding."

"Oh, Susan. I know how tough parents can be with their demands. My father, Folke Andersson, was a super famous archaeologist who taught me a lot but was never satisfied. He felt I could always achieve more. Then there was my maternal grandfather, Eduardo Beccera, world-renowned linguistic archaeologist. Both of them constantly live in my head, especially

Folke, scrutinizing and advising me. I still seek their approval and compare my work to theirs. My shoulders ache from the weight of wearing the family mantle of fame and glory," Marcos said with emotion.

"Well, it's a different story entirely for me. I view myself as a total, professional embarrassment to my parents. When I announced psychiatry as my primary specialty, both acted as if I had shortened *their* life spans. They equate shrinks to charlatans parading as doctors performing voodoo-like, primitive rites—practitioners on par with witch doctors. Then, when I began to investigate the psychic world, I felt like I contributed, without a doubt, to my father's early demise. I feel like I nailed down his coffin lid."

"I see. I'm sorry to hear that. Most parents would be proud," Marcos said earnestly.

"Yeah, well, I don't have most parents and never did. Due to my parents' utter dismay, I have maintained my certification as an internal medicine specialist to prove to them that I could practice real medicine."

"Meaning?"

"Never mind—just skip it, please."

Shifting topics, Marcos said, "I remember you once mentioned your grandmother was responsible for you becoming a psychic. How did that happen?"

She grinned and her shoulders relaxed. "My grandmother was quite gifted in the psychic realm, but my parents made her hide it from me and the rest of the world. In her later years, she recognized I also had the gift, and she encouraged me and told me not to waste it and not to pay any attention to my parents. She even told me it was my calling."

Marcos listened with genuine curiosity. "I see. You're an only child, Susan?"

"So I was told. And you?"

"Same."

"Well, we have in common that we've missed something not having siblings."

Marcos sighed and looked out over the dunes across the sound. "So, what are *your* goals and dreams? I don't like the thought of you catering to the empty, self-indulgent needs of the rich and famous for the rest of your career." Once he said it, he worried he might push her away by delving into sensitive, personal history.

She snapped back, "Just what do you mean?"

"What I mean is there are people out in the world who have basic needs such as food, shelter, and security, or what I call their pursuit of happiness. The rich and pampered exhibit all kinds of phony neuroses you have to make up words to describe. Frankly, I don't feel sorry one bit for your *celebrity* patients, some of whom likely make ten million dollars or more per movie. I don't understand why more of them don't choose to do more for those less fortunate." Marcos did nothing to hide his highly judgmental stance on the subject.

"That's what I plan to do," said Marcos. "I want to make a difference in people's lives. So, I've already started squirreling away some money in a trust fund in Belize. I intend to start a foundation to help others with various, humanitarian projects."

Marcos had struck a deep chord with Susan, and her face lit up while he spoke. "I had no idea you had this side. To tell you the truth, part of the reason I'm in Baja is my voyage of self-discovery. As you no doubt surmised, I'm not satisfied with what I'm currently doing, and I certainly don't want to do it for the rest of my life. I'm keeping my options open. As I mentioned, psychic archaeology, with heavy emphasis on psychic, could prove to be a new direction for me."

"Here we go. You and your psychic archaeology," quipped Marcos, whereupon he changed the subject to suggest they go *dig up* breakfast.

"Okay, Dr. Cranky. I'm game."

They hiked to the top of the dune where they had parked the Navigator and turned to take a last look over the lagoon and bid their friends adieu. It could not have been more breathtakingly perfect. A huge male whale emerged from the water, waving its gigantic head from side to side. Called spy-hopping, they had witnessed a last-minute gift from the whales. They rode back to the hotel in quiet appreciation of all that had happened.

Susan squeezed Marcos' hand and said, "Thank you for that wonderful surprise."

He kissed her lightly on the cheek before they entered the hotel lobby, famished. At the reception desk, Marcos inquired if there had been any word from Robert Powell. They still didn't expect him until that evening. After breakfast, Susan returned without delay to her room, and Marcos went to the car to collect the bedding. He delivered her sheets and blankets and told her he needed a siesta due to a lack of sleep the night before.

***

At lunch, Marcos guiltily admitted he wished Powell would show up so he could collect information about Dave. He was crankier than usual. "Damn! I really need to meet with Powell sooner. The insurance company's clock is ticking more audibly than before. I need to get on with my mission, personal enjoyment notwithstanding. The pressure is getting to me, Susan."

"Marcos, I have an idea. Since Robert Powell will not be back until this evening, let's go back to the lagoon this afternoon to watch those incredible creatures. They had such a calming effect on us. Lord knows we need calm before tomorrow's storm. We have a boatload of work ahead of us. Another hour or two won't make that much of a difference. We'll be collecting Dave soon," Susan said.

Despite his love of all things cetacean, Marcos was reluctant to be away from the hotel. *What if Powell returns early? I could miss him*, he thought. *Don't want to disappoint Susan, either. Decisions, decisions. Fy fan!* "You win. I'll leave word at the desk for Powell that we will return in two hours, tops. We must hurry."

When they arrived at the lagoon, most of the whales had already begun their migration north to the Bering Sea, swimming in tandem with their young. Susan urged Marcos to travel further north to catch a better view. But after a few kilometers, the car got stuck in a steep, barchan dune. It took Marcos a half hour using a tire inflation technique to clear the sand. *Wasted time that we don't have*, he thought. *Sorry, Dave. I'm coming.*

Then the unexpected happened. From a scenic promontory atop a dune overlooking the entrance to the lagoon, they watched a colony of sea lions frolicking in the water just offshore in a display of contagious playfulness. The lumbering bulls amazed them. They enjoyed each other's company and belly laughed a lot.

Marcos' mood shifted drastically as he pointed north. The sea was calm as the sea lions continued to romp and play hard. Out of sheer instinct, Marcos futilely yelled at the sea lions to get out of the water *muy pronto* as Susan looked at him in puzzlement.

Alarmed, he shouted, "There's a killer whale out there!" Knowing there was nothing he could do to reverse the course of nature, they waited in sad fascination for the horror of the inevitable event that would soon follow. The huge dorsal fin surfaced in plain sight, and Susan watched as it took its bearing and the huge nine-meter-long creature fixed its sights on an unsuspecting, young sea lion. The killer whale smashed into the juvenile seal with such force that the crash was audible onshore. Circling, the killer whale came around and, with its cavernous mouth open, scooped up the sea lion that disappeared, unlike Jonah, forever.

Susan reacted with tears after witnessing the carnage. "I have never seen anything that gruesome," she said, gasping for air.

Marcos grabbed her hand while they hurriedly headed back to the car. "I am so sorry you had to see that on the heels of our high after the first visit." *I knew we shouldn't have come back*, Marcos thought. *Another death scene is not what we need. Helvete!* Marcos glanced over at Susan who was visibly shaken. "Let's just focus on getting back to the hotel to meet with Powell."

The wheels turned in Marcos' head during the short walk back to the Navigator. Given the series of events thus far, he wondered if they had been witnesses to what he referred to as the cycle of life. Or was something else going on? He hadn't seen a killer whale at Scammon's Lagoon, ever.

They returned to the Navigator somewhat depressed. Marcos asked, "You don't suppose the angry spirits had anything to do with that bloody scene, do you? Everything was beautifully calm then wham! Am I getting paranoid, Susan?" Marcos asked. *Folke?*

Susan turned in slow motion and faced him. Clearing her throat, she spoke in hushed tones. "I don't know, Marcos. I didn't pick up any vibes, but I wasn't tuned in at all in that way. We can't assign every terrible act to the spirits, but anything is possible," she said, shuddering.

They both shook their heads, sighed, and climbed into the car. Silence filled the space between them as they drove back to town.

***

Back at the hotel, they took a short nap before dinner since Powell had not returned. *Powell had better damn well be back by dinner*, Marcos thought as his growing concern about his timetable gnawed at him again. However, he loved taking his siestas like this—a real luxury. He drifted off into a peaceful slumber right away.

Later, he awoke terrified in a cold sweat from a nightmare in which some unknown, sinister foe had stalked him. He sensed it had been an emissary dispatched by an angry spirit and shuddered as he tried to shrug off his fear. *I must face the fact I could have unleashed something horrible by chasing the meaning of the rock art*, he thought, afraid of the answer. All the unanswered, haunting questions paraded in neon lights before his eyes—*had Dave succumbed to these forces—had they killed him—and blast it, what had Dave been up to?* He intellectually sought the answers but emotionally did not look forward to the truth. *I wonder if I'm a coward. Pappa, I am so sorry. Förlåt!*

Marcos had not recovered from his exhaustion when he joined Susan in the hotel restaurant for dinner but chose not to discuss his experience with her. If he dared speak about it, it would rise to an admission of the reality of it to himself. They ordered margaritas and studied the menu. They both selected a traditional dinner of red snapper a la Veracruzana with flan for dessert and relied on the food and drinks to lift their spirits and provide temporary respite from everything.

In between bites, Susan slid in, "You know, I have to admit I'm still horrified by the killer whale attack on the poor, defenseless sea lion. I can't expunge the image from my mind, angry spirits or not. I can handle buckets of blood at the hospital, but the defenseless sea lion? What's the point? Why does there have to be so much killing in the world?" Susan teared up.

"Survival," said Marcos unequivocally. "With that thought, I think we *must* consider something or someone killed Dave for survival. Chilling concept or not." *Oh God, I've said it*, Marcos thought.

"I guess it's just against my entire value system as a doctor. I took an oath to save lives not to destroy them. I could never intentionally kill another person—could you?"

"No, not usually, but I certainly would for self-defense or defense of another. Perhaps I could have saved Dave if I'd been here," Marcos said thoughtfully.

"I hope it will never come to a test. It would be difficult to live with, I imagine."

Marcos kept eating and did not respond. As they were sipping their coffee and Kahlua, the desk clerk approached their table.

"Dr. Andersson, I didn't see you, or I would have told you sooner. Mr. Powell decided not to spend the night here. He had important business in San Ignacio tonight. I saw him leave over an hour ago."

Marcos thanked him for the news and cursed fluently in Spanish, red in the face. "At this rate, I'm never going to catch up to the guy." He had already wasted too much time waiting around for Powell. While he hoped Powell might have crucial information concerning Dave's death, time had grown shorter. He mentally reviewed what Joyce and he had discussed—soon the insurance company would close its file on this case. Sooner than that, Dave's body had to be disposed of according to Mexican law. Only a few more days remained to solve the puzzle.

Marcos heard the hotel phone ring in the distance. It reminded him of the call from Dave—the garbled recorded message on his answering machine beseeching him to come to Mulege. Then there was the part about *bopow* or something like that. Jarred by a blinding flash of insight, his mind made the connection—Dave's message was about Bob . . . *Bopow* . . . Powell.

"Susan, I'll explain on the way, but we need to leave at once," Marcos said after his revelation. "As much as I hate driving at night in Baja, I feel a sense of urgency to go to San Ignacio and catch up with Robert Powell before he takes off again."

***

Susan understood the pressing nature of their hasty departure and convinced Marcos she had been yearning to drive the Navigator and would be pleased to do the driving as long as it was not off-road over dunes and other hazards. Marcos gladly passed his key chain to her with his assurance the drive would be pavement all the way and a mere ninety kilometers, give or take. If all went well, they would arrive in an hour and a half, in time for a restful night's sleep.

Susan rubbed the triangular-shaped amulet on his key chain with her fingertips. It was cold to the touch. She stared at it for several seconds with all her medical and psychic might.

TEN
San Ignacio

According to Marcos, he and Susan would not miss much by way of scenery. They were about to drive through the bleak, barren Vizcaino Desert, a landscape of almost lifeless, scattered Joshua trees until they reached the oasis of San Ignacio, their destination.

Susan kept her eyes glued to the road south, as it dipped, rose, and conformed to the lazy relief of the land. She repeatedly ascended from one *bajada* and descended into another, trying to maintain focus.

"Aahh!" Susan screamed, making Marcos jump. A figure with outstretched arms loomed suddenly out of nowhere in the headlights. "I'm going to hit him!" she said, the graphic realization that she would smash into the person etched on her face. Relying on raw instinct, Susan swerved enough to avoid striking him straight on but glanced him with a blow sufficient to throw him over the hood of the car. She and Marcos both recoiled as the man's head slammed with cracking force into the windshield. Marcos had a brief, lurid glimpse of the man's face contacting the windshield, blood splattering across the surface. He grabbed the dashboard with white-knuckled hands and shut down for a few seconds. *No, no, no! This is bad for us*, rattled around in his head.

Susan stopped the vehicle in a panic. They both raced to the body to see if they could help the injured stranger. As soon as they reached his mangled body, they realized it was no use. He no longer needed their help. The accident was a grizzly sight with blood everywhere. The impact with the windshield had crushed the stranger's face. That made the second, inconceivably gory event in Susan's life in one day. She collapsed into Marcos' arms wailing. When she regained her composure sufficiently enough to speak, she forcefully demanded to inform the authorities.

"Are you crazy?" gasped Marcos. "Do you know what would happen if we did? Mexico follows the ancient civil code—guilty until proven innocent. The authorities would arrest you on the spot, try you for murder, and you would spend the rest of your life in a Mexican prison with absolutely no chance of release. You would be the victim of every inmate and jailer and his cousin for the rest of your life, and with no family to feed you, you would either put out or starve to death. No, we can't tell anyone about this. Help me pull the body off the road so we can get out of here. NOW!"

Susan assisted Marcos in between sobs. Marcos wet a rag and cleaned the blood off the car and cracked windshield the best he could. Feeling the need to put as much distance as possible between them and the scene of the accident, they climbed into the car and, with Marcos driving, took off rapidly for San Ignacio. Susan's desire to inform the police lingered, but Marcos insisted vehemently they could tell no one, ever. The situation truly posed a moral and practical dilemma. If they had to live without telling the authorities and knowing she had taken another human being's life, it could very well destroy her life. It had not been her fault, however. *The only good thing was there were no witnesses*, Marcos thought.

"What about the man's family?" Susan wanted to know. "Maybe we could find out who he is and give the family some money or something."

Marcos opposed the idea as it would be an admission of guilt unless they could do it anonymously. He preferred not to go anywhere near the victim nor to know anything about him.

"Couldn't we get a good attorney who would be able to prove to the court it was an accident and get us off?"

Despite his valiant attempt, Marcos was unable to help Susan fully comprehend the Mexican legal system and soon grew impatient with her stubbornness. Finally, he yelled at her that there was no way they could report the accident and avoid prison for the rest of their lives. They arrived in San Ignacio but not as Marcos had hoped. He had wanted to share this very special place with Susan without more death hanging over their heads. This was the *third* death now. It was time to consider a disturbing possibility—the unfortunate accident was in some way connected to the angry spirits.

When they checked in at the desk of the San Ignacio El Presidente, Susan pulled Marcos aside and said, "Marcos, let's get a room together tonight. I can't bear to be alone. Besides, I doubt if either of us is going to get much sleep."

While checking in, Marcos asked the clerk if he had registered a Robert Powell at the hotel. The clerk replied in the affirmative but stated Sr. Powell had already departed and did not plan to return until late. In their room, Marcos and Susan continued to discuss their plight in hushed tones until they fell asleep fitfully in separate beds.

***

Neither of them slept well, and both woke up the following morning feeling bone-tired and drained of life. Before sitting down for breakfast, Marcos inquired about Robert Powell only to learn he had gone out earlier that morning but not checked out of the hotel. Over breakfast, Marcos and Susan still debated their alternatives, including going to Santa Rosalía to board the ferry over to Hermosillo as soon as possible to leave the peninsula right away. They were so far down into Baja that even turning around and going back to California would be a major undertaking and not a quick enough exit. They could charter a plane, but they didn't want to leave the car behind as evidence that the authorities could use to trace them. Luckily, the accident had not damaged the Navigator aside from the badly cracked windshield. Marcos went back outside to make sure he had removed every trace of blood. In the pitch dark of night, he had been unable to clean properly and could still see blood splatter here and there. Feeling paranoid, he wondered if anyone had noticed. If they had, no one had said anything yet. However, the accident could have occurred at such an early hour that maybe the *policia* had not yet discovered the body. Marcos summoned Susan, and they jumped into the car. Despite his earlier misgivings, he said, "I think we need to return to the accident scene to determine the status of the body."

"Do you think that's a good idea? Maybe you were right—we should just stay as far away from this thing as possible and get out of here as soon as we can."

"Let's just check it out. Maybe we'll learn something new. Then we can decide what we're going to do."

As they rounded the bend approaching the exact spot, they saw flashing lights. A Mexican highway patrol car loomed ahead along with an ambulance. They spotted the corpse on a stretcher heading toward the ambulance. The police waved them down and greeted them.

"*¿Qué pasa aqui?*" Marcos asked the officer politely.

"Where are you going?" asked the officer. "And where are you coming from?"

Marcos informed him they were just coming from San Ignacio and were on a day trip to El Arco.

Satisfied, the officer grunted as he stared at the broken windshield. "What happened to your windshield?"

With his heart in his throat, Marcos shrugged it off and said it had happened when a passing truck had thrown a rock, a common enough occurrence for that area.

"I think you might be able to get it replaced in Guerrero Negro. Call José Pico. He's my brother-in-law."

Marcos thanked him but could not resist inquiring more about the victim from the police officer's point of view. "Is that a dead person there, officer?"

"*Sí*, we have a murder victim," the officer said with professional disinterest.

"Murder? What happened?"

"Well, the victim was shot twice, and the murderer then ran him over with a car, trying to make it look like a road accident. It's very clear the bullet wounds were the cause of death."

Susan and Marcos were incredulous, exchanged looks of relief, and murmured their condolences as the officer waved them on. Vehicles backed up behind them now. They wanted to dance a jig and celebrate the strange turn of events which shifted any blame from them to the real killer. They couldn't believe their good fortune, relieved to be in the clear. Marcos wanted to stop the car in the middle of the road and dance in celebration. He had no desire to leave Baja.

He had no desire to go to El Arco either, but he felt they had to carry through with what they had told the officer—in the unlikely event he checked. The identity of the man and the individual who shot him hovered over them along with the plethora of unanswered questions thus far. Marcos deduced the killer had shot the man shortly before their vehicle struck him and might have observed him and Susan hit the man. *Oh God, a new wrinkle*, Marcos thought. *An unidentified witness may still be out there. We're not in the clear after all. ¡Ay, caramba!* He cautiously shared his new worry with Susan.

They had a light bite to eat at a local dive in El Arco as the situation still weighed heavily on their minds. The new variable promised frightening implications. They poked their way back to San Ignacio. By the time they passed the fateful spot, the police and ambulance had left the site, and somebody had placed a small white cross on the side of the road to mark the fatality, as is often the custom in Mexico with the victim's family. That strongly indicated the victim had lived close by. The windshield would have to wait in line.

***

At the hotel restaurant late in the evening, word of the accident had reached San Ignacio, and everyone buzzed about it. Their waiter told them the whole story of the mysterious murder, eager to be the bearer of this breaking news item. Marcos and Susan listened with interest as the waiter embellished the story and made it out to be a great mystery. Marcos asked if anyone knew the identity and hometown of the man. The waiter told him the man's name was Pedro Garcia and that he lived on a little *rancheria* outside of El Arco. The waiter speculated that Pedro had been sleeping with another man's wife, a common motive for murder in that area. However, the waiter didn't know the identity of the killer nor did the *policia* yet. He added that the *policia* were most likely checking into his theory.

Marcos thought the shootings strange as Mexican law prohibited its citizens from possessing firearms unless they were hunting weapons. The poverty-stricken locals could not afford to purchase and register hunting rifles.

The waiter offered yet another theory, which did not surprise Marcos. He excitedly hypothesized that the man had found a lost treasure and someone had killed him for it. For a minute, Marcos harkened back to colorful stories of Spanish pirates loaded down with precious caches from Spanish and Filipino galleons. The pirates had put in on the coast to bury their treasures from plunder in the Far East and on the high seas, even bringing back gold from South America.

After dinner, Marcos invited Susan to join him at the bar for a nightcap. They were sleep-deprived from the night before, exacerbated by the stress of the day. Marcos was extremely agitated that he had been unable to catch up with the illusive Powell all day.

"I feel like I'm dragging my big feet," he muttered to himself, annoyed. While they sipped Conquistador brandy and savored its bouquet, a portly gringo of medium height with a ruddy complexion, a mop of unruly, dishwater-blond hair, and several days' growth of beard entered the bar and sat down at a table near theirs. He ordered, and when his drink came, he looked in their direction, raised his glass, and offered, "*Salud.*" Susan and Marcos saluted in return by raising their glasses and returned to their private conversation.

The man got up, came over to their table, and without asking, joined them. Marcos and Susan abruptly turned away, in no mood for company. The brash stranger affronted them with his rumpled clothes—an ugly, straw cowboy hat, Hawaiian shirt, and moss-green cargo shorts. Instantly, the man asked if they had heard about the *accident.* Marcos caught the man's choice of the word accident when everyone was talking about the murder.

"Why, I reckon the situation may not a' been what it appeared to be," the man sneered while Marcos tapped on the table in response and Susan rubbed her forearm. "I'm a thinkin' further investigation might reveal some interestin' new facts, if'n you git my drift."

Marcos stopped tapping, spun around, and got right in the man's face. "Like what?" Marcos asked in a gravelly tone.

"Interestin' thing ya have there," the man said, pointing to Marcos' key ring with the amulet. The man pounded down the rest of his drink, sprang up, and left without another word except for his all-knowing parting gaze over his shoulder.

"I don't like that guy," said Susan as she placed her hand on Marcos' shoulder.

***

A loud knock on the door invaded the calm of getting ready for bed. When Marcos answered, he found only a note on the floor. The note was in English and presented a terse message—*How did your windshield get broken?* There was no signature. He decided the note's author was the man in the bar who could have witnessed the accident, or worse, was the murderer who wanted something.

Deciding to investigate, Marcos waited until the wee hours of the morning when he felt everyone would be asleep then crept out without disturbing Susan. Out in the parking area in front of the hotel, he found a red Bronco with Arizona plates, the only other vehicle without Mexican plates. It had to belong to the gringo in the bar. Marcos tried the doors—locked. He then retrieved a piece of wire from the Navigator and fashioned a hook, slipped it through the window of the Bronco, and popped open the lock in a few seconds. After that, he examined the car and in a flash discovered a 30.06 rifle with an infrared telescopic scope under the back seat wrapped in a blanket. Marcos examined the rifle and determined it most certainly could have been the murder weapon. With that powerful weapon, the shooter could have effortlessly hit his target from quite a distance. The infrared scope would have easily enabled the shooter to witness the Navigator strike the victim. With more questions than answers, Marcos slipped out of the car, locked the doors behind him, and returned to bed for another sleepless night with his dark thoughts uncontrollably bouncing around his mind.

***

At breakfast the next morning, Marcos divulged to Susan what he had discovered in the car. Before she could comment, the gringo entered the restaurant and gave them a cheerful good morning salutation.

"Mind if I join you on this beautiful day?" Not waiting for an invitation, he sat down on an empty chair at their table. The waiter presented him with a menu. While he studied the menu, and Marcos and Susan studied him, he commented in a blasé manner, "Someone broke into my car last night."

Marcos said, "That's too bad. Anything missing?"

"Curiously, no. All appears to be as I left it," the gringo said.

"What exactly brings you to Baja?" Marcos asked. "Hunting, perhaps?" He wanted the gringo to know he had seen the rifle, already certain his rummaging around was known to the man.

"Maybe. Why do you ask?"

"Well, people don't usually carry a concealed 30.06 in their car unless maybe they're going to do some kind of hunting, and I just wondered what kind of hunting you had in mind," said Marcos with a calculated tone. Not waiting for an answer, he blurted out straight off, "You killed Pedro, didn't you? Why?"

Without taking his eyes off the menu, the gringo casually replied, "So, what if I did?" He cleared his throat. "You know, I'm in Mexico to raise capital for a business venture. Might the two of you consider a contribution to my cause?"

Marcos declined out of hand. He wanted to choke the slimy lout with his bare hands but refrained, using all his willpower.

The sleazy gringo looked straight at Susan, drooling and lusting after her. "Let me introduce myself. I'm Robert . . . Bob Powell from Tucson. I'm in mining. I already know your names. I got them from the desk clerk who said you'd been askin' 'bout me. Why?"

Shaken by the revelation, Marcos took a few deep breaths before he could respond. "Because I want to ask you some questions about a friend of mine, Dr. Dave Pearce, an archaeologist. You knew him."

"So, what if I did?"

"Did you know he was found dead at an archaeological site a few days ago?"

"Not surprisin' a'tall."

"What precisely do you mean by that?"

"He was messin' 'round on private property where them stupid paintin's is located. What he saw in them's beyond me. I've seen kindergartners draw better'n that. Them ranchers 's gettin' mighty sensitive about people pokin' 'round where they don't belong, 'specially where the rock art's concerned."

"Why are they so sensitive about the rock art all of a sudden?"

"Cuz it's their land, and they don't need nobody telling them what to do with it. The government's talking 'bout makin' them rock art sites some kind of national park or somethin' like that."

"Isn't preserving the art a good thing?" asked Marcos.

"Not for them ranchers it ain't. And another thing. That friend of yours was goin' off the deep end. I think them pitchures was driving him nuts. Why lately, the minute you'd bring up the art, he'd start shakin' and quakin' right out of the blue with a look on his face worse'n if he'd seen a ghost. He was turnin' into a nut case. Don't know what happened. He used to be a normal sorta guy. I kinda liked him, the way he'd tell me where them rock art sites was at and all."

"Why do *you* want to know where rock art sites are located?"

"Zeolites. You find rock art, you're gonna find zeolites, most likely." Bob rose noisily to leave. "I'd advise you to reconsider my offer of investin' in my mining operations. Maybe Susan here would like to make a nice little down payment right after breakfast." He cackled.

Marcos shot out of his chair and struck the loudmouth all in one motion, knocking him to the ground. Expecting retaliation, Marcos readied himself to counter any blow.

Instead, Bob just snickered and rubbed his jaw, seemingly unruffled. "Marcos, did you notice anything a missin' from your car?"

The remark startled Marcos. He had not and wondered to what the troglodyte was referring. "Come on, Susan, let's get out of here," Marcos said, grabbing her hand and leading her out. Bob stood his ground and merely smiled as they departed. Instinctively, they made a beeline to the parking lot and unlocked the Navigator. Nothing appeared to be missing. Marcos shook his head at Bob's earlier question. Susan walked around the car calmly, looking for telltale dents, blood, or anything out of the ordinary.

"Marcos," said Susan, "come here!" She was in the vehicle's front staring red-faced at the hood of the car. She pointed at a blank spot where the Lincoln emblem once appeared prominently on the hood.

That was the missing object. They returned to the restaurant to confront Bob, but they found he had already departed. By the time they ran back to the parking lot, his car was gone as well. If it were not for the possibility of things getting messy with the Lincoln emblem, Marcos would have reported Bob to the authorities instantly. He *had* to get that emblem back, and they *had* to get to Mulege to get Dave's body.

***

Exhausted after two sleepless nights, they hit their beds that evening and didn't awake until the sun shone brightly through the window. They could hear the raucous crowing of roosters around town rudely penetrating their consciousness. The angry spirits had thankfully spared Marcos this time.

"Well," Marcos interrupted the silence, "I've decided to stay. I owe it to Dave. I can't leave now."

"Good. I'm staying with you. You need me to examine the body and make an authoritative report. You also need me for the rock art."

"I'm glad you're here, Susan," said Marcos as he took her hand and squeezed it. "But I'm not sure I *need* you for the rock art."

"Again with that. You need me more than you know for the rock art. There are angry spirits you must appease. I think it's a matter of life or death. You *need* me for that."

Marcos shuddered to think of it.

Invigorated by a good night's sleep without nightmares, Marcos announced that he needed to get up into the mountains to show Susan some spectacular, aboriginal paintings known as murals because of their bigger-than-life size. He wanted to find out if she might learn something from those paintings because they were similar to the ones where Dave had died. Maybe they could find a connection—he thought it worth a try.

"But what about Robert Powell?" Susan asked.

"I don't know. I'd just as soon get far away from him. I'm hoping he won't turn us in to the police since we could implicate him." He shook his head. "I don't know, but I don't think we can do any more about it right now. Best to refocus. We need to help Joyce and Dave."

"I so agree. Let's get going." She gave him a reassuring smile.

From San Ignacio, they headed east for several kilometers while Marcos scanned the desert for the dirt track that headed north up into the mountains. He pointed out the craggy peaks of the Tres Vírgines while keeping a vigilant eye peeled on the horizon.

At last, he found the *carretera* heading north. Mile after mile, they ground sluggishly through the desert, passing the occasional *cardón* or stand cacti with pitaya fruit. The fruit from those stalky cacti had provided sustenance to the aboriginals. Some isolated ranches existed in the area, and scrawny cattle grazed with chollas stuck to their noses. At an old well, they stopped to sip some of its cool, refreshing water from the depths of the earth. They wet their bandanas and wound them back around their necks.

Continuing through the desert, they ascended the peneplain and arrived at a conspicuous feature in the typography consisting of a tumbled basalt flow from an ancient volcanic eruption. Halfway through it, Marcos stopped and got out. Susan didn't take long to discover the staggering, huge petroglyph site—an entire field covering many hectares. Almost every boulder featured some kind of artwork on it. She had a wonderful time examining more and more interesting designs of all kinds, including fish, way out there in the middle of the desert. Her favorites were those depicting macho guys who at first blush appeared to have three legs until she looked more closely and realized the middle legs represented huge phalluses.

"Hmm. These guys were super well-endowed," Susan said.

Marcos beamed and said he had developed a scientific theory that accounted for the extinction of the culture there. As the culture had evolved over time, men's and women's bodies had developed at different rates. At some unfortunate point in the evolutionary process, women had become anatomically unable to handle the men's size and had to refrain from lovemaking. As a result, the women bore no children, and the race eventually died out. "What do you think of that one?" Marcos posed the question with a smirk.

Susan rolled her eyes and shook her head. "I'd say the men had delusions of grandeur, Dr. Andersson."

Having satisfied themselves with observing hundreds of petroglyphs, they pushed on deeper into the desert. At the base of precipitous mountains, Marcos parked the vehicle and grabbed the canteen. They headed up a side canyon, respectfully avoiding the cholla as Marcos warned Susan that they would jump up behind and zap her. They stopped for a breather and swigged some water. As Susan turned around to survey the scenery, she let out a yelp. She had inadvertently backed into a cholla and had at least ten vicious thorns sticking into her backside. Marcos smiled widely and told her he had warned her and apologetically insisted she drop her pants. "Trust me. I have extracted thorns from a substantial number of students' and colleagues' body parts over the years during field work. You might say I have conquered the thorny problem. Ha!" *Wow! That time Folke actually broke a smile*, Marcos thought. *Bra.*

Unamused, Susan asked, "How can I drop my drawers with these things sticking in my rear?" Susan moaned.

"First, we'll have to pull them out the best we can, but some are going to break off, I'm afraid."

Standing in a compromising position with her bare bottom exposed, Marcos got out his Swiss army knife, sanitized the blade with a lighter, and began digging out the spines. When he finished his excavating, he gave her a friendly, but cautiously encouraging pat, avoiding the sore areas.

"Pull up your pants. You shouldn't go around with them down like that. What would people think?" he said, gesturing with exaggeration.

"What people?" Susan wanted to know. "You're the only one here, and I wonder what you think . . . with your perverted sense of humor."

Marcos enjoyed a belly laugh and cautioned her to be more careful in the future.

They climbed up a steeper grade, which was the entrance to a box canyon. Marcos took an abrupt turn to the left and headed north. Before long, they were climbing hand over hand up a cliff face with only roots and rocks for perches. Marcos emerged onto a shelf with an overhang from the cliff above him. He turned to give Susan a hand, which she happily accepted.

While catching her breath, she looked up and gasped. There, high on the ceiling of the overhang, beautiful, bigger-than-life, polychromatic figures of desert big horn sheep, deer and both male and female humans greeted her gaze. Curiously, the breasts of the females protruded from their armpits. Marcos commented the women were lying on their backs, their breasts flopping out under their arms.

"Were these women related to the well-endowed men?" Susan asked.

"Well, that's difficult to determine because animal skins modestly conceal the men's body parts in the murals," Marcos said.

"Yes, I can see that," Susan said.

"The theory is that the early missionaries thought the area had been inhabited by a race of giants owing to the size of the representations in the murals. It was a race of superior morality represented by the coverings. These male representations are unlike the natives the missionaries actually encountered during their efforts to convert them." Looking beyond the cave ceiling and the art, Marcos noticed for the first time a white deposit spilling over the side of the cliff—possibly zeolites. "Susan, see the white deposits? If they're zeolites like Bob Powell described, this area could be in terrible danger," Marcos said gravely.

Susan nodded her head in agreement and said, "I think that's a real consideration."

As they admired the incredible, monumental artwork, Susan said, "How do you think the natives managed the logistics of getting so high onto the cave walls to paint such magnificent works?"

Before Marcos could answer, two shots rang out from somewhere down the canyon, and bullets ricocheted from the cliff wall, spattering them with rock chips. Instantly, they hit the dirt and lay among goat droppings, waiting for the next round of shots. Nothing happened. Cautiously, Marcos crawled over to the edge of the precipice and peered out over the desert below, watching for movement. Far in the distance, he thought he caught a glimpse of movement but nothing distinct.

They waited for an eternity until they heard another shot from farther down the canyon. Marcos caught a fleeting impression of red movement through the thick paloverde, which must have been Bob's red Bronco. The weasel had followed them and shot at them. If Bob had been aiming to kill them, he could have done so easily. *Worse. He's toying with us*, Marcos figured.

"What now?" Susan asked.

"I'm totally open to suggestions. The only way out of the canyon is the way we came. And likewise, that road is the only way in. If that's Bob, he could be waiting to ambush us and attack at will." It gave Marcos a sick feeling of helplessness, having no weapons. They were sitting ducks. It reminded him of being back once again in the swirling vortex of the spirit realm.

After another hour, Marcos saw what he thought had been the red Bronco leaving through the dense undergrowth in the arroyo bottom, and he was certain Bob had departed. Nudging Susan, he said, "Let's try now." Reluctantly, they left the incredible murals behind and haltingly descended the cliff back to the floor of the canyon, feeling like open targets as they awkwardly climbed down. Marcos still feared Bob would set up an ambush somewhere on the way out.

Arriving back at their parked car, Marcos discovered Bob had shot out one of his tires, which was the last shot they had heard. Fortunately, they had a spare, and Marcos wasted no time in changing out the flat tire. Throwing the ruined tire into the back of the Navigator, he noticed the tire had been penetrated by three cholla spines and would have leaked and gone flat soon as the spines worked their way in. *Pesky cholla.* He shook his head.

Reaching to the floor of the car where he had stowed it, Marcos picked up his key ring by the amulet and instantly cried out in pain, dropping it with a thud back on the floor. "Ouch, that was hot. It must have heated up sitting in the car. The sun's sizzling today," he said as he examined his hand and noticed a red welt where the amulet had left its mark. Susan gave him an odd look but said nothing.

"Okay, I have a plan," Marcos said. If Bob plans an ambush, I don't think he'll do it before we get to the Hernandez ranch. That's the fenced-in ranch we passed on our way in. I think we can stop there and enlist the help of old Raymundo Hernandez and his three sons. They know this country intimately, and we've helped each other out over many years of friendship."

Susan managed a nod, still shaking slightly. "I trust you," she said.

Marcos drove ahead with extreme caution, stopping at the top of every rise to sneak out of the car and survey what was ahead with his binoculars. After determining that it would be safe to travel to the next promontory, they started cautiously, taking the back way to the Hernandez hacienda away from the main road.

Worried that maybe Bob had reached the hacienda first with some evil intent, he parked the car in a pitaya thicket and approached the hacienda on foot with Susan. They assumed a vantage point a hundred meters from the house, watched, and waited. Nada. After about five minutes, Miguel, the youngest son, emerged from the house and walked with no apparent concern toward the corral. Angling through the cover of the bush, Marcos converged with Miguel at the corner of the corral, startling him as he whispered his greeting.

When he detailed out the situation, Miguel assured him they had not seen Bob, but they knew him and collectively didn't like him. Bob had approached them some months before about getting a patent from them for mining rights on their property, which they had refused to give him.

Asking Susan to stand guard undercover and warn them if Bob approached, Marcos went into the house with Miguel to explain their dilemma to the men. Soon the men emerged from the house each carrying a 30-30, which all the ranchers around owned, most likely unregistered. They devised a simple plan. They would proceed just as Marcos had, cautiously, but with superior firepower. They were confident they could avert any ambush Bob might have in mind for them. Marcos felt more secure in their superior knowledge of the terrain where they could expect likely danger and defend themselves accordingly. Raymundo stated if Bob were to ambush someone, it would be near El Pozo.

They advanced cautiously, Susan and Marcos in the Navigator and the Hernandez men in their old Chevy pickup. When they reached the rise above El Pozo, they all got out and eased up to the rim overlooking the community well. From the rocks to the east of the well, they heard a shot ring out. Bob had discovered them. Raymundo gave the signal for all the men to fan out. With enough cover, they eventually surrounded Bob's position so he wouldn't have a chance. Now the advantage was in their favor.

As they maneuvered into position and stayed out of sight the best they could, they heard the distinctive sound of the Bronco revving up and taking off. Marcos peered from his position and could see the Bronco making a hasty retreat to the hard road. Bob would conceivably not give them any more trouble that day, now that he knew Marcos had reinforcements. The Hernandez men accompanied them back to the hard road just to make sure.

When they reached the highway, Marcos thanked them and presented them with a large box of 30-30 shells to show his appreciation for their efforts, efforts that could very well have saved their lives. He kept such things on hand, knowing their value in barren Baja. What puzzled Marcos was if Bob had actually wanted to kill them, he easily could have done so before they had noticed his presence. He thought once again that Bob must be toying with them and expressed his concerns to Susan.

"Of course he's toying with us. He wants our money. He's trying to scare us into investing in his zeolites mining operation," Susan said.

Marcos stood fixed in place and looked into her eyes. "You're right. Well, enough of that noise. Let's hurry to Santa Rosalía and inform the authorities about Bob and implicate him as the murderer." While he was not comfortable about driving on to Santa Rosalía with the possibility of another ambush, he had to risk it. But he realized that reporting Bob to the authorities could backfire on them, placing them under suspicion for their involvement in the death. The concept gelled in Marcos' mind—Bob could also have killed Dave given the importance of the zeolites. Dave's work had the potential to threaten Bob's zeolites operation. Marcos accepted that theory as being more logical than the angry spirit stuff. *That's quite a relief,* he thought.

***

It was a letdown for Marcos when they viewed the Sea of Cortez, albeit a dramatic approach winding down from the altiplano. The view paled by comparison to the breathtaking overlook above Bahía de los Ángeles he had wanted to show Susan earlier. Once they reached the coast, it was only a short distance to the town of Santa Rosalía, which in its heyday had been an important mining center and bustling port. At present, only a few mines remained open with one processing minimally. However, the rusty vestiges exemplifying its former glory still attested to a busy place on the otherwise sparsely populated coast.

Marcos had originally thought of pushing on to Mulege to spend the night, but informing the authorities was now his immediate goal. He and Susan found a small hotel just off the main street. It reflected a flavor of French influence due to the French mining interests that had inspired the architecture. Marcos pointed out a metal church by Eiffel of Eiffel Tower fame who had designed and prefabricated it for use in France's tropical colonies. Years later, the Boleo Mining Company operating in Baja had it shipped to Santa Rosalía where the authorities had assembled it with pride and preserved it as an important landmark.

The next order of business was to locate the *policia* and make a report. Marcos and Susan decided to walk to the police station only three blocks from the hotel. When they got there, they found it closed. Inquiries informed them that the police were out investigating a boating accident but, if truth be known, were out fishing, and no one knew for sure when they would return. Mañana was the consensus. Discouraged and tired, they returned to the hotel and grabbed large cups of black coffee in the quaint, lobby café. While waiting for service, their adversary, Bob, entered with an ear-to-ear smile on his face.

"Well, fancy meetin' you and Susan here," said Bob, as if nothing had happened.

"What the hell are you doing here?" asked Marcos venomously.

"Oh, just passing through and saw your vehicle out front and thought I'd check to see if you had any change o' heart on that investment opportunity I was a tellin' you 'bout."

"Not a chance," said Marcos.

"Oh? Well, now let me show you some incentive I happen to have right here," Bob said as he touched his breast pocket.

"What do you mean?" asked Marcos.

Bob snickered, took a Polaroid photograph from his pocket, and handed it to Marcos. Marcos and Susan gasped when they recognized the Lincoln insignia smudged and caked with a thick crust of blood. Bob's eyes twinkled as he indicated it would be an easy matter, even in Mexico, to show that the blood on the missing hood ornament matched the blood of the dead man. Maybe Marcos needed to reconsider. Two hundred and fifty thousand Yankee dollars each could be enough to get Bob's operation started and would be a good investment for many reasons.

Marcos' stomach turned. He felt relieved that he had not been able to report back to the police, but he was unsure of what to do. One thing for sure—he had to get the Lincoln emblem back along with Bob's rifle. There presumably was not another 30-06 within a thousand kilometers, and it would amount to conclusive evidence regarding the murder weapon.

"Why were you shooting at us today, you jerk?"

"Just lettin' you know I mean business. You almost got the drop on me though, didn't cha?"

"Bob, you had better clear out of here before I do something we'll both regret," seethed Marcos through his teeth.

Bob cocked his head confidently and got up, winking at Susan with unbridled lust.

*****

Marcos and Susan retired to their room and debated through most of the night what to do about Bob and their tenuous situation. As expected, Susan wanted to make a clean slate of the whole thing and get it out into the open. Marcos stressed that her approach would likely backfire on them. The last thing he wanted was the both of them to spend the rest of their days in a Mexican jail as he remembered Bob's parting, "Ya have three days to arrange your finances. If ya don't pay up, I'm turning the evidence over to the *policia,* and you'll be enjoyin' the hospitality of a Mexican jail the rest of your lives."

Marcos unleashed his fury on the innocent coffee table, upending it, and then smashing a wine bottle and glasses to pieces. *Herregud! I just let my anger get to me, exactly not what a good scientist should do*, Marcos thought. *What a mess.* "So sorry, Susan. I rarely get that angry. I let Bob get to me. My family would not be very proud." *Förlåt, pappa!*

Standing a few feet away, Susan observed Marcos through his rant. "Here, I'll help you pick up the pieces while you cool off."

Marcos just swore a blue streak in Swedish through gritted teeth.

ELEVEN
Robert Powell

"Okay, then," said Susan, exasperated and picking up glass shards, "let's just throw some money at this guy and get him off our backs. I can probably scrape up some cash and borrow some quickly enough. Maybe you could do the same?"

Marcos waved away the suggestion. "Don't you understand? He'll never leave us in peace and will just continue to hound us forever. He's a human leech. We *must* get my hood ornament back. Susan, I just know Bob had something to do with Dave's death, too. Hey, why don't you unleash your psychic powers on him? Put a hex on him. You know, a real whammy."

"You don't know what you're saying, Marcos. It's unthinkable for me to invoke the *dark* side. It beckons all kinds of problems. And I don't appreciate your trivialization of my psychic abilities."

"Yeah, well, I'd say the dark side has already reared its ugly head here, wouldn't you?"

"If so, no need to make it any worse. *No*, that's *not* an alternative, Marcos," Susan said, stomping her foot in protest.

She pondered the situation a while longer and thoughtfully offered a solution. "Marcos, have you seen the way that sleazebag looks at me? How about I make myself appear interested in him to distract him—the oldest play in the book. Then you could go through his car and his room and recover the gun and the hood ornament. They must be in one place or another."

"Even the thought of that creep touching you makes my skin crawl," said Marcos, covering his eyes with his hands.

"Don't worry, nothing will happen. I can take care of myself. I'll just make him think it might be possible. Then you can signal me when you find the hood ornament, and it will all be over."

They agreed it was the best plan they could come up with on a dime. In truth, they realized it had better work because they only had four more days to get to Dave's body.

***

The next morning, Marcos made a big production of having Susan kiss him goodbye in front of the hotel and wave goodbye to him, saying enthusiastically she couldn't wait to see him that night. Marcos repeated it in Spanish. Alluringly attired in a tight T-shirt and short shorts, Susan was ready to play her role.

Marcos drove out of town. He peered over his shoulder to check for a tail then veered off the road and pulled deep into a cavernous, abandoned, milling shed. He successfully concealed his car from prying eyes. Then he hiked back to town, taking a circuitous route along the ridges overlooking the town. Cautiously, he returned to the hotel and entered from the rear, certain nobody had spotted him, as it was still early in the morning. Marcos waited in a closet in the hallway off the dining room. He could observe Susan sitting at a table alone, sipping a cup of coffee while reading a novel. Before long, the door opened, and Bob entered with an ear-to-ear, smug smile on his face upon seeing Susan alone.

"Well, darlin' where's our boy, Marcos? Did ya wear him out last night?" Bob asked.

"Don't be vulgar," Susan said with contempt. "He's away for the day on business."

"Well, 1 hope he's arrangin' to get the investment money we discussed."

"That is a likely possibility," said Susan without commitment.

"May 1 join you, darlin'?" he said as he sat down without Susan's response. Bob motioned for the server and ordered *huevos rancheros* and coffee. While he ate with knife and fork in different hands, elbows on the table, smacking his lips, and Susan cringing with every bite, he gawked at her with his tongue hanging out as it wagged side to side.

"Well now," Bob gurgled between bites and a big gulp of coffee, "ain't that convenient. What d'ya say 1 take ya out on a little excursion and show ya the sites? There's some interestin' old minin' operations around these parts that 1 could explain to ya and show ya just how 1 intend to resurrect them with your investment money."

As coyly as she could muster a reply, Susan agreed it might be a worthwhile way to spend an otherwise lonesome day. Bob's lascivious, craggy face beamed with sheer delight at the prospect.

"Just let me finish up here, grab something from my room, and we'll be off." Bob nearly toppled the table leaping up in his haste. Neither Marcos nor Susan had realized Bob was staying conveniently in the same hotel with his vehicle nearby. He ascended the stairs, and Susan discretely followed. A few minutes later, she slipped back into the dining room and whispered to Marcos in the closet, "He's in number five, just down the hall from our room."

Seated back at the table, she waited for Bob to reappear. When he returned, Marcos could see Bob had attempted to tidy himself a little by shaving and changing into a clean shirt with a new orange bandana around his red neck. In great, good humor, he helped Susan out of her chair and took her by the arm, leading her to the exit. "First, we'll go to the old stamping and crushing operation. There's some equipment there 1 think 1 can use, and we should be able to get it goin' again for a few bucks, then we can go for silver as well as zeolites."

***

Marcos was unsure whether to follow them or go to the room first. He obviously had no car, and he didn't know how far they were going. He now didn't appreciate the turn of events and decided the best course of action was to go to Bob's room first. He found the room had one of those old-fashioned locks, like on his bedroom door as a child—each key worked in every lock in the house. On a whim, he tried his room key in Bob's lock. With no resistance, it opened easily.

Marcos entered and rummaged through Bob's meager belongings. He rifled through all the drawers—nothing. He lifted the mattress and looked around for other possible hiding places to no avail. He lifted the toilet tank cover and peered in hoping to find something. Nothing there. Marcos concluded that Bob wasn't stupid enough to hide anything in his room. He bristled with anger, slamming the door shut behind him with a crash and hustling to track down the car.

Remembering that Bob had mentioned the old stamp mill, he went downstairs and asked the front desk clerk for directions. The mill was three kilometers out of town to the west—too far to walk and not enough of a time window to get his vehicle. Instantly, he made up his mind to enlist the services of the only taxi in town and asked the clerk to call for him. After some discussion on the phone, the clerk informed him that the taxi driver regretted that another family had engaged him to drive them to Mulege that day. Marcos implored the clerk to tell the driver if he could only spare him five minutes, he would pay triple the normal fare for just a five-kilometer ride. He slipped the man at the desk a hundred *peso* piece as a token of his urgency. The *pesos* did the trick, and the driver would wait out front in a couple minutes.

In the cab, Marcos told the driver he planned to surprise some old friends, so he didn't want them to see him approach. When they arrived in the vicinity, the driver dropped him off and pointed out a path that would take him onto the site undetected. Marcos gladly handed over the agreed-upon fare and jumped out of the car. Following the path the driver had indicated, Marcos soon spotted Bob's car, devoid of Bob. Two things concerned him. First, he wondered if Susan was still all right, and second, he wanted to make sure he was undetected while he rummaged through Bob's car. He needed to determine their whereabouts before anything else.

***

During the drive to the stamping and crushing operation, Susan witnessed Bob's transformation from a redneck dullard to a sophisticated, self-educated mining engineer. He enthusiastically regaled her about ore strikes, prospecting for them, and determining the ore-bearing deposit. She learned about projecting the contents, the best locations to mine, and the expense and profit ratios of the whole operation. Submerged in mining operations, Susan forgot for a few seconds how much she detested Bob. Regardless of what she thought of him as a person, however, she admitted he was professional and competent in his area. Thus far, he appeared to be more interested in the mining operation than in her. She didn't know whether to be relieved or insulted. At least he had made no advances. Susan hoped Marcos had discovered the emblem in Bob's room and would soon find them.

Those were the thoughts going through her mind when they arrived at the site. Bob suggested they go up to the office where he had some charts to show her. On the way up, they passed a small, corrugated iron shed with the words *Peligro Dinamita* written in flaking and fading large letters on each of the four sides.

"What does that say?" Susan asked.

"It says, *Danger Dynamite*," Bob translated.

"Dynamite," echoed Susan, stalling, "I've always been fascinated by those movies where people set off charges of dynamite and blow up something."

"So, ya like ta see things blow up, do ya?"

"It fascinates me."

"Well, maybe if yur a good girl, I'll give ya a little show afterward."

As soon as they reached the broken-down office, Bob closed and locked the door behind them, which made Susan suddenly feel alone and vulnerable. With purpose, she glanced around the sparsely furnished, dusty office for a weapon she might employ in her defense if it should come to that. Bob led the way to a small bunk along the far wall. He dusted it off, sat down, and patted the mattress as an invitation for her to join him. She pretended not to notice his actions.

"What were you going to show me?" she asked, attempting to avert him from his obvious intentions.

"If ya come over here and sit on my lap, I may be more convinced to git out some sticks," Bob said with a leer.

Susan could hardly ignore the lewd implications and tried to say without disgust, "Hey, if you play your cards right, there will be plenty of time for *some activity* later, but first I want to learn all about this operation if I'm going to be an investor in it."

Temporarily appeased, Bob went to a cabinet and took out a chart, which he unrolled and laid out on a drafting table. She approached the table where he was intently poring over the map, again in a professional manner. He started explaining to her the strikes and dips and how he was able by taking a few core samples to determine the structure of the deposit and estimate its contents.

"That all sounds very scientific," she observed, trying to sound impressed, "but there might be other ways to determine the lode too—and other locations as well."

"Like what?" asked Bob with genuine interest.

"Well, you don't know very much about me . . . yet . . . but one thing you should know is that I have some ability with psychic powers, and while I've never enlisted these powers for personal gain nor specifically addressed them to such things as finding the location of mineral deposits, I feel quite certain that it might be worth a try."

"Hmm, okay, little lady, let's see whatcha can do." Bob retrieved a large chart of Baja from the corner, unrolled it, and tacked it to the wall. "Now, s'pose ya start pointin' out where ya think we might find them zeolites. I already know where a lot of deposits are, so I can check out if you know what yur doin' or not."

Convinced through experience that her psychic abilities would not fail her, Susan withdrew into a state of high meditation and turned herself over to the higher powers, asking for their guidance. When she felt ready, she took another deep breath, approached the map, and pointed out several locations that gave her positive vibrations. Bob made Xs on the map with a pencil wherever she pointed. When she finished a few minutes later, she felt exhausted. Bob studied the distribution of Xs.

"You're pretty good, missy. Ya found a heap o' sites, some I know, and some I don't. What might surprise that boyfriend of yours is you also located a bundle of them paintin's. Do ya see what's going on?"

"What do you mean?"

"Well, haven't you figured out wherever ya get rock art, ya most likely find zeolites? Them old Injuns liked ta paint on basalt. Basalt's volcanic, and so's zeolites. It's formed in association with basalt. It's the white, foamy stuff that forms on the top of basalt flows."

"Fascinating."

"Well, them paintin's is a bit of luck, cuz it makes zeolites easy to find. That's where that archaeologist fella come in handy. He'd tell me where them rock art sites was, and I'd usually find zeolites there."

"So, that's why you were working with Dave?"

"Yup, too bad what happened. I coulda used him more."

"What do you mean exactly?"

"You know, him dying and all. Leastways, he's prolly outta his misery now. Hated ta do it, though."

"Hold on there, Bob. Explain what you mean, *out of his misery and you hated to do* what?"

"Well, when he found out I intended to blow all them lousy paintin's to smith-a-reens, he came on the site and refused to leave, thinkin' it would stop me from dynamitin' them squiggles on the rocks. He started what he called communicatin' with the spirits. Guess he thought he would turn 'em against me, but it musta backfired. He started screamin' and carryin' on, floppin' on his back like a stuck pig. He was one scared *hombre*. Never seen such fright on a face as that. I could tell he'd given up hope. They had him good and wasn't lettin' go. He begged me ta shoot him. I took pity on him. Hated to do it, though. He reckoned them spirits was gonna tell him all about their art, what it meant. Said he was on the verge of them tellin' him. He was afeared and excited all at the same time."

"You killed Dave?" gasped Susan.

"Mercy killin'. You'd a done the same thing if you got any decency in ya."

"Incredible. You admit you killed Dave because he seemed possessed by spirits. Why do you want to destroy rock art? I don't understand."

"Simple, missy. The Mexican government's makin' noise 'bout protectin' the rock art. The rock art's where them zeolites are located. They make a national monument of 'em and we're plum outa luck for minin' zeolites. Ya git it?"

"Oh, my God," Susan said as recognition dawned on her.

"Got most of them ranchers lined up on my side now. Most of 'em is broke. Devaluation hit 'em hard. They need cash. Zeolites equals cash. That rock art ain't ever gonna help nobody. Ya know, *they* killed Dave, poor devil. That's the way I look at it. Them ranchers is lookin' forward to gettin' dynamite so's they can blow up all the rock art on their ranches. Then the government won't have nothin' ta protect. Dynamite shipment's comin' soon, missy. Then kaboom!"

"But what's the big deal about zeolites? Isn't that what they use to make kitty litter?"

"Some, but there's real money in these here Baja zeolites. Special properties, ya know. You could make gasoline with Baja zeolites, and alcohol, acts as a *catlist*. Tell me there's not a fortune here. You're just lucky I'm invitin' ya to invest. I'm gonna make you a rich woman. You'll thank me afore long. Well, heck, this could shake up them snooty Arabs, good and plenty. Could be the end o' OPEC as we know it."

Bob's information had stupefied Susan to such a degree that she hardly noticed he had positioned himself next to her. He encircled her with his arms and forced a sloppy, unwanted kiss on her lips, trying to force his tongue into her mouth. Without warning, his powerful arms released her, and he reached out and pulled up her top around her neck in one motion, exposing her perfectly fitted, silk camisole. He stopped to admire the statuesque figure in front of him. Instinctively, Susan covered her chest with her arms as she evaluated the situation and then pulled down her top. She could fight him, but she needed to stall so that Marcos could find the Navigator emblem. She didn't doubt Marcos would arrive, eventually. Doing the first thing that came to mind, she surprised Bob when she started laughing.

"Hey, Bob, don't be so hasty, we have plenty of time. If you want to get me going, why don't you set off some of those dynamite charges. That would give *me* a charge, and maybe then, I'll be able to give you an even bigger charge. Dynamite turns me on, Bob."

"Okay," he said haltingly with amusement. "Tell ya what. Why don't ya just slip out of them shorts for me like a good little girl? Give me some incentive, ya know?"

Provocatively, Susan undid the button at her waist and teasingly slid down the zipper. Delaying the end of the show as long as possible, she let her shorts fall to the floor in slow motion while she moved her hips. Humming, she pulled her top over her head, twirled it a couple of times, and tossed it casually on top of her shorts. She stood before him in her expensive, black lace panties and camisole, wheels turning as she contemplated her next move.

Bob ogled and drooled at the same time.

Next, with a look befitting a temptress, she placed her fingers in the elastic band of her panties and confidently strutted back and forth in front of a mesmerized Bob who enjoyed the show propped up on one elbow. Adrenalin pumping, Susan wet her lips, pasted a smile on her face, held her breath, and planted a kiss squarely on Bob's fleshy lips.

"There," she said coyly. "I've kept my part of the bargain, now you keep yours. Be a good boy and set off some fireworks for me. You'll be glad you did. You'd better make it a good show, however."

***

Tripping over himself, Bob speedily unlocked a cabinet over the desk and took out a plunger and large reel of wire. He deftly stripped off the insulation on the wire and hooked the exposed ends around the terminals of the detonating device. He started to leave when he realized that he should take his rifle with him. Bob slung it over his shoulder, unraveled the wire, and departed, whistling as he locked the door behind him. He unlocked the door of the dynamite shed, removed two sticks, cocked his head in hesitation, and took out two more. He approached the exposed cut after unreeling the wire as he progressed toward the hillside at the back of the site and found a core hole where the crew had earlier extracted samples. Bob plunged in two sticks of dynamite then affixed and secured the wires to the detonating cap. He glimpsed back at the office and waved at Susan looking like a vintage calendar girl posing in the window observing him. He busied himself setting the other two charges.

**

Marcos had observed the two go up the trail to the office, and he figured he had some time out of sight to get into Bob's car. He promptly found a piece of baling wire and unlocked the vehicle in no time. Bad news, he couldn't find the rifle. He forced open the locked glove compartment hoping to discover the Lincoln insignia but did not. He tore into the spare tire compartment with no results. He removed the back seat. Nada. He opened the hood and examined the engine compartment, even the air cleaner. Nothing. Nothing in the headliner either. As a last resort, he slid under the vehicle on his back and peered up under the chassis, feeling every place for something concealed from his view. Satisfied the insignia was not in or on the vehicle, he dusted himself off and concluded that Bob must still have it on him.

Cautiously, he inched toward the office, attempting to conceal himself. "Am I seeing what I think I'm seeing?" he mumbled to himself as he caught sight of what he thought to be a half-clad figure in the window. Marcos blinked his eyes realizing it was Susan peering out the west-facing window, waving to someone. *Oh brother, things are way out of hand,* he thought. *I need to speed things up—at least she appears to be alone and unharmed unless she's faking it with the idiotic smile on her face. Who's she waving at? Bob?* At that moment, he cursed himself as a true man of action and hated that he had no clear picture of the goings-on.

Ignoring caution, he took off at a full run. Marcos ascended the path to the office and breathlessly pounded on the door latch. Locked. He lunged desperately against the door with his full weight and force. The entire, flimsy structure of the rickety office shook without the door giving way. A second time, he hurled himself at the stubborn door, which refused to budge. Trying again with all his might, his other shoulder connected with the door with greater impact. The frame splintered profusely while the door gave way, and Marcos crashed headlong into the room. Susan rushed to him, but Marcos bypassed her, making a beeline to the window in time to see Bob. Alerted by the commotion, Bob had retrieved his rifle and was running at full speed toward the office. Then Marcos spotted the plunger and lunged for it.

A blinding explosion rocked the office on its foundation. The concussion whooshed past, but the office protected them from the full force of the blast. Glass from the windows flew through the air, a small projectile cutting Marcos above the eye and leaving a small but bloody scalp wound. Dazed, he took a few moments to reorient himself after the thunderous blast. He located Susan on the floor rolled into a ball, covered with blood. Stunned, she reached out to him as he bent over and scooped her up into his arms—to comfort her, shield her, and protect her.

"Are you okay?" he asked in a shaky voice.

Susan didn't reply but clung to him crying with her head against his chest. He pulled her to her feet, offering his loose outer shirt for cover-up.

"Well, one thing you can give Bob credit for is he knew how to set a dynamite charge properly. However, he shouldn't have wired up that plunger."

"Yeah, but at least he didn't get the *charge* he was hoping for," said Susan, wiping the blood out of her eyes.

Determining Susan had no serious injuries, Marcos went over to the sink to wet a rag and wipe away the blood from her surface wounds. He gathered her intact but dirty clothes, handing them to her with a smile of sheer relief. As soon as Susan dressed, they left the office and trekked back to his car in the abandoned mining shed, leaving Bob behind under tons of detritus.

With a clearer perspective, they speculated about their next moves and if the townspeople would consider the blast to be unusual or hopefully a common occurrence. They considered ditching Bob's car but couldn't explain the fact Susan had left with Bob from the hotel. Nagging questions hung in the air. What was Marcos engaged in prior to showing up at the mining site? Where in the hell was Bob? Why did Bob abandon the Bronco at the mining site? Had Bob actually been at the site? Why was the detonator in the office? The authorities would likely ask these and other difficult questions. Surely, all fingers would point to Susan and then by association to Marcos. It was all risky business. They nodded at one another and let the chips fall where they may and let fate take its course. After all, Bob had certainly furthered his own destruction.

***

Back at the hotel, after hastily cleaning up, they descended upon the dining room and sat at the table as if nothing had happened. Hesitating then looking askance at them both, the server asked, "Will Señor Powell be joining you?" Susan said they would not be waiting for Bob, who was up at the mine doing some test blasting. She added that since she hated loud noises, she had come back on her own and had met Marcos, who had been out doing some archaeological scouting, and he picked her up on the road. She asked the server if she had heard any blasting from the direction of the mine. The server waved her hand as if to dismiss it, indicating it was commonplace with Bob around, and no one paid any attention whatsoever. Everything appeared normal. Marcos and Susan picked at their lunches—they lacked appetites. Each felt tremendous pain in every crevice of their assaulted bodies.

Marcos was a clutter of lividness, gladness, and sorrow when Susan enlightened him about her conversation with Bob and its revelations about Dave—how he had died and specifically the association of the rock art with zeolites. He shook his head, fought his tears, and suffered the aching in his gut in silence for a few moments. "When you examine Dave's body, do you think you can provide evidence of *murder* rather than *suicide?*"

"If what Bob told me is true, it'll be a piece of cake."

"Fine," said Marcos. "Let's go find that body. Time's wasting. We can send your report via express post to the insurance company. That ought to get Dave's wife her due at least and save their house. Let's pack and get out of here. We can be in Mulege for dinner. Then we can deal with that shipment of dynamite and see if we can save the rock art. We're going to have to do some serious conversing about Dave learning the meaning of rock art by communicating with the spirits. That must have been the breakthrough he mentioned to his wife."

Marcos flinched at the thought of what he had just said.

"Must have been," agreed Susan.

As they left the hotel and headed to the car, Susan spied a curious creature walking down the sidewalk with a comical amble and semi-sideways inclination to its short-legged shuffle. To Susan, it looked like a genetically aberrant form of a small, hairless pig, somewhat cute in its homeliness. "What in the world is that?" she asked Marcos in amazement.

Marcos stopped in his tracks. Open-mouthed he stood in veneration.

Susan did not understand why he would have such a reaction to this harmless-looking, ugly, little creature.

"*Herregud!*" exclaimed Marcos. "That's a Mexican hairless, barkless dog called a *Xolo*. The Aztecs included them on trading expeditions to use for food along the way. They also put them at the bottom of their beds to keep their feet warm during cold nights in the mountains. I thought I was seeing a piece of animated ceramics. In all my travels throughout Mexico, I've never seen one of these creatures. Let's follow it and find out where it came from."

The dog aimlessly scurried around town then went to the door of a neat, little frame house not a block from the hotel where someone came to the door and let it in. Marcos went to the door, inquired about the dog, and returned with a contented look on his face. He told Susan people bred the dogs in Ensenada and that the homeowner gave him the name of the top breeder. Marcos vowed to get one of the crazy little souls of the ancient Aztecs to match the ceramic one sitting on his hearth at home.

As his thoughts gravitated briefly to the fate of the Aztecs, he had great difficulty with expunging thoughts of Bob's fate from his mind and leaving their situation to fate. *Not very scientific*, Marcos sadly noted and surmised that the *Xolo* had appeared at their feet out of nowhere like some kind of sign or, God forbid, an omen. *What next?* he asked himself while the bloody history of the Aztecs flooded his mind.

TWELVE
Personal Insights

———————

Marcos and Susan enjoyed the 112-kilometer drive from Santa Rosalía to Mulege along the coast of the Sea of Cortez with its cerulean waters. Without acknowledging it aloud to each other, thoughts of Dave's fate plagued them both.

Their destination, Mulege, was an oasis similar to San Ignacio with a Spanish mission from the eighteenth century. The mission stood as a sentinel in the west overlooking the lagoon to the east. The prison, another imposing structure watching over the small town, some people mistook for a church. A long-standing tradition in Mulege was that—anyone convicted of a crime would spend nights only in the prison and would be free to work and be with their family during the days. In the whole history of Mulege, only one prisoner had escaped but soon returned of his own volition out of guilt. Marcos deemed it an enlightened form of justice.

They passed by the town on the highway and drove south for a couple kilometers to the turnoff for Hotel Mulege owned by gringo Jeff Stevens. The hotel offered both rustic and luxury accommodations. As they looped back north to the hotel from the turnoff, they paralleled the dirt runway for small aircraft. Most of the hotel's customers were private pilots who flew down to go fishing. The runway was essential to the hotel's operations. Accordingly, the hotel also had a radio for communicating with the pilots, and it served sufficiently as a communications network for all of Baja. It was Baja's early Internet. By standing near that radio, listeners didn't need CNN to tell them what was happening in Baja or the world for that matter.

Marcos and Susan parked in the hotel lot and strolled into the courtyard spotted with palms, jacarandas, and bougainvillea in various shades of purple, orange, red, and pink with blossoms swaying in the gentle breeze. As they entered the lobby through a stone archway, they could hear the short-wave radio blaring. It was a news clip concerning the accident in Santa Rosalía. "Authorities pulled the body of Robert Powell, an American miner, from the debris resulting from an accidental dynamite explosion."

The local authorities had pieced all the details together, ingeniously deducting Bob had set a charge, and while returning to the office to detonate it, a large map binder had fallen from the shelf, landing squarely on the plunger, sending Bob to meet his maker. Unbelievably relieved, Marcos and Susan squeezed each other's hands tightly, acknowledging they were in the clear and affirming the old reprobate had met a just end. The tension they had been living with for the past few days melted away, and they finally relaxed and collapsed into nearby chairs.

Jeff walked out of the kitchen and greeted Marcos. They chatted about local events. Intent on their conversation, Marcos neglected to introduce Susan to Jeff. When he realized his breach of etiquette, he corrected his faux pas without hesitation. Jeff welcomed Susan with more than passing interest and a bucket of charm. Susan blushed slightly with all the gracious attention from the handsome gringo with his south-of-the-border manners and flare.

***

Marcos, without even thinking about it, asked for one room instead of two. He didn't feel it would be wise to leave Susan alone at this point. Besides, he realized he wanted to be with her. He found he enjoyed her company thoroughly, and they had been through a lot together. He would do his best to comfort her. Holy crap, he had even seen her half-naked. At the time, and under the circumstances, he had not paid too much attention. Now, he realized just how stunningly beautiful she was. Something he had not felt in a long time stirred within him. That surprised him greatly. Despite his feelings, the unresolved doubts about her lingered in the back of his mind. And she still reminded him of someone.

"Thanks," Susan said.

"For what?"

"The one room." She gave him a sheepish look. "I guess I assumed we'd share a room again but then realized that wasn't necessarily the case. I don't want to be alone after what happened."

"No problem," he said, becoming more smitten by the moment. "Jeff, excuse us. We need to settle in and maybe grab a siesta before dinner."

"Hey, you two, tonight just happens to be the big weekly barbecue with a fiesta, mariachis, and our world-famous barbecued pig. Please accept my personal invitation. You won't want to miss the food or talent," Jeff said with pride.

"Thanks, Jeff. It sounds wonderful," Marcos said. "We accept with enthusiasm, don't we?" Marcos turned to Susan with a huge grin.

Susan smiled back, turned to Jeff, and said, "*Sí, sí.*" She grabbed Marcos' hand as he whisked her off to their room where their bags were already waiting.

Susan went into the bathroom to take a shower. She called Marcos to bring her the soap. Unwrapping the soap, he passed it over the top of the shower curtain. He could see the outline of her voluptuous body silhouetted in the shower curtain. He felt aroused.

Impulsively, he asked, "Do you believe in the conservation of natural resources?"

"You bet. I'm a regular donor to all kinds of environmental causes. My favorite is the Palouse Land Trust because I like the way they operate. They're doing so much to preserve natural environments."

"Good," said Marcos as he stripped off his T-shirt, dropped his shorts, and stepped into the shower.

Susan kept showering and accepted his presence matter-of-factly without reaction as if this was an everyday occurrence. Marcos took her in his arms, and she allowed him to hold her tightly. While the warm water sprayed their bodies, the dirty residue of all that had transpired washed away, purifying them. They both needed that and understood it intuitively without having to speak of it. The act was cleansing and therapeutic. After toweling each other dry without speaking a word, they flopped naked on top of the bed with their legs intertwined and fell asleep peacefully.

The sad lament of a Mexican *ranchera* ballad and the waft of the pungent scent of roasting pork floating through their open window heightened Marcos' hunger. In no time, they had thrown on some clothes and headed to the patio to join the rest of the guests.

Marcos placed a few chunks of barbecued pork on his plate and grabbed some small corn tortillas from the comal, scooped some salsa on the side, and helped himself to the salad. Susan followed his example. They retired to a table where they could enjoy their meal and talk in private. Marcos placed a bit of the meat on a tortilla, put some salad on top, and ceremoniously sprinkled salsa over the whole concoction. He enjoyed every bite and repeated the process several times until he was satiated. Susan, less enthusiastic, hesitatingly consumed a taco or two.

"So, how do you like the pork? Does it live up to Jeff's hype? Through my travels, I've noted that some people don't like pig cooked this way. Do you want me to get you something else?"

"That's okay. I can handle this. Funny you should mention it, though. In my earlier kosher days, pork never came near my lips. Gave that up. I don't practice any religion these days. I decided religion is not for me. I'd prefer to follow my spiritual path through my work. And I'm finding Baja quite spiritual. So, this meat is quite tasty, but I don't eat too much meat of any kind as a rule. It's not all that healthy for you, Dr. Andersson." Susan wagged a finger.

Marcos listened but didn't feel the slightest guilt while he savored the tasty pork. Making no usual excuses, they left the gathering after eating and returned to their room. As they crossed the patio, an old man of obvious Indian descent, offered some beads for sale. He motioned to Marcos who stopped to examine the wares, thinking he might buy something for Susan and help the old man out. As he checked out the various strands of beads in different colors of seeds and shells, he unconsciously fondled the amulet on his key chain.

The old man nodded toward the amulet. "Do you know what that is?" he asked in Spanish.

Marcos shrugged. "It's just something I picked up in the desert years ago."

Standing erect and fixing Marcos with a hard stare, the man said, "People should know what things are before taking and keeping them."

But Marcos was eager to get back to the room and didn't pay any attention. He gave the man a dollar and thoughtfully picked out a shell strand for Susan.

With the old man's parting words, he insisted Marcos return the artifact where he had found it or bad things would happen to him. His comment confounded Marcos, but he tucked it away in the back of his mind for future reference true to his academic routine. As he walked away, he held the amulet up to the light, turning it repeatedly, subjecting it to his learned archaeologist's scrutiny. Nada. He could not *see* anything of note. He wondered what Folke would *see*.

Once inside the room, Marcos poured them both a good measure of Kahlua for a nightcap and settled into a chair. Susan sat on the edge of the bed, sipping the mellifluous, dark liquid she had grown to appreciate on this trip.

"Marcos, before anything happens that either one of us regrets, I think we need to talk. We've spent some nights together in the same room in the same bed. I told myself no man-woman stuff was going to happen on this trip, and you seemed to be a trustworthy person. Now, with all that's happened, I must admit that I've taken comfort in you and enjoy being with you. You are a remarkable man, Dr. Marcos Andersson, and I think I'm falling for you, if I may be so bold. I've never met a man like you before, and you feel *right* to me."

Marcos could not believe what he was hearing but allowed her to continue without interruption.

"But there are so many considerations. First, I have no idea how you feel about me. I might be making a perfect nuisance out of myself, but I need to know where you stand before we can move ahead, if that's even in the cards. Then I asked myself, what's the point? You have your life in Idaho and your adventures around the world. I have a very busy life in Los Angeles, and my practice is important to me.

"I'm not sure that our lifestyles could ever blend or that either of us would want to change the way things are. I can't see what possible compromise we could make. Yet, if you must know, I still entertain the romantic notion that one day a prince charming will sweep me off my feet and we'll live happily ever after. I suppose all women hold that fantasy since girlhood. Stupid, isn't it?

"Then maybe there's the issue whether to have babies. I'm not sure about that one myself. Nevertheless, I wonder if you are that prince charming and if that is what I want. I don't know. I wonder how you feel about all this, Marcos. I fear I am putting you on the spot. It has occurred to me that you never meant for any of this to happen either. Heaven knows you said *no* enough times whenever I proposed coming along with you. We may have ourselves in a fine mess, big time. Even so, it's our relationship I'd like to get some perspective on now. Then again, I know we're here to get Dave, and here I am confronting you."

A flushed Marcos squirmed in his chair and took a heavy swig of Kahlua.

"And there's another thing. Before anything can develop between us, or between you and anyone else for that matter, you need to release yourself from your grief over your wife, and realize that you have to get on with your life and that it's okay. I don't think your wife if she was as wonderful as you say, would want you moping around the rest of your life. She would want you to be happy, but you aren't allowing yourself to be happy to your fullest potential. Marcos, I'd like to take a stab at making you happy, but first you must exorcise the demons in you. So, what do you have to say about my monologue? I hope I haven't made a royal loser out of myself."

"Wow, that's a lot in one speech, and a lot to process." Marcos swallowed making a gulping sound. "You leave me swirling. Where do I begin? Well, you're right about the sex. It's the last thing I had on my mind. No, you haven't made a loser or an idiot out of yourself at all. I'm glad you brought up all this because it has certainly been on my mind too. I'm flattered you feel that way about me, Susan. In case you couldn't tell, you are very much on my mind. Things are turning out way differently on this trip than I had envisioned. For instance, we haven't been able to visit all the sites in the San Francisco Mountains that I had planned for because of that cretin Bob. In addition, I find myself still in sheer terror over what we may have unleashed in the spirit world. I don't know what to make of Andrea's death, Dave's death, and even Bob's. It could all have been a combined omen, a warning, or whatever, and we're not heeding it."

"Let's talk about that later. First, I'd like to know how you feel about what I've just told you."

"Well, you know I didn't want to have anything to do with you and all your psychic nonsense. I have to admit now that I find myself quite attracted to you. Maybe circumstances have thrown us together, forcing us to seek comfort in one another. I've considered that too. While I'm sure that contributed, when I think back on it, I realized I was having those feelings in Guerrero Negro before our whole world view was altered in moments that night on the highway. As for changing lifestyles, I'm fond of mine, and I can't even imagine living in Los Angeles or anywhere else in California again. I've been there, done that. I feel somewhat the same way about kids.

"When Carole couldn't have children, I figured there were already enough kids in the world, and maybe I could do something for those who already exist. I think I'm too old to be a full-time Dad. Do you have any idea how much responsibility it is to raise kids and how much they tie you down? No, I'm sure that I wouldn't want to go through fatherhood at this point in my life. I wouldn't mind being a grandfather, though. Yet I would never want to be the one who deprived you of experiencing motherhood. It's a precious thing, and children are to be treasured. So, we both have lots of things to consider here."

"What about Carole?"

"Wait, I want to tell you something else first. One of the things I envy about you is how much you help people every day in your line of work. I hope to be able to do the same somehow but maybe help many people at the same time one of these days. Therefore, I surely wouldn't want to deprive you or others of that either. No, you have not made an idiot out of yourself. If anything, your bringing up these critical issues makes me respect you more. I'm glad you did because I didn't quite know how to do it."

"Carole?"

"Yeah, well, you're right about my wife and grieving. It's something I've been working on in my way in my own time. I suppose just taking the step to come back to Baja and to have joined up with you is a giant step for me. I know you're right when you say that my wife would want me to be happy."

"Marcos, whether you end up in a relationship with me or anyone else, you have to get over that last hurdle and let go of her. It was a beautiful chapter in your life. No one can ever take it away from you. However, you have to build on it to complete your mission and fulfill your purpose. I think it would be flattering to your wife for her to know that because of your relationship with her you honor the institution of marriage and would like being in that kind of relationship again."

"I'll be all right. It just takes time."

"You know, one of the services I perform as a psychic is to help people contact their departed loved ones." Her eyes sparkled as she talked about the comfort and relief she had provided clients whenever she channeled communications from the other dimension with loved ones. "I can't help wonder if you could benefit from such contact. If so, I'm a bit conflicted over whether I should be the one to assist you with that. Questions of professional ethics could leave us both doubting if I would try to help you get over Carole primarily to meet my own self-serving ends."

At a professional level, Marcos understood Susan's ethical and personal conflicts. Over time, he had stacked up enough of them himself during his tumultuous career. Nevertheless, he had never attempted to contact Carole before, the possibility of which simultaneously intrigued and terrified him. He opted to sleep on that one for a while, but he could address some of what she said.

"One thing is for sure. I think I would feel more comfortable if you were not the one to assist me for all the reasons you stated. In the meantime, I think I'm making significant progress in letting go. Just to hold hands with you awakens feelings in me I didn't expect to have again. You have unearthed them, brushed them off, and exposed them to the light of day. So, thank you, Dr. Cohen. I hope you don't use the same techniques with all your clients."

"Your archaeological references are not lost on me, Dr. Andersson. I appreciate a little professional humor. I'm glad to be of help as well. Let me reassure you, I don't use those techniques with any of my clients."

"Well, Dr. Cohen. I am neither one of your clients nor patients at this point," Marcos reminded her with a chuckle.

"Marcos, I must admit something to you," Susan said clearing her throat. "You have not just awakened feelings in me but have given me new feelings I've never experienced before. Compared to you, I haven't been as lucky to have experienced a blissful marriage or even a significant relationship. I'm actually treading new waters with you. It feels wonderful and exciting but at the same time frightening for me."

"How so? Can you explain more to me?" Marcos asked.

"Frankly, I don't want to be hurt, nor do I want to invest a lot of energy into something that has no hope of going anywhere. Yet I adore having you hold me and can't believe the comfort of waking up in the morning and having you next to me. I have lovingly shared the experiences of the adventure with you, even the insane ones. Face it, our adventures have taught us valuable lessons."

"After our rocky start, I also have enjoyed experiencing Baja with you as well. You are a valuable asset," Marcos said.

"Again, I am so very sorry for my earlier, clumsy behavior," Susan said.

When Marcos stepped into the shower with Susan earlier that afternoon, she didn't know what to do. Her prudish side had wanted to scream and toss him out—her adventurous side had wanted to grab him and pull him in—her do-nothing side did zero. Susan let Marcos know that sometimes it was good to have a do-nothing side because it allowed things to unfold naturally without interfering. If any hope existed, it demanded that Susan act proactively in the relationship. Susan was by nature not a passive person.

"Marcos, I want you to be that knight in shining armor on a white horse. I want you to sweep me off my feet and carry me away. But let me back up a bit, please. Marcos, one of the things I had hoped to accomplish personally while I was in Baja was to focus on what I wanted in life. I've been feeling lately as if I'm digging myself deeper into a rut, and it doesn't feel right. Seeing the way you live your life so carefree and yet with such genuine concern for others intrigues me. Maybe, somehow, we could join forces, but I don't have any picture of how. Do you?"

Marcos said, "You could come back to my ranch in Idaho with me and watch the grass grow for a while. It's very peaceful there, but it gets lonesome. I'd like being able to share that with someone."

"Watching the grass grow would be nice for a while, but after a short time I would either slip into boredom or go bonkers without something to sink my teeth into."

"Hey, you could split logs, remember?"

"Dr. Andersson's simple cure-all."

"Well, there's more to do there than that, but you'd have to come and find out for yourself."

"Well, I'm curious. I've never been to Idaho. Tell me about where you live." She turned an eager face to him.

Aiming to impress, Marcos sought to fascinate her with ranch and house details and his new life in Idaho, admitting that the isolation brought an element of loneliness. The changing of the seasons, however, provided interest and scenic texture for him.

"Hmm . . . I'd like to curl up in front of the fire with you on a cold winter night," Susan said. "Marcos, your place sounds wonderful and impressive in many regards. I would have expected nothing less coming from you. You painted a real picture for me, and I can visualize it. I'd like to come visit someday."

"Doctor, you have my most cordial invitation any time you like. I'd be honored to have you as my guest."

"Thank you. First, however, we need to bring our present undertaking to a satisfactory conclusion, and we need to do something about how we're going to handle our relationship."

"Susan, I advise you to go with your do-nothing side and just let things unfold naturally, and we'll just watch what transpires. I wholeheartedly recognize that neither of us should make any promises at this point because it would be imprudent to do so. I truly get it that you earnestly want to be proactive in a relationship. But I once read a Zen master who had written that doing nothing in itself is a form of action," Marcos said thoughtfully.

"Interesting," Susan said.

"Besides, we won't be doing *nothing*. We have a lot to do before this journey is over, and it seems to keep becoming more and more intense. Let's just let nature take its course."

"Hmm . . ."

"I'm so beat, and tomorrow we have to deal with Dave's body. Do you mind if I crawl into bed beside you?"

Marcos asked himself if Susan suspected that despite his growing affection for her, his Zen approach was code for his reluctance to commit. *Can she hear my inner voice of doubt when it comes to her forthrightness*, he wondered? *I know she's holding back vital information.*

"Dr. Andersson, I thought you'd never ask," Susan said softly followed by a few moments of total peace.

THIRTEEN
Mulege

———

Marcos awakened to the homey sound of cock crows, looked up at the thatched ceiling, and remembered where he was. He had survived another night but wondered how much longer he could endure this. He turned to Susan and smiled at her, appreciating her presence. Then he leaned over, grazed her with a gentle kiss, and said in a pleasant voice, "*Buenos días* and *God morgon*."

Marcos did not look forward to the day and could hardly imagine seeing his closest friend dead. Dave had been so full of life and had so much yet to offer. He had contributed brilliantly to his field of studies and was revered by friends and foes. Despite that, however, Marcos anticipated returning to his old haunts in search of new meaning. If what Bob had said contained a modicum of truth, Dave had had a consequential encounter with *vengeful* spirits. Marcos could still not fathom what could have angered them enough to scare people to death. Perhaps it was something akin to his own nightmares in which the spirits captured him without an escape. That morning, he had experienced just that.

Marcos had no idea where Dave's body was. Generally, Governor Ramiro had told him it would be in Mulege waiting for him. At breakfast, he asked the hotel owner, Jeff, where the morgue was. Jeff shook his head at the thought of their little town having a morgue. He said death and funerals were family affairs. Every family took care of its funeral arrangements. There was no funeral parlor either.

He had heard something about the death of the archaeologist and was sorry to hear it was Marcos' friend but had no idea where the body could be after all this time. It had to be somewhere equipped with a freezer or cold storage unit. That pointed to a meat processor perhaps, but there was no such thing, and no butcher shop in town had a large enough cold storage space to house a human body.

Marcos was about to call Ramiro when Jeff suggested they try one of the commercial fishing outfits in town. The owners didn't have actual cold storage buildings but rather flash freezers on their boats. They kept their catch cold that way until they delivered it to market. After a few calls, Jeff reported that Garcia-Lopez had preserved the body on one of their boats and, growing tired of storing it, were about to hold a burial at sea because it was taking up precious cargo space. They had only kept it thus far as a personal favor to the governor. Unfortunately, the boat was at sea and would not return until late that night. Elena, the wife of Martin Garcia, promised to radio her husband's boat and tell him not to dispose of the body. Marcos and Susan would be able to see Dave first thing the next morning.

Marcos performed mental gymnastics to block Dave out of his mind for another twenty-four hours. He welcomed the reprieve and bided his precious time by taking Susan to visit nearby rock art sites. *Dave would like that*, he thought. He thanked Jeff for his help and went to get Susan for breakfast. Of all the places in Baja, this was Marcos' favorite breakfast spot. He ate eggs sparingly but could not resist the tortilla española, a scrambled, baked egg dish smothered with peppers and onions, fiery salsa, and melted cheese with a corn tortilla on the bottom. What made it special were the potatoes cooked with the eggs that absorbed the chili flavor. Sometimes the dish included bits of bacon and other times ham for added flavor and texture. Marcos and Dave had shared their love for good food. *This meal's for you, mi amigo!*

Even though he demolished his breakfast, Marcos was antsy to depart because he had so much he wanted to show Susan. "I know a wonderful rock art site in this area. Thinking through our options, we can either sit around the hotel and dwell on all the horrible possibilities of what we'll face tomorrow or suck it up and continue our archaeological studies," Marcos said.

"I think that's a great idea. Each time we visit a site, we have another opportunity to gain knowledge about the rock art to help you find the meaning. I think Dave would want us to do just that," Susan said with a wink.

They drove back into town, crossed a bridge, and took a side road that led under the bridge, and forded the shallow lagoon. They went up a steep grade past native huts and corn patches and emerged at the top of the hill overlooking the town. A beautiful old building greeted them, still in service and well maintained.

"Oh, Marcos. Is that one of the Spanish missions? Please, can we stop for a few minutes and take a look?"

Marcos pulled over and came to a stop in front of the seventeenth-century mission. Before entering the imposing stone structure, he took Susan by the hand around to the side of the building as he mysteriously searched for something. Finally, his eyes lit up, and he made a beeline to some scraggly-looking weeds growing along the side of the building. The leaves resembled something like geraniums but were much softer and velvety. "Here, let me pick a couple of these rare leaves for you to look at." He picked two leaves and unabashedly plastered them on the sleeves of Susan's T-shirt. They stuck like Velcro.

"Jeez, Marcos. Do you ever ditch your lame sense of humor?" Susan scolded. "I really can't tell if you're playing around or trying to illustrate some kind of botanical point." When she tried to remove the leaves, she had a difficult time pulling them off, leaving tiny bits of green clinging tenaciously to the fabric.

"Oops! The leaves don't normally stick that much. Sorry," Marcos said with a slight stutter. "Hope your shirt's not ruined." Marcos thought to himself, however, the leaves were reluctant to disassociate themselves from such a beautiful host. He let out a naughty chuckle and shook his head, quite amused with himself. "Seriously, Dave used to stick the leaves all over himself and pretend he was the Hulk of archaeology. Yeah, you had to be there." Marcos' voice trailed off.

Marcos had discovered that this was the only place in the world where these plants grew. After reasonable diligence, he had never found them anywhere else in Baja or even in Mulege. In scientific pursuit, he had taken samples to botanists at the University of California who had been unable to identify them. If the university were to name the plant, he thought it quite appropriate to be named after him as the explorer who had made the discovery. The natives called them *pega pega*, which meant sticky sticky.

They entered the cool, stone sanctuary and admired the primitive paintings on the walls and the marbled decorations with an imposing altar. "Take a moment to reflect on how impressive this edifice must have been to people who had known only brush huts for shelter," Marcos said. "As one might expect, the missionaries effortlessly convinced the people of the superiority of their God. No doubt, the missionaries had strongly believed it themselves. As an anthropologist, I have always straightforwardly questioned if their God were so loving and powerful, how could he have allowed all the Indians to perish? After all, they were also his children." Marcos sighed at the thought.

Lest they become depressed over these musings, Marcos showed Susan the lime kilns where actual limestone was rendered to make the mortar that held the blocks of basalt together in the mission. A promontory beyond the lime kilns afforded a magnificent view of the whole oasis below them with its ubiquitous palm trees and the lagoon leading out to the bay—a lovely and serene sight. Only the prison on an opposing hilltop unnaturally punctuated the landscape below.

"Can we stop at the prison for a few minutes, Marcos, since it's nearby?" Susan asked.

"Of course," Marcos agreed.

The prison appeared abandoned and in great disrepair. It housed no inmates at the time, but it stood ready to receive guests should the occasion arise. They shuddered to recall the incident with Bob that might still implicate them and result in incarceration. They departed a little less happy shortly after that.

Next, they headed south of Mulege, following the rugged coastline overlooking the Sea of Cortez with its incredible vistas. Marcos pulled the Navigator off the road in the middle of a basalt flow extending down to the ocean. They hiked up along the huge boulders that had tumbled down the slope. To Susan's delight, she discovered a garden of petroglyphs decorating almost every available surface of every boulder. They lingered there a couple hours, examining the artwork and enjoying themselves in the sun.

"Susan, do you see? There are a few new motifs to be inventoried here, including a variety of fish, insect-like creatures, non-objective designs, and anthropomorphs. Cool, huh?"

"You bet. I can only imagine how many people carved here."

Below the petroglyph site, a small, lovely, semi-circular bay glistened in the sun, not surprisingly called Media Luna or Half Moon Bay. The sun, directly overhead, reflected fiercely off the rocks, creating the perfect interlude to cool off. They drove right down onto the beach. While Marcos removed his shirt and shorts, he heard a splash behind him. *A pelican, no doubt, diving for fish*, he thought. It was Susan playfully splashing in the water and motioning him to join her.

In his boxer shorts, he dove in and swam up to her and into her arms. Surprised by her naked body, he hugged her, feeling her pressed against his chest. He knew she could feel his arousal as she drew him even closer. Marcos invited her to try floating on her back, knowing that with the ultra-buoyancy of the supersaturated saltwater in the Sea of Cortez, she would practically float on top of the water. After a refreshing swim, they toweled off each other, but they could still feel the salt adhering to their bodies. It was a little itchy and annoying, but they dressed and drove south down the road for a mile or so.

Soon, Marcos pulled off and headed down a dangerously precipitous rock-strewn trace of a road into a small valley. At the bottom, he parked, and they walked toward the cliff to the east. As they hiked up out of the arroyo, they could see the mouth of a small, stained rock shelter looming ahead—their destination. Marcos headed straight for it with Susan in tow. Suddenly, she screamed. Marcos turned to see her frozen in her tracks. A large, coiled rattlesnake rattled a warning, ready to strike.

Marcos said, "Don't even move an eyelash."

Susan remained frozen in fear. Without hesitation, Marcos knelt and picked up a large rock, which he expertly aimed and lobbed at the snake. It was a lucky shot—smashing the snake's head and disarming the deadly threat to the woman he was beginning to care about. He reflected on the thought of losing her, and it was more than he could bear.

"Given your medical expertise, I don't have to tell you that a snakebite in a place like this could be deadly with no available serum. Snakes have been a hazard of my profession and a major threat in the field. We rely solely on the application of moist compresses, keeping the patient calm, and marking the edges of the swelling until we can get help. That's exactly what I had to do with Dave on a remote dig years ago. God, nearly lost him that time," Marcos said. He whipped out his knife and sliced off the head of the snake, nimbly avoiding the fangs dripping with deadly venom.

Next, he cut off the rattles and presented them to Susan as a memento. He then sliced open the belly, gutted, and effortlessly flayed the long, tubular reptile. This he presented to Susan who accepted it with reservation. He placed the meat in a plastic bag, intending to make a rattlesnake belt for Susan and to eat the meat for lunch. "I don't like to kill anything unless I eat the meat. I don't want it to go to waste and for its life to have been in vain."

"Well, then maybe we should have eaten Bob and with that act destroyed the evidence." They cracked smiles, but both agreed, however, that Bob's life had already been in vain and eating him would bestow an undeserved honor.

Inside the rock shelter, they could clearly make out a representation of a red, life-sized coyote pictograph. "Dave and I named this Coyote Cave in honor of this very pictograph," Marcos said. Several black and red pictographs of fish and turtles also decorated the surface. "The rock art reflects the exploited resources in the various environments. As you can see, the ancient dwellers strew tons of clam and oyster shells around the surface and the entrance."

When Susan grew pensive, Marcos could see her gradually entering a trance. He disengaged from her while she received whatever information she could about the cave. Marcos shivered to think of himself entering the spirit world and the terrifying vortex he had previously experienced that still haunted him. He had set his keys on a rock next to him. Unnoticed, *the amulet glowed red.*

When Susan returned from her meditative state, she donned a big smile. "Marcos, I learned a vast amount of information from the spirits that I need to sort through. First, though, I am delighted to report this is a happy place. The people who occupied this site looked forward to visiting on their yearly round of gathering and using the available resources. The cave represented a place of abundance to them, which allowed for a seasonal gathering of more people in one place. For the rest of the year, they had to scour the meager environment in small bands of family groups. The coyote had been a sacred symbol to them—they were the people of the coyote clan," she announced.

Marcos listened intently with an occasional nod. The smile on his face reflected the utter satisfaction he felt upon hearing the details he and Dave had sought for years. "Susan, I'm so impressed you were able to receive that level of detail about this site. You're proving to be so resourceful," he said with bright eyes and a wicked giggle.

Back at the hotel, Marcos presented the bag of rattlesnake meat to the cook, asking him to prepare it for their lunch. Sautéed in butter with a little garlic and doused in lime juice and salsa, the meat in fresh corn tortillas made incredibly delicious rattlesnake tacos. The other guests didn't seem to share their enthusiasm, however. At first apprehensive, Susan jumped in and got in the spirit and wanted to take part in this important ritual to celebrate the life of the snake. It made good sense to her. No surprise, they tasted to her like chicken tacos.

The time for that long-awaited shower and siesta was perfect. Absent hot water, the lukewarm water felt deliciously refreshing as they soaped and caressed each other's bodies in the shower. It felt fantastic to rid themselves of the itchy salt. Feeling clean and refreshed, they laid down on the bed in one another's arms and fell into a well-earned, peaceful slumber.

***

Marcos and Susan ordered shrimp for dinner with a bottle of chilled Santo Tomás *vino blanco*. In the past, he had delighted in gorging on the abundant shrimp of Baja until he had learned how much cholesterol they contained. *What a total downer.* It seemed that everything good had some evil attached to it. *What a world of temptations we live in. Det är så sant.*

Their in-depth conversation during the meal centered on rock art. Marcos assumed an academic posture. Now that they had visited several sites with pictographs and petroglyphs, he asked Susan about her sense of the difference between the two. She was a bright student and responded resoundingly that she had discovered quite a difference, especially using the accumulated details provided by the spirits. While there were some common elements between them, they were quite different within their cultural context.

"But that's based on my observations. What I learned today, what the spirits spoke to me, adds more context. A specialist, a man with great power and vision, created the large drawings on the caves. The spirit guides assisted him to produce those very drawings. In contrast, common, everyday people, regular men, created the petroglyphs. Those were magical and had primarily to do with hunting." Susan even impressed herself.

Marcos asked for clarification. "Do you mean every time a guy would go hunting, he would carve a sheep on a rock to bring him luck?"

"Well, in theory, yes, based on the principle of like produces like."

"Seriously? If a man had carved an animal every time he went hunting, there would exist millions of petroglyphs everywhere—not enough walls in caves. While there certainly exists a plethora of them, the numbers would be inconceivable over hundreds or thousands of years."

Susan smiled wryly and cleared her throat. "No, they didn't carve them every single time. Once the carvings brought luck in the hunt, the people would honor them with offerings. When carvings no longer brought luck, the people would carve new ones, resuming the cycle."

"Well, that explains the animals, but what about other things such as meandering, non-objective designs, and anthropomorphs? Did you gain insights about those?"

"The non-objective designs were often like maps showing where the animals were to be found. Sometimes they commemorated a successful hunting strategy."

"And the human figures?"

"Those people had enemies. There was warfare. They depicted their enemies, just like the animals, to bring them success in battle. They honored both the powerful male and female shamans."

Everything Susan had presented made sense to Marcos on a certain level. He said, "However, I guess you can appreciate my frustration in not being able to corroborate your findings with hard, archaeological data. Listen, Susan. I can't believe I'm going to say this. I mean that if someone had said something like this to me a couple weeks ago, I'd have thought he was a kook. Okay . . . all right, it's true, isn't it?" Marcos shivered. "Dave's breakthrough was going to facilitate his communication with the spirits of the rock art to learn the meanings."

"Yes, that is *precisely* my theory, Marcos." Susan spoke with an unwavering look into his incredulous, tired blue eyes.

He proceeded with caution. "Let me speculate a bit. Bob Powell's plan to destroy the rock art in his avaricious quest for zeolites angered the spirits. The spirits must have taken it out on Dave because he was *present* and open to communication. They had been able to reach him, which they had accomplished without differentiating the good people from the evil people. I think I understand. I don't particularly like it, but that's the way it appears." Marcos shuddered with his next thought. "Susan, the spirits consider all of us the enemy!" That edgy factor left Marcos anxious to the core.

"Wait a minute. Take heart. I think we can convince them we're the good guys," Susan said.

"I don't know, Susan. What about the rattlesnake today? Do you think that was a warning, an omen? Yikes, it could have actually killed you."

"As Freud would say, perhaps it was *just* a rattlesnake. But thanks for saving my life."

Marcos thought as fast as he paced. He asked Susan about Andrea and Bob—three deaths thus far, including Dave. "Do you suppose we became agents for the spirits to do their bidding when Bob died?"

"Anything's possible. I don't know that for certain. I do know that we must make some kind of peace with the spirit world to heal the wound and to restore order and balance in the realm *between the two worlds.*"

"How in this world are we going to do that, no pun intended? Can we do it before we become the next victims?"

Susan shook her head. "I don't know yet. I just don't know. A way *will* reveal itself, though. You'll see when the time is right."

"Oh, fantastic! We'd better figure it out while we still can," Marcos barked. "I have a confession. Sometimes I'm afraid to fall asleep at night, scared to death that the unspeakable spirits will come to me in my dreams and drag me into their dimension, rendering me incapable of escaping."

"Oh, you poor baby." Susan gently stroked his arm. "I'll protect you, but you have to sleep with me," said Susan winking at him.

That night, they slept in a peaceful, trusting embrace. For the time being, the terrifying nightmares spared Marcos. But wondering when and if they would return made it almost as bad as having the nightmares, for it consumed his waking consciousness as much as the sexual tension. That, he could have sliced with his fabulous Swiss army knife.

***

Marcos had received a message from Jeff the night before that he was to come to the pier at five a.m. to retrieve Dave's body. The message was clear that the boat would not wait should he arrive late, and the crew would unceremoniously bury Dave's body at sea. The legal time for retention of the body had elapsed. Without hesitation, he and Susan found their way to the pier in the darkness before dawn.

Due to a local epidemic that had killed the fish, the fishermen had to travel farther and farther up the coast fishing each day, and they were busy preparing to get underway. Señor Garcia greeted them cordially and invited them on board for coffee while he ordered the crew to extricate Dave's body from the flash freezer below deck. Before they half finished their coffee, the body, wrapped in many layers of plastic, dangled from a hoist that swung it out over the pier. It spun around in the air near the back of Marcos' Navigator, playing out like a macabre scene from a bad horror movie.

Marcos took another gulp of the strong coffee and threw the rest overboard. Handing the cup back to his host with thanks, he offered to pay Garcia for storing Dave's body. Being a man of honor, Sr. Garcia raised his hand, refusing further payment because the governor had already sent him a check. He seemed proud of that and didn't want to compromise the gesture. The crane operator followed Marcos' hand signals as he and Susan wrestled Dave's cold, hard body into the back of the vehicle.

"So, what's the plan?" Are we taking Dave's body to the hospital or somewhere else?" Susan asked.

"There is *no* hospital. This is what we're going to do. There's no place we can perform a normal autopsy. I think we should hustle out to the site where Dave died as far as we can before the body thaws too much. You can perform a rudimentary procedure there, documenting it well with photographs. In addition, while you're doing your thing, I'll collect firewood for a funeral pyre. When you're done, we'll cremate Dave and send him on his way to wherever he's going next. I'm well aware this is not up to Hoyle, but let's hope this will release him from his horrible torment in the spirit world and help Joyce with the insurance company mess." Marcos felt a biting chill as he matter-of-factly outlined the gruesome plan.

He knew the site well where Bob had killed Dave. He and Dave had visited it together countless times. He remembered how the paintings appeared on a cliff face of a sheer basalt flow in a steep canyon. Above the basalt outcropping lay a thick layer of what looked like white ash—zeolites, Marcos now realized. In reality, Bob could have merely scraped off the top of the deposit instead of destroying the entire site. *What a lunatic,* he lamented. But there was more to it than that, and the government was involved.

190 VENGEANCE OF THE VANISHED ONES

They drove hard for two long hours through the desert to reach the site. Marcos was reduced to tears when he faced the destruction. The beautiful paintings of bighorn sheep and deer outlined in black and filled with red no longer existed. The hunters, represented by figures painted black and red vertically and wearing elaborate headdresses, had vanished. The handprints of white and ochre that adorned the walls had vaporized in the dust. All the magnificent, ancient art was gone, buried under tons of overburden caused by Bob's infernal explosives. Marcos gritted his teeth and muttered, "Bob's death and burial were a fitting end after what he perpetrated here." He couldn't imagine that anyone in any realm could have destroyed such treasures. *Folke, this would totally finish you off,* he thought, shaking his head.

With much respect and caution, they took their time removing Dave's body from the car and laid it on a clean tarp on the ground, cutting open the multiple layers of the plastic shroud. Marcos braced himself but gasped when he saw what he expected to be his best friend's familiar face. His stomach knotted on the verge of vomiting, his breath came in heaves, and for a moment, everything spun around him. A grotesque mask stared up at him as he reluctantly pulled back the plastic. Dave's frozen face like Andrea's reflected the horror Bob had described—a living nightmare that surely would have killed him if Bob had not. *Perhaps Bob's act had been merciful after all,* Marcos contemplated and then dismissed. He didn't want to *see* anything else and realized his thinking was craziness. He left Susan to perform her medical examination while he gathered firewood.

As Marcos set about his work with a chainsaw he had borrowed from Jeff, he sensed the presence of something malevolent. He didn't like it, so he worked faster. He wanted to get out of that place as soon as possible, sensing evil had settled in after its destruction. Instead of a beautiful site of murals, it was now a locus of foreboding—a place of angry spirits and death. Naturally, they would have experienced outrage at the destruction of their rock art, but that was clearly not all. Marcos knew with every fiber that he and Susan had to discover what *precisely* Dave had done to unleash the spirits' unbridled wrath.

Listen to me, thought Marcos. *I'm talking as if I believe in all this supernatural nonsense now. That's the trouble—if you believe it, it makes it real.* Nevertheless, it was impossible not to believe after all that had happened and all that he had experienced.

Marcos worked feverishly cutting firewood and stacking it in a rectangular structure with enough room on the top to place Dave's body. He cut extra to pile on top of the body to make sure it burned to ashes. He wasn't sure how much he would need only having studied funeral pyres before. It was hot drudgework, but he didn't care. He needed to work hard to keep his mind occupied and focused instead of allowing it to wander and fixate on the spirit realm. He wanted nothing more to do with angry spirits if he could help it. Instinctively, however, within his dark recesses, he realized that an impending faceoff would soon make an appearance. He was weak and unprepared to encounter it.

Dave's body had thawed enough for the unorthodox autopsy about to take place. Thankfully, it didn't smell. Before leaving to gather firewood, Marcos had urged Susan to work as swiftly as possible. He planned to send Dave efficiently and humanely on his way.

***

Susan didn't have much to work with and had assembled a few implements she thought would come in handy from the kitchen and the workshop of the hotel. She needed to establish and document forensically that the cause of death was not a self-inflicted bullet wound.

Susan found a single wound in Dave's heart. She extracted the bullet with great difficulty from the still semi-frozen flesh. The lack of powder burns and the angle of entry of the 30.06 rifle bullet ruled out suicide. She documented it all photographically, took measurements, and wrote copious notes. Susan hesitated, thought, then stared down at her extremely cold, aching hands. *Unfrickinbelievable. Never thought I'd perform an autopsy under such medieval conditions. Modern medical science be damned!*

Three hours later, she brushed back her hair, wiped the perspiration from her brow, and called out to Marcos that she had finished. Together they dragged Dave over to the pyre and, with great difficulty and all their combined strength, hoisted him on top. Both of them disassociated themselves from seeing Dave as anything other than a corpse in order to complete their impossible task. Marcos sprinkled some gasoline over the wood and threw on a lit match. With a flash, the pyre ignited and blazed, contributing to the already unbearably hot atmosphere. The plastic melted—the clothes ignited. He witnessed the flesh on Dave's face turn red, orange, and then brown as the fire increased in intensity. The funerals of the Vikings crossed his mind.

Marcos could not bear observing the disintegration of his friend like that. He took heart, in that, just for the occasion, he had brought with him an atlatl Dave had carved and given him as a present. Together they had heaved many a dart with it, proclaiming themselves world champions if ever the Olympics featured hurling atlatls as an event. Marcos felt there should be some kind of ceremony but was not prepared, never would be, and did not feel adequate. His few words were to wish Dave well on his journey to wherever he would go next and to thank him for his friendship and his inspiration. Clutching the atlatl, he finally made a solemn vow he would do everything in his power to make amends with the spirit world, learn what he could from the spirits about the rock art, and produce some kind of publication so that Dave's efforts would not be in vain. He also promised to look after Joyce.

Marcos knelt with his eyes closed while uttering his last words of memorialization and farewell. Even when he stood twenty feet from the fire, he could feel its intense heat. The flames had fully swallowed Dave's body—he could no longer see his friend and felt as if his spirit must have already departed if it had not done so before. With tears streaming down his cheeks, he threw more wood and the atlatl at the fire until he collapsed sobbing. Susan, bleary-eyed, comforted him in her arms stained with Dave's blood.

When the fire fell to embers, they worked hard for another hour and a half to place stones over the ashes in a mound that would be Dave's physical resting place forever. Marcos gathered up some of Dave's ashes for Joyce and the family. *Dave, my dear friend, I hope you approve.* He dusted himself off then photographed Dave's monument for Joyce and the kids for family closure. His complete body fatigue rolled over him like an asphalt compactor.

They returned to the hotel in silence. Susan meticulously prepared her medical report and dispatched it to the insurance company via express delivery that afternoon. In a state of deepest bereavement, Marcos allowed himself, for a brief moment, to feel satisfied he had found Dave's murderer and had avenged his death. *Mission accomplished, thank God*, he thought, words he respectfully had used so many times before when completing critical fieldwork.

***

Marcos pulled himself up onto one elbow and jolted out of deep sleep. Cold and sweaty, he cringed from a pounding headache and painful back strain as he steadied himself with his feet planted on the floor and padded to the bathroom. He switched on the light and stood staring in the mirror at his weary face with deep, dark circles under his eyes. *¡Caray! I look like I've aged twenty years*, he contemplated sadly. His cold, moist skin reminded him of Dave.

Marcos frantically splashed cold water on his face but could no longer ignore the consuming doubt that he had not unearthed the entire truth. His mind flashed on his father. Reluctantly, he admitted to himself aloud in the mirror, "Folke, I need your help now more than ever. I have a strong feeling I am missing something. *Pappa, hjälp mig, snälla!*"

He waited a few minutes before stepping backward from the mirror—he had been *looking* at the problem but not *seeing* it. That needed to change.

FOURTEEN
Bountiful Rock Art

It dawned on Marcos that his knowledge of the local history in Mulege was critical for his next steps. After the *revolución* of 1910, throughout most of Mexico, the government had subdivided huge, private landholdings, often as expansive as 400,000-plus hectares, and gave them to the peasants as communal properties known as *ejidos.* Baja, however, had escaped this process for the most part. Those in charge had considered it a forgotten place where few people desired to live. Because of this, many ranchers in Baja had retained their property, some of which had emanated from Spanish land grants four hundred years before. The limited numbers made Marcos' essential job of contacting the ranchers relatively easy.

The largest and most influential landowners were Gustavo Figueroa with 75,000 hectares and Huberto Ballesteros with 50,000 hectares, both ranchers in the Mulege area. Marcos recalled Dave's wife, Joyce, telling him that Dave had planned to meet with Gustavo. She had urged Marcos to speak with Gustavo since he may have knowledge about Dave's activities in Baja. Hacienda Figueroa was originally a Spanish land grant quite palatial in its day. Due to hard times through the centuries, the family had to sell off some of the lands. Unlike the Figueroa holdings, Ballesteros' land remained in the original landowner's family for only two generations. Huberto's grandfather had made a tidy profit running liquor by boat from Ensenada to San Jorge during Prohibition. With the profits, he bought the land from another family. The land was passed on through the generations, ending up under Huberto's ownership.

Marcos knew a considerable concentration of major rock art sites resided on those lands, and with them came major sources of zeolites. Ballesteros derived his only income from the scrawny cattle he raised on the barren, desert land. Figueroa and Ballesteros, as well as the other ranchers in the area, were desperate for cash. The devaluation of the *peso* had hit them hard, resulting in mortgaged lands teetering on the rock face of foreclosure. All the ranchers resented the idea of the government designating the rock art sites on their land as national monuments with no compensation. They felt the rock art belonged to them because it was on their land and the national government had no business telling them what they could or could not do. Of course, if the government had offered them fair compensation for their rock art sites, the situation might have played out differently.

To a man, however, the rancheros were in favor of mining zeolites as a precious source of badly needed, quick cash—the sooner the better. And as a result, the rock art was an obstacle to their goal rather than an asset, and they held no interest whatsoever in archaeological patrimony. For quick relief, most rancheros had enthusiastically embraced Bob Powell's plan to dynamite the rock art sites to put a permanent end to government interference. But now that Bob was dead, they had no inkling of how to proceed without him.

Sitting at breakfast, stewing over what to do, Marcos overheard a conversation that made his blood boil. That self-serving Interior Minister Delgado had sent an emissary, Roberto Peréz, to tell the ranchers the dynamite would be forthcoming soon and Powell's plan would move forward. But it hadn't arrived yet, and the rancheros were getting impatient and anxious. The delay was good for Marcos, along with one other thing he learned— even if they had the dynamite, they didn't know how to use it and were afraid of it. Powell had promised to dynamite for them.

Marcos already knew Huberto Ballesteros. Once a dashing, handsome fellow, he was now a slovenly, feckless degenerate who reportedly bathed once a month. His face was that of a sorrowful, repeatedly kicked dog. The skin on his cheeks sagged terribly on his deeply furrowed face. His paunch forced him to waddle when he walked—or was it, perhaps, the gluttonous consumption of liquor? Over the years, the vats of booze and mountains of fatty foods had placed quite a strain on his diminutive, five-foot–two-inch frame. His rank, bodily odors preceded him as he often stumbled through town on his way home drunk during the wee hours. His western, cowboy-type attire was filthy from falling and sleeping where he dropped. Huberto rarely changed or washed his clothes, considering that a waste of precious water and detergent. Although he owned a hacienda on his ranch, he lived in a shack at the edge of town most of the time. He kept a peasant woman who lived in a lean-to at the back of his shack and cooked for him. He paid, fed, pushed her around occasionally, and demanded sexual favors. The woman had no family and no place to go, so she tolerated the *perro podrido*. Rumor had it Huberto had married once, but his wife had escaped and run away with a truck driver from El Paso. He had no children, at least none he claimed as his. At forty-six, he was bitter about life and eternally obnoxious.

Huberto had once boasted about his huge dreams. His father had saved enough money to send him to Mexico City to the university. He had partied and flunked out the first year but had remained for two more, knocking around with his friends until his father's money had run out. It had broken his father's heart when it became obvious his son would not graduate from the university and become a lawyer. His father had become so enraged over Huberto's plight that he had disowned his only son. Only on his deathbed had Huberto's father finally forgiven him and bequeathed him the ranch.

Until his father's death, Huberto had struggled, working as a ranch hand, a truck driver, and a cattle buyer. He had saved enough money to buy two trucks so he could transport cattle to market. But he had quit working altogether when the ranch became his, and he lived off whatever income the cattle brought, which was not much since the herd had dwindled from lack of decent care and veterinary attention.

Due to the potential zeolites deal, Huberto had a way out of his hole and a way to resuscitate his image.

Marcos had met Huberto Ballesteros once before when Marcos had asked permission to visit a stunning cave site on the Ballesteros ranch and had not been very impressed with the man. He had determined back then that Huberto was in a downward spiral. Marcos felt sorry for the wretched fellow and wished he could help Huberto somehow.

With the current situation, it was imperative that Marcos enlist Huberto's help. When Marcos tried to find Huberto in town, people said they hadn't seen the guy in a couple days and assumed Huberto had gone to the ranch. Marcos and Susan were determined to find him there the next morning.

"Hey, señor, do you know anything about dynamite?" a young man asked Marcos as he turned back to the hotel.

Marcos stopped in his tracks and turned around. "Not much. Why?"

"You asked about Huberto. He says if the dynamite ever shows up, he's going to set it off himself and get rid of all that rock art. He's tired of waiting."

Marcos ran his fingers through his hair. "Hmm. That's very interesting. *Gracias.* If you see Huberto before I do, tell him that's not a good idea."

The young man shook his head and rolled his eyes. "*¡Ni hablar!* I could tell him, but he thinks he's smarter than the rest of us. He won't listen."

***

The next day, they were up early, enjoying their delicious breakfasts, ready to embrace the day. "What do you say we get a move on and hustle to the Ballesteros ranch," Marcos said anxiously.

"I'd say that sounds like a good idea," Susan said with a nod. "I'm ready to go when you are."

"Great. I need to determine if I can sway Huberto's opinion and save the rock art. As an added attraction, there's a wonderful site far to the west of Mulege I'd like you to see. It's up in the rugged sierra over difficult terrain, so we need plenty of time to reach that destination."

"I'm game," Susan said, stroking Marcos' arm. "Here's hoping we pick up more clues about the rock art."

From the hotel, they traveled about five kilometers north of town before turning off onto a dirt track heading west into the desert toward the mountains. Bouncing and grinding their way through the treacherous chollas over rocks and streambeds that were flash flood traps, they meandered toward the mountains. Passing through a lush forest of paloverde, they began their ascent. As they crossed a rocky, dry riverbed, a beat-up old pickup approached them. Marcos had to swerve to the right to avoid the passing vehicle. As he did so, they felt a horrible bump. He had hit a large rock with force. Expecting the worst, he jumped out to inspect the damage. The other vehicle stopped, and two ranch hands came over to see what the trouble was. Instantly, Marcos realized he had hit the rock so hard it had bent the wheel and broken the seal in the tubeless tire. They were losing air in the right rear.

"*¡Traigame una piedra grande, hombre, prontisimo!*" yelled Marcos at the approaching ranch hand. "Bring a large rock, quickly!" The man complied with a perplexed look on his face. Marcos grabbed the rock and began pounding on the rim, beating it back into shape and restoring the seal. He had fortunately reacted with enough speed to preserve a safe level of air pressure so they could continue without having to put on the spare. *Oh my God*, he lamented, remembering he had forgotten to replace the tire Powell had shot out. *How could I have been so careless? Must take care of that as soon as I get back to town.*

Marcos produced some cold beers from his cooler and tossed a couple to the ranch hands, thanking them for their help. They nodded their heads heartily.

"Hey, señor," said one of the ranch hands, "we now call you the gringo who fixes tires with rocks."

Marcos clapped his hands with restraint, shaking his head. "Do you guys know if the *patrón* is at the ranch?"

The same ranch hand said, "No, señor, we not see him in a week. We worry a lot."

The two men bade Marcos and Susan, "*Vaya con dios.*"

"If you happen to see the *patrón*, please tell him to get in touch with me at the hotel. *Es muy importante. Adiós, amigos.*"

Marcos, somewhat troubled, consulted with Susan, "As long as we're here, do you think we should go on up to the cave site? Or do you want to go back—given the tire and the absent Huberto?"

"We've made it this far. Let's keep going," Susan said with a nod.

Soon they were on their way again up the mountain, down into the valley on the other side, and up another mountain. They followed a narrow track leading into a valley with a stream meandering through it. At that point, they were unable to go any further, even with a four-wheel drive. A burro would have had difficulty in such terrain. Marcos parked and secured the useless car near the stream under a tree.

The two hiked up the canyon under large ficus trees providing them sparse shade. The temperature had risen to well over one hundred degrees in the sun. As they came out into a *potrero,* the high valley ahead split into two more valleys. "Are you doing okay?" Marcos said.

"Sure, as long as the canteen holds out and I avoid the cacti."

They kept up the climb, with Marcos helping Susan scramble up the rubble of an ancient lava flow. After taking a drink from their canteen, they rounded a cleft heading up a steep incline over large boulders.

Two huge *cardones* stood as silent guardians at the entrance of a large rock shelter that easily exceeded thirty meters at the mouth and went back into the mountain another fifteen meters. It sported a high ceiling, perhaps eleven meters at the apex. The sun now in the west on its descending journey, cast a perfect light on the incredible, life-size figures painted everywhere on the ceiling.

The ghostly white anthropomorphs could have been skeletons without the bone structure. Breasts on the female figures protruded from their underarms. "A bit crudely represented here, the women are actually lying on their backs like the other site," Marcos said.

"In my opinion, the renderings result from the creator's inability to produce frontal representations artistically," Susan added.

"Very astute, Dr. Cohen."

The male figures appeared either with transverse red and black paint dividing their bodies vertically or horizontally at the waist. Many of them were black on top and red below while others had the same colors reversed. The animal inventory included deer, turtles, coyotes, and pumas. The renderings were reminiscent of the figures they had already seen at other sites.

"I still stand in awe of how the ancient artists painted these figures so high on the ceiling of the cave," Susan said.

"I know, me too. As I've said, the use of *ocotillo* or *cardón* splines to create scaffolding was both practical and ingenious," Marcos said with authority.

Internally, his archaeologist's mind overflowed with myriad unanswered questions, which had multiplied during his many studies. Who exactly produced these paintings? Could anyone in the tribe paint them? Did the act of painting require initiation into the culture as a participating adult? Or was it merely the more spiritually enlightened individual, such as a powerful shaman, who created these works? Were they the result of a vision quest? Were they historical documents depicting actual events? Did the creators perceive them in a vision?

As usual, the inability to *dig up* the evidence frustrated Marcos. He would have expected to excavate the answers about an extinct culture as an archaeologist. Thus far, that had not been the case. The situation had disappointed him time after time—two decades worth to be exact and counting.

Marcos dreaded not knowing if he dared to tamper with the answers to his questions, out of fear of releasing some evil attached to the paintings—transferring the evil to himself. *On the face of things, it seems Dave already released it somehow. Now, it's my job to assuage the ancient spirits and restore order and harmony,* Marcos reminded himself as a shiver rippled through his body.

Susan pointed to another set of strange symbols the natives had carved deeply into the wall. "They look like parentheses," she said.

"They're likely female genitalia painted to represent some kind of fertility symbol."

"Marcos, I detect your frustration and want to do *something* to help you," she said. She took him by the hand, leading him to a large, flat boulder where they could sit in the shade of the entrance to the cave. "Don't worry so much. I'm quite confident we'll gain more knowledge here, too. As you can tell, I don't share your apprehension."

Marcos made the conscious decision not to enter into a meditative state. He couldn't handle it just then. Frankly, he wasn't even sure it was a good thing for Susan to do as he looked on while she entered the cave alone.

After what seemed like hours to Marcos, Susan came back from her communication session. Beaming ear-to-ear, she said, "Marcos, I have much to tell you. I learned only a respected and knowledgeable shaman could have achieved these powerful and sacred drawings. The information gleaned corroborated the fact that those ancient Michelangelos did, indeed, build scaffolding of *cardón* splines lashed together with cactus or palm fiber. After preparing their natural pigments and animal fat, they fasted for two days and two nights and painted the revelations from their visions. In some cases, they recorded past events to teach future generations the truth, the meaning, or significance of the representations. In other cases, they could have been millennial prophets who depicted a future of plentiful game, water, and plants," she said catching her breath.

"Please tell me more. I've been waiting years to discover such vital information," Marcos said excitedly.

"Sure. A sad event had occurred—some type of altercation as depicted on the ceiling. We can see that some of the people have arrows and spears sticking out of their bodies. As I understand it, during some point in the conflict, one individual had twenty-one projectiles protruding from him. The opposing war chief and each warrior had been obligated to shoot an arrow into the enemy. Because the victors had been the occupants of the region of the cave, it became a shrine for them—a powerful spot for many generations. They portrayed the women as fertility symbols to ensure the efficacy of the culture and that the future generations would live in abundance. The inelegant fertility symbols had underscored that depiction. The game on the walls represented a kind of homeopathic hunting magic to ensure like produced like in the hunt, a matter of affirmations and positive thinking." Susan smiled as she focused on Marcos. "Thoughts?"

"That's incredible. I can't believe you received all this information. How did it come to you exactly?"

"That's the thrilling part, Marcos. I've contacted a guide who was very helpful in wanting to answer my questions. He hasn't told me his name yet, but I think he's on our side. He did warn me that there are angry spirits who harbor evil intentions and that I must be very careful to avoid them at all costs."

"Yeah, but how do you avoid them? That's about all I seem to bump into, which has me petrified. I didn't even try to take part today. Maybe I should just leave it to you and not try to get involved. But I don't want you to meet the same unthinkable fate as Dave and Andrea!"

Despite his apprehensions, Marcos was quite pleased with the information Susan had revealed. It all appeared valid as it fit the pattern of cultures at that level of evolution. Of course, he couldn't prove a word of it and would incur the sheer contempt of contemporaries within the professional milieu were he bold enough to produce scholarship based on her revelations. It struck him as a bona fide, scientific conundrum.

Hand in hand, they made their way back to the vehicle. When Marcos turned the ignition key, he felt unusual heat from the amulet but surmised it should be hot from sitting in the sun. Observing the amulet more closely, he thought it even glowed red from the reflection of the sun through the windshield. *Man, this hunk of expensive Lincoln steel certainly absorbs heat*, he thought, chastising himself for not having left the windows cracked. Instinctively, as if he were back in Los Angeles, he would have locked the car down. For that, he chided himself.

***

The track they followed led to the ranch house and its outbuildings. The road split heading into the mouth of a tiny canyon Marcos had not yet had the opportunity to explore. Impulsively, he turned up the canyon, thinking he would kick it out a bit and perhaps discover more rock art there he had never studied before. Rounding a bend, they instantly entered a box canyon. Marcos retrieved his heavy-duty, field glasses, and he and Susan hiked to a promontory above the surrounding brush so they could study the basalt walls of the canyon. He excitedly expected to find rock art on them since the conditions were ideal with exposed basalt surfaces with a heavy patina.

Starting at the end of the canyon, he adeptly surveyed the rock walls using the field glasses. Moving toward the east, about the center of the canyon, he found a large cleft in the wall obscured by a shadow. It could have been a lava blister—a cave. He pointed it out to Susan, offering her the binoculars. It was approximately one hundred meters away.

"Let's check it out," Marcos said, grabbing Susan's hand.

As Marcos approached, he confirmed his suspicions. The cave appeared to have some depth to it. There must have been another road branching off the one they had taken into the canyon because obscured in the bushes he saw a parked truck. Battered and layered with dust, the old Ford F150 guarded the cave entrance fifteen meters away. Then he recognized it as Huberto's, or at least he remembered seeing Huberto in a similar one several years before. Marcos lifted the hood to check the engine—stone cold and most likely had been so for a while. Perhaps Huberto had gone hunting for bighorn sheep in the mountains. Marcos walked to the rear of the vehicle, looked into the bed, and stopped abruptly. Every muscle in his body tightened.

"Susan, look at this."

"What?" she asked as she came around to the back of the truck.

Marcos leaned into the bed and lifted the lid of a wooden box filled with sawdust and some red sticks of dynamite. Rummaging around, he instantly calculated that at least two were missing. "Oh damn, he intends to blow up the rock art sites!"

With the dawning realization that the nearby cave could be the target, Marcos rushed to the entrance, stopping short at the mouth. Diminutive red figures of deer and bighorn sheep adorned both sides of the entrance along with a couple animals painted in white, upside down with spears extending out from them. He could see paintings on the rock of the shelter as well, but what grasped his full attention was Huberto, stiffly lying on his back, legs spread, arms straight up above his head with a stick of dynamite in each hand. Frozen in a moment of horror, the screams from the grotesquely gaping, extended jaw echoed in the silence. Susan crept up behind Marcos and let out a muffled gasp.

Marcos recorded the grisly scene with his digital camera and then removed the dynamite from Huberto's hands. He returned to the truck and gingerly seated the dynamite back in the box. Removing the box, he took it to his car and carefully padded it in the back seat.

"He intended to blow up that cave," Marcos said. "Wait a minute. That gives me an idea."

He removed the two sticks of dynamite he had just placed in the box and put them back in Huberto's hands exactly as he had discovered them.

"Why did you do that?" asked Susan.

"You'll see," was all Marcos said.

***

The ride back to town passed mostly in silence with Marcos and Susan each separately immersed deep in thought. Besides, it was too bumpy to carry on a decent conversation, even though Marcos went extra slowly, taking care not to disturb the dynamite. Before returning to town, Marcos turned off the highway onto a dirt road heading east toward the sea. He stopped at the edge of a cliff overlooking the Sea of Cortez thirty meters below. First, he pulled the cord fuses and caps out of the sticks of dynamite. He then smashed the box with a large rock, set the defused dynamite on top, and set the pile on fire. Within seconds, he kicked the burning pile over the cliff and watched the contents plummet sizzling into the sea. Explosion averted.

In town, Marcos drove around aimlessly for a while until he spied the truck of Huberto's *vaqueros* parked in front of a cantina. He parked with a thud and said, "Hot? Let's go grab a couple cool ones and break the sad news."

When they entered the cantina, cheers of olé and bravo broke out, confusing Marcos and Susan at first. Marcos' reputation had preceded him. The two *vaqueros* they had encountered in the desert were there and had been telling everyone about the loco gringo who fixed tires with rocks. From that moment on, the people addressed Marcos as Don Piedra, which was like addressing him as Sir Rock, an honor of dubious intent.

Marcos ordered a round of drinks. He waved his hands to gain everyone's rapt attention and informed them he had some unfortunate news to tell. He removed his digital camera from the pocket of his cargo shorts and turned it on to display the image of Huberto Ballesteros graphically on the screen with his face contorted by fear and anguish with dynamite sticks ensconced in his hands. Marcos asked them to pass the camera around so everyone could have a good look as he told them he had just found Huberto dead in a pictograph cave on his ranch. Marcos emphasized the guy had died because he had planned to blow up the cave to destroy the rock art. That had no doubt angered *the spirits of the ancestors of the ancient ones*, who had produced this beautiful art.

In retaliation for the unthinkable act of destruction, the angered spirits had taken Huberto's soul with them to the underworld and left his earthly remains to rot. Marcos suggested to the awestruck assemblage, "This is what it must be like to die without your soul." He paused for effect then added, "This is not the only soul claimed by the spirits recently. I believe the same spirits claimed the soul of archaeologist Dr. Dave Pearce, leaving him to die at the site where he was excavating. To the north, a woman who dared to tamper with the spirit world had died in the same fashion.

"This fate awaits anyone foolish enough to tangle with the angry spirits. Bob Powell, the zeolites miner, died under tons of rock—a suitable end for someone so evil as to encourage others to destroy the ancient art in the name of their immense greed," said Marcos, barely speaking above a whisper. He looked around at the disquieted faces as he spoke with measured words, pacing himself in between deep, deliberate breaths. As a final shot, with certainty in his voice, he said, "These unnecessary deaths should serve as a warning to anyone who seeks to disturb the ancient spirits or, worse, destroy the rock art."

Having delivered the pithy message, Marcos and Susan left the silent gathering in the cantina, knowing the listeners would soon promulgate the message as fast as if Marcos had blast emailed it on the Internet. Any rancher who attempted to tamper with the rock art would have to consider the consequences, and the evidence was abundantly convincing, especially for anyone the least bit superstitious.

Marcos hoped his presentation would serve as sufficient warning, but he had already learned so often in the field that avarice was a powerful motivator. Perhaps he could better sway Gustavo Figueroa, the most powerful, respected, and influential rancher in the region. Then Sr. Figueroa could convince the others not to destroy the rock art. Again, Marcos recalled Dave's wife, Joyce, had mentioned that Dave had expected to meet with Sr. Figueroa.

FIFTEEN
New Exploration

———

Marcos arose the following morning in darkness, eager to visit a new rock art site he had never before studied and also hopefully find Gustavo Figeroa. He brought Susan a cup of coffee from the restaurant, but when he offered it to her, she moaned. Something had wreaked havoc with her stomach—tainted shrimp from the previous night's dinner she concluded. Urgently, she rushed to the bathroom and violently heaved the contents of her stomach into the toilet then returned to bed weakened. She no sooner lay down when the strong urge sent her rushing to the bathroom to sit on the toilet this time.

After relieving her bowels, she vomited again, barely reaching the bathroom sink. Humiliated, she declined Marcos' offer of help. She cleaned herself and fell into bed miserable, obviously in no shape for the activities Marcos had planned for the day. He commiserated with her and told her he would return with something to set her right in no time. He gently broke the news to her that she had a touch of Montezuma's revenge, a common malady of people unaccustomed to traveling in Mexico. Susan weakly moaned in response, burying her sweaty face in the pillow.

A closed *pharmacia* greeted Marcos upon his arrival in town. He made a few inquiries and found the proprietor enjoying his breakfast in a restaurant nearby. Graciously, nodding with understanding, the pharmacist opened his shop and supplied Marcos with some *vioenteroformes* to treat Susan's condition.

Susan showed no improvement when Marcos returned, even though she had visited the bathroom twice during his absence. "Marcos, I strongly suspect my condition is the work of the angry spirits. I vow never to disturb them again if this misery visited upon me would cease and desist already."

"I'm sorry, but I can assure you this malady has nothing to do with the spirits. It's some disagreeable bacterium." He handed her a couple of *vioenteroformes* tablets and a bottle of water, demanding she take them and promising they would make her feel better lickety-split.

"What are you giving me, Marcos?"

"*Vioenteroformes*. They're magic. I've given these to people who thought they were going to die in the morning, and by noon they were scaling pyramids."

"Good Lord, Marcos, are you trying to give me cataracts? These are what we call *entero vioform* at home. We haven't prescribed this stuff in years."

"Maybe a sustained regimen would, but all you need is a couple, and poof, it's all over. Trust me. Here, let me help you." Marcos gave her the pills and held the water bottle for her.

"Well, if they'll help me get rid of the *revenge*, I guess I'd make a contract with the devil. I hope you're right. I've never felt so ill in my entire life. As a doctor, I have no patience for being ill myself."

"Don't worry. You'll be just fine. Get some sleep. I'm going with one of the servers at the restaurant to see a site he told me about this morning. It's not too far. I should be back in time for lunch. I predict you'll be all healed by then. Just relax and allow the medicine to do its job, and try to get some sleep. Drink lots of water. Doctor's orders," Marcos commanded.

He handed her another bottle of water, kissed her lightly on the forehead, and departed.

Part Indian, Alex, a local and the waiter at the hotel restaurant, waited for Marcos on the patio.

"*Buenos días*, Alex."

"*Ese carro está chido*," said Alex, as he commented on the Navigator appreciatively, never having been in such a luxurious vehicle.

"*Gracias*, Alex. Had a problem with one of the tires, though. I hope it will continue to hold enough air to get us back and forth. No time to pick up a spare."

Alex directed Marcos south of the hotel. After a few kilometers, they turned off the paved highway and headed west into the mountains. Soon the rocky, dirt track they had been following disappeared as they entered a canyon with perpendicular red walls of sculpted sandstone. Then they followed the streambed through natural swells of standing water, over rocky and sometimes sandy streambeds, until the canyon narrowed, and they could drive no further in the vehicle. On foot, they waded through a *tinaja*, a natural cistern of water up to their armpits. Marcos held his backpack with the camera equipment over his head. As he looked up toward the sky, he felt the sensation of the narrow canyon walls closing in on him, giving him an uncomfortable feeling. He was relieved when they left the water and the canyon expanded again.

As they traipsed along, Alex kept a running commentary on the plants he saw and told how his mother, a full-blooded Indian, would use them in her cooking and for medicinal purposes.

"Alex," asked Marcos curiously, "did your mother ever teach you anything about the meaning of the rock art?"

"Not too much, Dr. Andersson. She would warn us not to play near the *pinturas*, for they were sacred and powerful, and we must respect them and never, ever touch or harm them in any way because the guardian spirits would hurt us."

"Guardian spirits, huh? Do you believe there are guardian spirits still protecting them after all these years?"

"I think it must be so, Dr. Andersson. I remember some young guys who got drunk one time and started shooting at the *pinturas*. On the way back to town, their truck went off the road, and they all died in an explosion. People say it was those spirits who caused the accident, but I don't know for sure. *Sí, sí.* I think it best to respect them."

Alex veered out of the streambed and headed into the brush. Soon they were in a hollowed-out chamber on the east wall of the canyon. A huge rock protected the entrance to the shelter. On the face of the boulder were shields with various graphic designs. They went behind the rock and entered the chamber. Marcos caught a glimpse of mountain sheep depicted and a large, white deer upside down with a spear sticking out of its body. To the upper right was a panel of red handprints with one white hand beneath it. Again, there was also a series of what resembled closed and open parentheses, which Marcos referred to as the fertility symbols.

"Alex, would you mind leaving me alone here for a while?"

"*Bien*, Dr. Andersson, just shout out to me when you have finished. I'll hear you."

***

Marcos sat with his back to the rock, staring up at the renderings on the wall. He admired their simplicity of design and contemplated their astonishing power. Intellectually, he acknowledged that the moment was upon him to learn what the art would have meant to its creators. Honestly, he had grown wary of reliance on his imagination. He held respect for the renderings and appreciated being alone in this sacred place. *I so wish Susan was here to share the entire splendor with me*, he thought with mixed emotions.

Given that Marcos dared to appear at the shelter solo was an act of bravery given his nightmares that still plagued him. He was tense and cautious at first. Marcos' presence before the ancient art required of him deep, controlled breathing because he knew the fate of the others who had succumbed to the *vengeance* of the spirits. He found as he relaxed and sat calmly, a certain peace filled him. Marcos had a heightened awareness of the existence of strange, slightly stale air about him. He drifted absentmindedly into another realm, peacefully floating within a reverie that until the present, he had only experienced as a child. This time no spinning vortex beckoned him with evil faces flashing by and leering at him. Marcos experienced in this instance a calm communion with the spirit world.

Academically, he ran a short script in his mind, seeking explanations as to the difference between the two types of encounters while he thoroughly appreciated the tranquility of his present experience. It was an out-of-body experience complete with the sensation of floating—floating free of time and space, unencumbered by physical bounds. For a brief moment, Marcos felt the adrenalin rush of the hunt followed by the unfamiliar exhilaration of killing a bighorn sheep, the reverence of placating and thanking its soul, the pride of presenting the meat of his kill to his people, and the satisfaction from their appreciation. He was delighted to share the meat. He felt these things personally down into his core and faced what it was like to be an ancient hunter in this land long ago. His face flushed when he aimed his atlatl and experienced the Zen of knowing his dart had traveled expertly to the target.

Marcos returned to the present plane with the ancient knowledge he had gained. He had never during his life experienced the thrill of any hunt. He longed to know if modern hunters in possession of their high-tech riflescopes and powerful weapons experienced the same feeling, but he doubted it because they couldn't possibly share the same relationship with or respect for the animals they hunted. Their very existence did not depend on it. *No, it had to be an entirely different kind of experience*, he surmised. Surely, there was some kind of primeval similarity, but it could never be the same. He could hardly wait to return and relate to Susan what had transpired. He now believed his expedition was proving to be worthwhile after all. What Marcos had just experienced would be a lifelong lesson. Was it the case that rock art taught those individuals who were receptive to its messages? With that, he had a brilliant moment of academic clarity—*that most certainly had to be one of its functions*. He was beginning to *see* and not just *look*. He sighed more deeply than ever before. *Jag förstår, pappa.*

Marcos called out for Alex, who materialized without a sound. The two returned to the hotel with paltry dialogue because Marcos still reeled from his encounter in the shelter.

***

Susan had slept most of the morning. When she awoke, she felt almost human again. Marcos' magic pills had done their job. She showered and set out to see if she could get something light to eat, something her stomach could easily tolerate. Susan decided tea and toast would do nicely. The staff had closed the restaurant, but the waiter told her he could accommodate her at the bar. Susan entered the bar and spotted first off another customer sitting on a bar stool indulging himself.

"Well, hello there, gorgeous. Come join me. Care for a Bloody Mary?" asked the balding, disheveled man. He wore a Hawaiian-print shirt that hung over his striped, green walking shorts. She could see his black oxfords and white socks.

"No thank you, I'll just be having some hot tea and toast alone," she said to the man and the waiter.

"Well, at least come sit over here and talk to me. It would be good to talk to someone in English. These Mexican people here don't speak much English. My name's Connor—just flew in from L.A. That's my Cherokee airplane out there. Did you see that nice little four-seater? She's a real beaut, practically built her myself. They don't make them anymore, you know. She's my pride and joy."

"That's nice."

"So, what's a pretty lady like you doing in such an off-the-beaten-path kinda place all alone?"

"I'm not alone. My companion is off exploring an archaeological site at the moment."

"Would that be a boy companion or a girl companion?"

"Boy."

"So, are you an archaeologist too?"

"No."

"Just along for the ride, eh?"

"Yes, something like that."

"Archaeology. Yeah, I see stuff about that on the Discovery Channel. It's something the way those guys dig up dinosaurs and such. Old bones. Can you imagine people dedicating their lives to old bones?

"Guess I should introduce myself properly. Connor Chase. What's your name, honey?" he asked, extending his right hand while guiding it toward her with aid from his left because it seemed to wander.

"Susan Cohen."

"Not married I see. Jewish, huh? Well, what do you do if you're not an archaeologist, Susan?"

"I'm a psychiatrist."

"Whoa! So, it's Dr. Cohen, and you're a shrink. Well, excuse me. Ain't that just something?"

"And what do you do, Connor? I imagine searching for dinosaur bones is not your line of work."

"No way. I'm in real estate. Have my own office in Costa Mesa. Do darn well too. Guess you could tell by that plane out there, huh?"

"How wonderful for you."

Susan thanked the waiter who had set a cup of hot tea and a plate of toast in front of her.

As she buttered her toast, Connor said, "Well, Susan, or perhaps I should say Dr. Cohen, what do you say we go back to your room and you give me some shrinking. I have a problem I'd like to discuss with you. What do you say?"

"Sorry, I'm here on vacation."

"Come on, how can a doctor refuse a patient. I'm not a well man. You could help me. I'd even pay you."

"No. Sorry."

"Aw, come on. We could do a little shrinking together before your boy comes back and no one would be the wiser, and I'd be outta here in my Cherokee. I promise I'd leave you one happy lady. I've never had any complaints from the ladies, you know. You might be interested to know I have gained some pretty good skills, if I do say so myself. Most women are amazed after they experience a piece of the ole' Connor man."

"You are beginning to annoy me, Connor. I'd appreciate it if you'd just leave me alone. I'm not feeling very well."

"I told you, Susan. I can make you feel real fine. I've got just what you need."

Connor stood up, reached out, and took Susan's arm, squeezing it tightly, pulling her up off the stool.

"Come on, Susan. Let's go to your room now. You'll be glad you did."

Coldly, Susan said, "Take your hand off me, and don't you ever touch me again."

"Oh, and what are you going to do about it, little lady? Call the police? Come on, let's go. Your resistance is making me crazy. Is there a psychological term for that?"

Connor tugged her away from the counter and began leading her toward the door.

***

Ecstatic to tell Susan about his enriching engagement with the rock art, Marcos rushed to their room first upon his return to the hotel. Disappointed not to find her there, he took it as a sign that she must be feeling better. The pills had worked, but then he knew they would. He logically concluded she must have gone to the restaurant. Realizing the restaurant was not yet open for lunch, he thought he would check the bar since he had not spotted her anywhere on the grounds.

Marcos' eyes took a moment to grow accustomed to the dark interior of the bar after the bright sunshine outside. As his eyes adjusted, he could make out what looked like two people struggling by the bar. A man was clutching onto a woman by her wrist and attempting to pull her away from the bar. Then he recognized Susan.

Before he could rush to her rescue, he saw her plant her feet and whirl away from the man. His lock on her wrist broken, she lashed out at him, her right hand chopping him on the left side of his neck. Her left hand had already delivered a savage blow to the right side of his neck. Following that, a quick jab to his nose brought his hands to his face. Before his knees could buckle, she twirled and bashed him in the face with her foot. With a dancing kick, her foot caught him in the groin with a lightning strike. He went down groaning, clutching his crotch and begging for mercy.

The barman and three waiters all cheered and shouted, "Olé." Marcos, stupefied by her performance, stood simultaneously in shock and awe. He whispered on his own, "Olé, Susan," before hurrying to Susan's side.

"Susan! Appears you're feeling better," said Marcos.

"I've felt better, thank you. And that pig didn't help any. I didn't mean to come on so strong, but I rather lost it. I don't like men trying to control me like that."

"What did he do?" Marcos was curious to find out.

"He wanted to go to my room with me for a little fun and games. He told me he was quite a man, but somehow I doubt it."

"Jeez, Susan. I guess I won't invite you back to the room. I'm not sure I'm up to that brand of foreplay right now. Why don't we have a drink by the pool and wait for the restaurant to open? I have something quite exciting to tell you."

When they had ordered drinks and more tea and were comfortably seated in the shade of an umbrella by the pool, Marcos asked, "Where in the heck did you learn to do all of those moves?"

"What?"

"You know, you practically brought down that guy, quicker than a machine gun. It was awesome. I guess I didn't have to worry about you with Powell, did I?"

"I told you I could take care of myself."

"Indeed, but where did you learn to be such a formidable force?"

"It's about my only form of recreation these days. I've taken self-defense classes for several years now. I attend them religiously once a week. It's been good for me to release the tension, but I've never had to use it until today. Came in handy, though. Do you think I should apologize to the creep? I guess I kind of overreacted."

"Not by a stretch. He had it coming to him. I wish I could have given him a punch or two myself. Serves him right. Maybe he'll learn a lesson. Maybe I learned a lesson, too."

"And what lesson was that, Marcos?"

"Never underestimate a woman at face value for one thing. And I guess I'll be very careful about how I go about wooing you."

"Not a bad idea," said Susan with one eyebrow raised, her face cracking to a smug little grin as she daintily sipped her tea. "Now, what was the exciting news you were going to tell me?"

"Alex took me to a new site I'd never seen before in a beautiful, deep, red arroyo. I sat alone in this rock shelter, contemplating the pictographs. At first, I felt tense and concerned the spirits would capture me. Then as I began to relax and control my breathing, I could feel myself drift away, and I somewhat left my body and became one with the exact time and place of the paintings, entering the realm of the ancient hunter. I vividly experienced firsthand what it was like to be a hunter. I have retained that knowledge and still have all the sensations associated with the hunt. I learned that one of the uses of rock art was to teach the way of the hunter to young men. I *know* that now. There is no lingering question in my mind about that."

"That's fantastic news, Marcos. Congratulations! See, I said you *could* enter that realm, and now you've done it, successfully."

"Yes, this *one* time, but what about the terror that still lingers and haunts me from my previous experiences?"

Susan gently coached Marcos. "That is a separate problem yet to tackle, and you will. However, don't give up now. Remember your promise to Dave."

Marcos sat in quiet repose drinking his margarita and half listening to words of congratulations coming from Susan. What had happened to him in the shelter defied years of logical thinking and training as a scientist. As a hunter, his encounters were *real*—he still experienced the titillation and instant adrenalin high as he pursued his prey, atlatl in hand. *Dave, please hang in there with me. I'm still trying to fit the pieces of the puzzle together. ¿Qué pasa? You tell me?*

***

The next morning, they skipped breakfast and slept in late. Susan greeted the day back to her normal self. As they entered the hotel restaurant with incredible appetites, Alex rushed in from the kitchen to greet Marcos with a worried look on his face.

"Dr. Andersson, that man, Connor, and his friend, who had flown down with him in his plane, paid me a lot of money to take them to the site where we went yesterday. It was really bad, Dr. Andersson. The two men didn't appreciate the site like you did. No. They tried to chip off large sections of the rock art with their knives," Alex said somberly.

"Oh God, Alex. Did anything else happen? Go on." Marcos said.

"*Sí, sí.* It was lucky their knifepoints broke off in the process. But they carved some filthy symbols and their initials on the surface of one of the larger deer paintings."

"*¡Dios, mío!* So sorry you had to witness that mess, Alex."

"I know, Dr. Andersson. I begged them to stop, but they just made obscene gestures at me and kept on. I even warned them they would anger the guardian spirits of the rock art and that what they were doing was very dangerous." Alex sighed. "That only made them laugh more, Dr. Andersson."

Upon hearing this news, Marcos wanted more than anything to carve his initials on their backsides and make them bleed. He asked Alex where he could find them. Alex shrugged and pointed over at the runway beyond the hotel. They could hear the engine of the Cherokee revving as it readied for takeoff. Brakes released, the plane lurched ahead, gathered speed down the runway, and leaped into the sky.

In Spanish, Alex said, "Those guys are going to fly over the site to take pictures from the air and then continue south to Loreto to spend the night and fish the next day."

"Is that right?" was the only thing Marcos could think of saying.

Susan and Marcos intently observed the airplane diminish in size as it climbed and circled toward the mountains to the west and flew away in that direction.

But the three watched in shock when the craft inexplicably collided with a mountain peak. The sudden explosion turned the plane into a horrific ball of flames, which they saw before the sickening sound reached their ears.

"Maybe the sun blinded the pilot," Susan suggested, though they all knew what had really happened.

"Alex," said Marcos, "I'm counting on you to make sure each and every rancher learns the gory details about what happened today and why."

"*No hay problema*, Dr. Andersson," said Alex. He nodded his head sadly but knowingly.

Still shaking after what they had witnessed, Susan and Marcos made their way to the dining room for lunch, preferring something like food to distract them from their thoughts. Over salads and steaming bowls of *sopa de albondigas* and fresh homemade tortillas, Marcos said, "Much as I enjoy remaining incommunicado, I really should check my email."

"Yes, normal things," Susan said, smiling wanly.

Marcos smiled and nodded. "I might just need to provide buy or sell orders to my commodities brokers. I left stop orders on most of my positions—short on natural gas, long on corn contracts. It might be time to take some profits or, God forbid, cut my losses." He shrugged and sighed at the same time. The real world, as he knew it, seemed so remote now and insignificant.

When Jeff, the owner, came over to ask if they were enjoying their lunch, Marcos asked him if he could use the office phone for a few seconds just to grab his email. He wanted to download it now and would read it offline and respond later as appropriate. Jeff said he would be in the office waiting for him after their meal.

Marcos and Susan could not resist the delectable flan for dessert. Marcos broke the silence in between bites of the sublime confection.

"Susan, we've been through hell these past few days. I haven't thanked you enough on behalf of myself, Dave, and his family for your invaluable medical help. Without your excellent skills and attention to detail, I most likely wouldn't have met the local deadline for timely disposal of a body, as well as the insurance company's impossible deadline for closing the case. For that, I stand eternally grateful to you," Marcos said with a slight hitch in his voice.

"No thanks necessary. Just doing my part," Susan said with a big smile. "But I never in a million years could have predicted that I would perform an autopsy in such primitive conditions. Then there's Dave's icy cold corpse and the fact he had been murdered. One for my future medical memoirs, I say."

"I get it. I never in a million years thought I would preside over an actual funeral pyre. I have only studied pyres during my period of fascination with the Vikings. Dave, I am certain, would have gotten a kick out of that," Marcos said, his blue eyes dancing. "We shared a different brand of humor than most when it came to history and archaeology. I loved him for it."

Susan drew in a deep, slow breath. "Do you feel like you've wrapped things up here in Baja sufficiently?" she asked, cautiously probing.

Marcos hesitated for a moment. His brow was deeply furrowed. "Interesting you should ask. It's like you read my mind. I've been turning that exact question over and over in my head since Dave's burial. Honestly, I'm totally exhausted and not thinking too clearly at the moment. I need some time to rest, recharge, and continue to piece together the big picture."

"Any ideas?"

"Well, I don't know. Right now, however, I need to stretch my legs and check emails before my eyes glue shut from fatigue." Marcos shook his head. "I need to see whether my investments are still making money for me while I'm traipsing around Baja." When done talking and eating, he grabbed his mini handheld computer from the front pocket of his cargo pants, excused himself, and marched off to Jeff's office in anticipation of good news—for once.

***

Susan sat in deep contemplation while sipping another cup of herbal tea, waiting patiently and wondering where her life was headed and what in the hell to do about her plans for embarking on the new discipline, *psychic archaeology*. *I need Marcos' help with that*, she sighed. For an instant, she flashed on the amulet. *I think Marcos is withholding information about that crazy thing*, she thought. *But then again, I haven't been entirely forthcoming about all aspects of my life either.* While waiting, she ordered more herbal tea. Her thoughts grew heavy.

***

Some fifteen minutes later, Marcos emerged without a word from the office, sat down across from Susan, and began tapping through his email messages with his new stylus. The government-issued, state-of-the-art, pocket computer came in quite handy on his trip. Marcos was mostly pleased with the markets, but there was an oversupply of natural gas all of a sudden, which he had not expected. The price was tanking. *Better dump that turkey,* he thought to himself as he tapped out a message to his broker in haste. He had lost over five grand. *Oh well,* he was up triple that overall. Truth be known, he hated to lose any amount. With exhaustion gaining on him, he looked up at Susan and said, "It's time for a siesta after that great lunch and a bit too much investment news. What do you say? Everything else can wait."

Susan rose, nodded, and took Marcos' hand. "I think you're right."

Marcos walked Susan to their room with *no* expectations. He recognized his elevated level of fatigue and anxiety from head to toe and that he required decent sleep to face whatever awaited him. The battle waging in his head between unresolved issues and the grotesque image of Dave dead worsened his physical state.

As they stood at the door hesitating for a few seconds, they embraced more tenderly than before. Although Marcos fell comfortably into Susan's arms, he wondered if his weakened state and sadness over Dave's death triggered her reaction to him. *Perhaps she's fearful I'll have a breakdown,* Marcos thought for a moment. *Helvete!* He urged himself to expunge that thinking from his mind, calm himself, and try to enjoy the moment. He realized he wanted to be with her, badly. *Quit overthinking, you sad sack*, he thought miserably.

Susan held onto Marcos' hand as she gently pulled him into the room. They took a few steps closer to the bed and stood facing each other with their hands on each other's hips. Marcos rested his head on Susan's as she slipped out of her sandals and looked up at him. He could feel the heat on his face and neck. The first-time butterflies in his stomach surprised him.

Susan gestured to Marcos to lean down. She softly whispered in his ear, "Take my clothes off."

With no hesitation, Marcos took a small step back, gathered the bottom of Susan's T-shirt in his fingers, and gently pulled it up over her arms and head, tossing it gently on a nearby chair. The sight of her perfectly shaped, ample breasts amazed him. "My God, your breasts are beautiful," he said while he cupped them in his hands. Susan's gasps aroused him to greater heights, as he unfastened her shorts, giving them a slight tug and inching them to the floor.

The two kissed deeply with tongues passionately probing each other's mouths. Susan unbuttoned Marcos' shirt, sliding it down his arms onto the floor. Without changing position, Marcos hurried things along and removed his shorts and boxers together deftly in one motion, stepping out of them and kicking them aside with one foot.

Susan managed an appropriate chuckle. "I really appreciate a man with your level of coordination," she said softly as she led Marcos to the bed and guided him on top of her. He covered her face and neck in firm, hot kisses and nibbles.

Marcos was aware of his every heartbeat. He had been with Carole exclusively for a very long time after a series of unsuccessful relationships. They had grown sexually comfortable over the years, in harmony with what each other enjoyed and needed in bed. With Susan, he didn't want to appear too eager or make any moves that would make her feel uncomfortable. He had to trust his experience and instincts and let nature take it from there. For an instant, however, Marcos' left-brain recalled a couple of clumsy, first-time sexual encounters from his past where everything had been all sharp elbows and jerky moves. In reality, he wished the *theater of sex* in his head would remain dark during intimate moments.

Side by side, still catching their breath and basking in the afterglow, Marcos turned back on his side to admire better the object of his affection in the muted light of the candle on the nightstand.

"You are absolutely . . . so stunningly . . . beautiful," he said, searching for words, "in so many ways."

"Do you really think so, Dr. Andersson?" Susan said with a sexy smile.

"I think you are a fantasy I have not allowed to materialize. Are you truly real? Oh God, I never thought I'd ever know love again. It's been such a long time. It's wonderful to give and receive love. I've missed that, I now realize."

"I sure *missed* it, that's for sure."

"When was the last time you loved someone?" Marcos asked bluntly.

"When I said I missed it, I meant I missed it altogether, as in missed the ball, struck out. The love train abandoned me back at the station which leaves me a bit confused in matters of the heart. I've never said this to anyone before, but I *think* I love you. It somehow feels right being with you. I could so easily give myself to you. I guess I already have in a way. Our lovemaking is over-the-top incredible, and that was only the first time. Usually, the first time is less than hot, in my experience. Yet . . ."

"It was very good, no complaints on my end," Marcos said while a part of him wondered what she really meant by *she thought* she loved him. But looking at her bare body chased those fleeting concerns away.

"Hold me tight. I want to fall asleep in your arms."

"Gladly. Susan, I know many uncertainties still surround the situation here in Baja, but as I see it, we have each other, and our relationship has come a long way. We work well together. Those thoughts give me great satisfaction and hope for dealing with whatever comes."

"Me too," Susan said then kissed Marcos and nestled herself against his chest.

Marcos performed as requested and held Susan tight in his arms as they both fell asleep.

They awoke to the sound of the desk clerk pounding on the door. "Dr. Andersson, Dr. Andersson, I have an urgent message for you," the clerk said in a desperate voice.

"*Sí, Sí.* I'm coming," Marcos yelled back as he struggled into his shorts, tripping his way to the door.

The desk clerk shoved a telegram into Marcos' hand as soon as the door cracked open. Marcos tore open the envelope and stepped out into the hallway to observe the desk clerk scurry off. He turned pallid as his eyes focused on the scant message. *Fy fan!* He drew in a raspy breath, wadded up the telegram, and stepped back into the room. *Folke, I can't believe my luck!* ran through his head.

Susan sat up in bed. "Marcos, what's wrong? You're whiter than this bedsheet."

"Seems my services are needed straightaway in Guatemala."

***

Although Susan and Marcos had shared intimate details about their lives and professions during their adventures, Marcos had been unable, for good reason, to tell her everything. He particularly had never mentioned what he referred to over the years as his *side gig*— his association with government organizations like the DEA.

Susan had no hint of what was coming next.

About the Author

Lee Orlich Bertram is an American novelist and poet. *Vengeance of the Vanished Ones, Book One* is her debut novel in the Dr. Marcos Andersson series. Lee received her BA, MA, and PhD from the University of California, Irvine, and her JD from the University of Idaho. After a career in K-12 education, Lee began the practice of law in Idaho and Washington. In addition to writing and her practice, Lee teaches business and international trade law at Washington State University. She is multilingual, enjoys playing piano, sitting on corporate boards, cooking, studying archaeology and Egyptology, and originally hails from California from an immigrant family. Lee lives in Idaho with her husband and their feather and fur babies.

Note from Lee Orlich Bertram

Word-of-mouth is crucial for any author to succeed. If you enjoyed *Vengeance of the Vanished Ones, Book One*, please leave a review online—anywhere you are able. Even if it's just a sentence or two. It would make all the difference and would be very much appreciated.

Thanks!
Lee Orlich Bertram

We hope you enjoyed reading this title from:

BLACK ROSE
writing™

Subscribe to our mailing list – *The Rosevine* – and receive **FREE** books, daily
deals, and stay current with news about upcoming
releases and our hottest authors.
Scan the QR code below to sign up.

Already a subscriber? Please accept a sincere thank you for being a fan of
Black Rose Writing authors.